Holly heard the muted rumble of the motorcycle before she saw it, and the sound made her remember the feel of it between her legs a week ago, when she had felt as if her body was fused to Reyna's.

She got out of the car and waited. She tipped her head back to look at Reyna while she took off her helmet. The poor motel parking lot light was still sufficient to illuminate Reyna's eyes.

Reyna seemed to want to say something, and the words Holly knew she should utter were in her mouth, too. Then Reyna dropped her helmet and took Holly's face in her hands.

Hard, raw want coursed through her because her body didn't know better. But her mind knew she should pull away. She had rewritten her life in a month but some parts of her had not changed. She had only contempt for what Reyna represented and so she could not go to bed with her, not again.

She tipped her head back with a low whimper as she opened her mouth to Reyna. She was washed with desire and conflict, her head screaming at her to push Reyna away while her heart pounded with an escalating passion that made her arch hard against Reyna's thigh.

LOOKING FOR NAIAD?

**Buy our books at
www.naiadpress.com**

**or call our toll-free number
1-800-533-1973**

**or by fax (24 hours a day)
1-850-539-9731**

SUBSTITUTE FOR LOVE

BY
KARIN KALLMAKER

THE NAIAD PRESS, INC.
2001

Printed in the United States of America on acid-free paper
First Edition

Editor: Christine Cassidy
Cover designer: Bonnie Liss (Phoenix Graphics)

Library of Congress Cataloging-in-Publication Data

Kallmaker, Karin
    Substitute for Love
        p.   cm.
    ISBN 1-56280-265-8   (alk. paper)
    I. Title.

813'.54—dc21

*Maria, for whom there is no substitute
and to new friends*

Twelve Flowers were Their Gift To Say...

About the Author

Karin Kallmaker was born in 1960 and raised by her loving, middle-class parents in California's Central Valley. The physician's Statement of Live Birth plainly declares, "Sex: Female" and "Cry: Lusty." Both are still true.

From a normal childhood and equally unremarkable public school adolescence, she went on to obtain an ordinary Bachelor's degree from the California State University at Sacramento. At the age of 16, eyes wide open, she fell into the arms of her first and only sweetheart. Ten years later, after seeing the film *Desert Hearts*, her sweetheart descended on the Berkeley Public Library determined to find some of "those" books. "Rule, Jane" led to "Lesbianism — Fiction" and then on to book after self-affirming book by and about lesbians. These books were the encouragement Karin needed to forget the so-called "mainstream" and spin her first romance for lesbians. That manuscript became her first Naiad Press novel, *In Every Port*. She now lives in the San Francisco Bay Area with that very same sweetheart; she is a one-woman woman. The happily-ever-after couple became Mom and Moogie to Kelson James in 1995 and Eleanor Delenn in 1997. They celebrated their twenty-first anniversary in 1998.

Part 1:
Clay

Tenderness, roughness — delicacy, coarseness — sentiment, sensuality — soaring and groveling, dirt and deity — all mixed up in that one compound of inspired clay.

— Robert Burns to Lord Byron, 1813

Holly, Now

All Holly could think was, "I wanted this to happen."

Lips soft, as fragrant as her imagination. An insistent hand at her back pulled her into the embrace. Her arm wound around the smooth neck, hanging on so her senses could give way to a demanding mouth.

The music covered her moan but she knew there was no hiding the yes that swelled in her throat, a yes to a question that hadn't yet been asked. This yes tightened her spine and opened her mouth to beg for the question.

Finally, air again. She breathed deeply and was dizzy while her body responded to a knowing caress of her shoulder blades, her ribs, forward, until her breasts ached with yes.

In her ear, over the music and the throbbing of her pulse, the question at last. "Do you want to go someplace where we can be alone?"

She nodded. The hand at her back guided her toward the door, but she stopped abruptly. Looking up, into fathomless eyes the color of melting ice, she murmured, "I don't know your name."

She had to repeat herself with her lips brushing against the warmth of a pale earlobe.

Those endless eyes regarded her for a long moment, as if struggling with a decision. Then breath at Holly's ear sent a shock wave of gooseflesh down her spine.

"My name is Reyna."

1

Holly, 2 months earlier

Rain spattered against the window again and Holly
Markham glanced away from her work to consider the
storm's severity. High winds, streaming rain — a typical
southern California winter storm. An inconvenience, but
nothing more than that.

She took a moment to watch drops merging and
separating as they wandered down the pane. It seemed like
a random dance, but she amused herself by considering
what equation would express the movement of raindrops
down glass, taking into account the variable wind velocity,

the accumulation of grime, and the mass of each drop. Very few things in nature were truly random.

With a sense of minor reluctance, she returned her attention to the actuarial data spread over her desk. It wasn't nearly as fascinating as raindrop patterns, but anything to do with numbers never failed to hold her interest. Average medical expense for the most common workplace accidents, geographic incidence and regional health care prices were just a few of the variables that help set Alpha Indemnity's's worker's compensation insurance policy pricing. Clay characterized her job as the underbelly of modern business. He was right. But it paid very well and made use of her bachelor's degree in mathematics. She was not defined by her job. It was just a necessary evil.

A shadow blocked the light on her paperwork and she glanced up.

"The great man needs you. Same old, same old." Tori had a stack of new printouts under one arm. Holly recognized them as the growing presentation deck for the pricing committee's semi-annual meeting. It had been originally scheduled to be sent out next week, but late last night the deadline had been brought forward to tomorrow. Tori was swamped.

"I'll be right there. Have some M&Ms," she suggested, gesturing at the candy dish on her desk. Tori's expressive brown eyes were full of stress.

"Thanks." She munched appreciatively. "I don't remember it ever being this hard to break in a new actuary."

Holly shrugged. "His tension level is a bit high, isn't it?" She'd noticed Jim Felker's tendency to go into a tailspin every time some piece of information was unexpected, no matter how trivial or how easily resolved. Tori, in particular, had come in for more than her fair share of reprints and verifications.

"I'd give anything for your little trick with the numbers." Tori took a couple more M&Ms and headed for her desk.

Holly fortified herself with a few of the little chocolate pills and walked up the row of cubicles to Jim's office. Of

6

all the failings Clay had helped her overcome, chocolate — the miraculous fusion of sugar, caffeine and fat — was the one she'd never conquered.

Jim was in a tailspin, big time. "Holly, you just have to look at this mess. None of these arrays look right to me." What hair Jim had stood on end. His black-rimmed glasses were askew.

She examined the columns for a few minutes. Jim at least knew when to leave her alone. Arrays of numbers, grouped in regional sequences and presented with corresponding standard deviations — it was the simplest of math functions. Finally, she said, "The totals are fine. They seem reasonable based on the inputs."

"How can that be? Look at this column. Fifty items, everything starts with one and yet the total is nearly one hundred. That just doesn't make sense."

Patience — her one virtue that Clay agreed she had in plenty — came easy to Holly. "It's like the total at the warehouse store. I could get ten items, all of them under ten dollars. Statistically, given an even spread in the array with the assumption that nothing is under four dollars, I'd expect my total to be around one standard deviation — sixty-five to seventy-five. But it's always pushing ninety. That's because the spread isn't even. The items are under ten, but by pennies instead of dollars. So my total is statistically high."

Jim was looking at her as if she were telling him a long, involved anecdote about a vacation she'd taken as a child.

She pointed at the array Jim was using as an example. "The array is unusually weighted on the upper end. That's what seems strange to me. You've got very few one-point-ones and a lot of one-point-nines." It was no surprise to her that medical costs continued to rise on a per injury basis.

"So Tori didn't pull the right data?" He made a noise under his breath and shook his head. "Some people . . ."

"The download descriptors look right to me," Holly said quickly. "But these units might be moving up in a trend. Which means next quarter they could go up over two."

He made a note, but so quickly he almost caught Holly

rolling her eyes. He was the actuary — he was the one who was supposed to wonder why data was unexpected, not just assume that the totals on the report were wrong.

She smiled sweetly. "Did you need anything else?"

He gestured crossly at a stack of papers. "All these reports need to be reverified. I'll get Tori to do it. Maybe she'll get it right this time."

Poor Tori, Holly thought. "Do you want me to look through them? Maybe they don't all have to be reverified."

"No, no, they're all wrong. If she spent more time on her job than her personal life she might learn something."

Holly didn't quite know how to respond. She was the senior analyst and not exactly Tori's peer, so it didn't seem appropriate for him to be sharing his feelings about Tori's work with her. Sue was the unit manager who acted as the buffer between the actuaries' demands and the analysts' complicated statistics gathering and reporting. "I've never noticed that Tori spends much time doing anything other than work."

His expression grew conspiratorial. "Just look at the picture on her desk. It's pretty obvious what occupies her mind all the time."

Holly blinked. Whatever could he mean? Did Tori have something new on her desk? "I've always thought of her as pretty focused."

"Pretty?" He shrugged. "That's obvious, too. You have a boyfriend, right?"

Holly only had time to nod at this apparent non sequitur before his phone chirped and she was glad to leave him. She didn't know what he was referring to, but the tone had been unpleasantly shaded with dislike for something in Tori's private life. Was that why he seemed to be always on her case?

Her detour by Tori's desk to see if she could divine his insinuations was cut short by the muted hum of her Palm Pilot. She hauled it out of her trouser pocket — yikes. She was having lunch with Jo today and had nearly forgotten. She was going to be late.

She arrived at their usual restaurant only half-sodden

and was relieved to see that Jo was just settling into one of the booths they preferred.

"I was worried I was going to be late," she admitted as she dropped into the seat across from Jo.

Jo's easy smile was in full evidence. "You always say you're worried about being late. I don't know why you worry — you're always on time."

"I didn't used to be, as I'm sure you well remember," Holly reminded her. They'd known each other for eight years, since their freshman year at the Irvine campus of the University of California. Jo had known her before Clay's attempts to cure Holly of her many bad habits — among them a poor grasp of the passage of time — had shown any real success.

Maybe it was the flick of Jo's eyes to the window that warned Holly off the topic of Clay. It reminded her abruptly of how awkward last month's lunch had been when Jo announced out of the blue that she didn't want to talk about Clay anymore. Jo had never liked Clay. The feeling was mutual. But she'd never made an issue of it before.

"What do you feel like having?" Jo was studying the menu after the short silence and Holly followed her lead.

"A burger, if you promise not to tell —" She bit back *Clay* and finished, "on me."

"I won't tell." Jo was serious. "I'll never tell."

"Thanks."

They ordered and then were left to sip at their mugs of herbal tea. Holly thought of five things to say, but all of them led to the topic of Clay. Jo seemed unusually contemplative.

"How's Rod?" If they couldn't talk about her boyfriend, maybe they could talk about Jo's.

"I suppose he's fine," Jo said after a sip from her tea. "We broke up about three months ago."

Dumbfounded, Holly could only stare.

Jo answered the unspoken question. "It's not — I wasn't ready to tell you why."

Holly considered Jo one of her closest friends, even though when their schedules were busy they saw each other

9

about once a month. They'd liked each other almost immediately, and always seemed able to pick up exactly where they left off. She felt selfish for not asking about Rod the last few months and realized now it was odd that Jo hadn't mentioned him either. "And now?"

Jo shook her head with her lashes lowered.

"Is something wrong?"

The brilliant flare of Jo's smile was unexpected and it negated the tears in her eyes. "Nothing. Everything is right."

"I'm glad, then." Holly was completely sincere. "You don't have to tell me why if you don't want to."

"I'll tell you all about it — just not right now."

Reassured by the happiness in Jo's expression, Holly let it go, even though she felt unsettled by the mystery. They chatted about movies — Jo seemed to have been out a lot recently. Holly assumed she was dating again, but didn't pry because that would lead to the taboo subject of Jo's breakup. Jo was positively glowing the entire time they ate their meals.

"I can't believe you still haven't seen *Good Will Hunting*. It's been on video for ages. You're the only person I know who'd get the math." Jo pushed her unruly black curls back from her face.

"We don't watch a lot of movies." The plural slipped out before Holly caught herself. She munched on the kosher pickle and realized she'd inhaled the burger without even noticing. It never paid to skip breakfast. She eyed Jo's unfinished French fries.

"I know — you're involved in far more worthy pursuits, like reading deep books and weeding your organic cauliflower," Jo scoffed. "You ought to see it, though. You'd be rooting for the kid all the way. It won an Oscar for the writing, too, so it's not like it's crap. Here," she added, pushing her plate with the last of the French fries toward Holly. "Good thing I didn't have the grilled veggies, too, huh?"

"Thanks." She dabbed up some extra salt with a fry before biting off the end. "You haven't mentioned your dissertation — are you still waiting for a new advisor?"

10

"Yes. I had one, but then we got word that her entire department is being cut at spring semester. The war on public education never stops."

"That's terrible," Holly sympathized. "Now what are you going to do?"

Jo frowned at her tea. "Shit, I don't know. I'm glad I'm teaching part-time because it keeps the roof over my head. Hey, did you know the part-timers are starting a union? It's ridiculous that we don't have representation like the full-time staff. There are more of us."

"Maybe that will make a difference." It seemed to Holly that Jo was in a constant state of flux in her teaching job in the business department at U.C. Irvine, and certainly Clay fared no better in social science at Cal State Fullerton. She'd tell him about the unionizing at Irvine because it was something he would definitely be interested in. Part-timers' schedules were always being changed, classes added or taken away, or the number of students doubled or halved, all without notice.

"I don't have a lot of hope," Jo admitted. "But something has to give. They just keep firing the tenured people and expecting someone like me to provide the same quality classroom experience. It really cheats the students, particularly the undergrads. This is the University of California, for God's sake. Not to mention that us part-timers are treated like widgets, getting stuffed into whatever hole happens to appear. They wanted me to teach business statistics next semester."

Holly choked on her tea. "You?"

"Yeah — as if economics and business law are the same thing as statistics. Now you — I bet you could walk in the door, with no preparation, and teach a stat class to perfection."

Holly sincerely doubted that. "I'm way out of practice."

"Toss a coin two hundred and fifty times. What's the longest run of heads you're likely to get?"

"Seven. Why?"

Jo was shaking her head with a mixture of awe and pity. "It took me ninety minutes to figure that out last night. It was the first question on the first test I'd give to a stat class. And that's just business stat. I turned it down this morning. For someone out of practice ..."

"I just remembered the answer, that's all. It's a basic question." She calculated the tip, rounded up to the next dollar and added her own bills to Jo's to settle the check.

Jo pursed her lips. "You roll a die a hundred times. What's the likelihood that one number on the die will never come up?"

"One time in one hundred sets of one hundred throws." Holly was getting irritated. "What's your point?"

"My point is that you could be teaching — you could be on the road to research grants, publishing, mathematics department chair in any number of colleges. If you finished your Ph.D., Irvine would be wet for you — even Berkeley would be. And that's just two public schools. The private schools would be just as eager, and that's before any of them know you can also write an enlightening, engaging monograph when it suits you. You are the most patient person I know. You'd make a great teacher. Forget college, think what you could do in a high school. Teachers have more profound impact on a single life than any movie or book, than art, even. Think of how you could be living proof to the girls that women can be good at math."

Jo had to know she was on dangerous ground. Jo was the one who hadn't wanted to talk about Clay. Her silence must have warned Jo she'd gone too far.

"I'm sorry," she said gently. "I know your aunt tried to beat into you that math was unladylike. That having a brain would cost you any hope of getting a man."

"I got over it, you know," Holly said intensely. "You know I did."

"Yeah," Jo said, her voice quiet. "You stopped listening to your aunt. But in the end, didn't Clay tell you the same thing?"

Holly's tongue felt dry as sandpaper when she answered. "I don't want to fight about Clay. That is not what he told me."

Jo leaned forward suddenly, her eyes bright with an anger that surprised Holly. "What was his line? That math was anti-humanist? That the master's degree and Ph.D. you could have had from MIT were just 'illusory pursuits, pseudo-education'? But did he ever suggest you pursue some other educational field? Was his real problem that you were virtually guaranteed your doctorate when he hadn't been able to finish his dissertation in four years of trying? He never did finish it, did he? He has nothing but disdain for the practicality of mathematics but I assume he enjoys your paycheck just fine."

Holly slid out of the booth and didn't look back. She didn't want to listen. It was as if she didn't know Jo anymore.

Her umbrella was nearly useless in the wind, but she put it up anyway. The roar in her ears drowned out Jo's voice until Jo was right behind her.

"I'm sorry, Holly. I didn't mean to let it all out like that."

Holly kept walking toward her car. It was only when she had her key in the lock that she found her voice. "It sounded like you'd been holding that in for a long time."

"I have. I'm sorry because I know I hurt you."

"Do you really think so little of me?"

"No — of him. He's so . . . no. I've said plenty."

Holly turned to face Jo. Their umbrellas tangled in the wind and rain splashed across their faces. "He's made me a better person."

Jo bit her lower lip, then said steadily, "That's debatable. I'm sorry," she said again, when Holly began to protest. "I'm being a bitch, but listen. Do me a favor, okay?"

Holly nodded tightly.

Jo wrested their umbrellas apart. "I want you to see if you can go thirty minutes without saying, doing or thinking something and then wondering if Clay would approve."

Holly's lips trembled, and she knew that Jo would not mistake her tears for rain. "I don't know if I want to see you again."

Jo looked stricken. "Then I really am sorry." Her lips trembled. "I'll wait to hear from you then."

Holly had her door open when Jo spoke again.

"I thought I loved Rod, but then I grew up."

Holly glanced up, puzzled, but after a searching gaze, Jo hurried away.

A pall hung over the office when she returned to work, but she didn't notice it until she was seated at her desk. The scene with Jo had left her head spinning with . . . anger, mostly. Jo had no right to judge her relationship with Clay. Jo didn't understand. Nothing she had said was true.

She entered her computer password without noticing the unnatural silence and was confronted by more than a dozen instant message screens. Then she realized the only audible sounds were the beeps that heralded the messages.

She flicked through the screens with horror. Everyone wanted to know what she thought of the fact that Tori had just been fired.

She slipped down the silent row of cubicles to find Tori.

Tori was obviously trying not to cry, but her eyes glittered with angry tears.

Holly pitched her voice low. "What happened?"

"I missed the mail deadline on the presentation," Tori snapped, making no effort to avoid being overheard. "I was only told last night that it had to go today. And two hours ago he tells me to reverify everything and it's still supposed to go in the afternoon pouch. Which is impossible. Then he tells me I've had plenty of opportunities to figure out how he works and I'm not catching on. After four years, here's two weeks' severance and get out."

"I can't believe it." Tori had worked successfully with at least a dozen different actuaries. Jim Felker was the first one who had had problems with the quality of her work.

"Neither can I." Tori picked up the photograph she'd had on her desk since New Year's and added it to the others in the box she was packing.

With a sense of detached horror, Holly stared down at the picture. She'd studied it when she'd first noticed it because Tori looked fabulous. It had been taken at a New Year's Eve soiree, and she and Geena were both dressed to the nines, Tori in an evening gown that highlighted generous curves and Geena in black pantsuit that glittered with sequins. Geena's arm rested casually around Tori's waist and they looked happy and relaxed. The picture had been there for several weeks now, replacing an old one of the two of them in hiking gear. It was the only picture on her desk. What on earth had Jim Felker been referring to earlier?

With a sick sensation in her stomach, Holly put two and two together. God — he had meant Geena. He had described Tori as obsessed with her private life because Tori was gay.

"Did he . . . say anything else?"

"He said sometimes people just aren't compatible. He thought I'd be more . . . comfortable . . . elsewhere. Some-place other than fascist Orange County, I'm sure."

"Shit." Holly was willing to bet that the driver had thought Rosa Parks would be more comfortable in the back of the bus. She was well aware that Orange County was overwhelmingly conservative, but there was finally a state law that banned discrimination in employment against gays. How was Jim Felker going to get away with this? Where was Sue?

Tori looked at her sharply, then nodded. "Yeah, that's what I figure. I thought it was okay to be out, even in our little corner of California. I've been out the whole time. He's the one who's new. And it's not like I spend much time talking about my private life — not like some people." She sent a bitter gaze in the direction of Diane's cubicle. Diane was notorious for talking about her last tryst and devoting hours to arranging her next one. In Holly's opin-ion, Diane ought to have been reined in long ago. She'd said as much to Sue during a quarterly review. Diane wasn't half as productive as Tori.

She realized then that she would be the one expected to train Tori's replacement. She'd be the one reviewing all of the newcomer's work for three months.

It wasn't fair. Holly knew the inconvenience to her was nothing compared to what Tori was going through. None of it was fair.

"Don't leave until I get back," she told Tori.

As she walked toward Jim's office she knew what she

was going to do. She made up her mind all in an instant and then had the gratifying thought that Clay, for once, would applaud her lapse into spontaneous action.

She entered Jim's office without knocking. That was a first for her. She surprised Sue, their unit manager, in the midst of an angry exchange with a mulish-looking Jim. "Would anyone like my opinion?"

Sue didn't answer until the office door had closed. Then she pushed back the gray lock that had escaped from her habitual tight bun. "Holly, I know you're probably upset, but employee relations don't come under your purview —"

"Except when I have to help hire, train and manage the new person. You're throwing away someone who is very good at what she does, regardless of what the new kid on the block thinks." Holly was breathing hard and unsure where her courage was coming from. But she would not back down.

Sue, normally unflappable, seemed to be having a hard time controlling her temper as well. "As I *said*, this matter does not concern you."

"He shouldn't have the authority to fire her. That has always been a screwed-up policy. The analysts report to you, but an actuary can fire any of us."

"She missed an important deadline," Jim pronounced.

"An impossible deadline she only knew about for less than a day. And you had her reverifying data I offered to check over." She turned to Sue. "He fired her because she's gay. Anything else is just crap."

Sue favored Jim with a look that said she'd happily supervise torture designed just for him. She turned resolutely back to Holly. "Work quality has suffered."

Dumbfounded by Sue's defense of what Jim had done, Holly said with her last bit of patience, "Think about it statistically, Sue. One actuary in the more than dozen Tori has worked with finds problems with her work. Logically, the problem lies with the actuary, not with Tori."

Jim came to life. "That's dangerously close to insubordination."

"Are you going to fire me, too?"

"I don't know why you're defending her." Jim's whining

tone grated on Holly's last nerve. "It's not as if you're like her. You're normal. People like us shouldn't have to put up with her constant reminders about her sex life."

"In the four years I've worked with her, Tori has never referred to her sex life. Diane, however, spent a year in a work-hours-only cybersex relationship with some guy in accounting. A fact which I mentioned to you, Sue. Diane still works here, getting full-time pay for half-time productivity."

Sue was near an exploding point. She knew Sue had been with Alpha Indemnity for nearly thirty years, and yet Holly had never heard of Sue losing it over anything. "None of this is relevant — "

"I'll testify for Tori if she wants to get a lawyer. This is discrimination, plain and simple."

Jim said smugly, "It'll be hard to find a sympathetic judge for her kind in Orange County. She was tardy twice this month, too."

Sue slapped her hand down on his desk. "Will you just *be quiet*!" She swallowed hard and turned a steely gaze on Holly. "For the last time, this does not concern you."

"Tardy? What kind of joke is that? We all work late all the time!" Holly took a deep breath. This was unbelievable. She could hear Clay urging her on. It was the right thing to do. Talking to Felker wouldn't get her anywhere. She gave Sue one last try. "I've always respected you, Sue. I know it's not easy managing a group of highly paid, know-it-all professionals, but you do it well. Until now, you've managed to keep the relationships between us analysts and the actuaries calm. But this is too much. I can't believe you don't see how wrong it is. Tardy — that's just crap and you know it."

Sue said nothing, though her lips worked with anger and frustration. They shared a long gaze. Holly suddenly felt as if an equation she hadn't realized was incomplete had solved itself in her head. Sue the spinster, with no visible private life. Solve for the simplest answer.

More gently, Holly said, "Maybe you do." Something new flared in Sue's gaze. She's afraid, Holly realized. Tori is expendable as long as her secret is safe. "Maybe that makes you worse than he is."

Sue's mouth thinned to a pale line. "Don't make this harder, Holly."

Holly dismissed Jim with a flick of her eyes. "I'll make it simpler. She goes, I go."

2

Among Aunt Zinnia's many rules for the comportment of girls and women was: "Threats are promises. Decent women keep their promises."

Holly had made a threat and she had carried it out. With dignity and pride, she told herself.

"You didn't have to go and get yourself fired." Tori stared fixedly out the passenger window as they drove toward Tori's home in nearby Costa Mesa. One hand nervously fiddled with a hanging thread that had resulted when her sweater sleeve had snagged on something deep in her file cabinet. Sweaters can be replaced, Holly thought, but not one that so precisely matched the smoky topaz of Tori's eyes. Aunt Zinnia would categorize Tori's fashion sense as "smart," her second-highest compliment. The top was "classy," which was reserved for royalty and Jackie O. Holly had never achieved either level.

"Technically, I wasn't fired. I resigned." Holly turned up the wiper speed and slowed down a little. "Besides, you needed a ride home."

She meant it as a joke, but Tori shot her a guilty look. "Now I feel even worse."

"I'm teasing. I had no idea you were commuting with Geena. What were you going to do, wait in the lobby for three or four hours?"

"Geena could pick me up early —" The rest of Tori's answer was cut short by the chirp of her cell phone. "Finally! That has to be her."

Holly had no choice but to listen, though she pretended to be wholly absorbed in driving.

"I'm so glad you called — oh honey . . ." Tori choked. "I got fired. That fucking bastard Felker, that's who. I think I will — do you still know that lawyer? Holly says he was making all these remarks about us. Holly — Markham, yeah, the math whiz. You won't believe this — you still there? It's always bad when it rains. Anyway, she quit in protest. She's driving me home. No. No, I'm sure. Not family. Oh God, honey, I can't believe this is happening . . ."

She wouldn't be able to tell Clay about it until later tonight, even though he was probably home by now. His Thursday schedule was light. It wasn't exactly news she wanted to give over the phone. After she left Tori's she had a scheduled duty call on Aunt Zinnia. She stifled a grin. Aunt Zinnia would be appalled that Holly had quit over such a matter. I probably shouldn't be feeling quite so happy, Holly told herself. This is a tragedy for Tori. But it felt like a triumph to her.

Tori directed her to a 1920s bungalow not far from the 405 in northern Costa Mesa. She accepted the offer of coffee — they'd both gotten soaked putting their boxes in the backseat and trunk. Holly could not believe that she'd accumulated so much junk in six years. To add to their chill, her old Taurus had stopped providing heat a few weeks earlier. It really was time for a new car, but she hadn't yet broached the subject to Clay. Clay had strong feelings about buying something new when the old thing could be repaired. One of those sixty-five-miles-to-the-gallon hybrid cars was awfully appealing. Of course, being unemployed, perhaps it was not the best use of her savings right now. Clay was right, fixing the heater would be much cheaper and more responsible to the planet.

"You want to make that coffee Irish?" Tori hefted a slender bottle into view. "I've got some whipped cream, I think."

"Sure, why not?" Spontaneity seemed to be the watchword of the day. Red meat, alcohol and quitting her job; she was racking up quite a list. They sipped companionably and talked about everything except what had just happened. Holly was amazed that pressing research problems she'd been pursuing, that had seemed so important to complete, no longer mattered at all to her. She had walked away without a backward glance, at least where the work was concerned. The work was Sue's problem now.

She would miss her co-workers — the Friday night ice cream socials they had in the summer, the Wednesday afternoon popcorn parties. Monday morning she'd be craving the special high-caffeine blend they'd perfected just for the beginning of the work week. She would miss the birth of Romy's baby and the big celebration they'd been planning for Jamillah's retirement. She had e-mail addresses and phone numbers. She would make an effort to keep in touch. As she left, she'd also made a point of formally saying good-bye to everybody. Ng and Liz had been in tears while Sue had looked on, more grim with each passing moment.

"We'll both be able to find new jobs — I bet within a week," Holly observed when Tori began to look depressed again.

"I know — but I liked Alpha because it was so close to home. But now I'm leery of working for any of the other local companies. Felker belongs to the actuary society. What if he tries to get me blackballed?"

Holly said honestly, "I wouldn't put it past him. He was

21

always hinting that there was something wrong with you. Not your work, but you. I was too obtuse to put two and two together. For me, pretty ironic."

Tori's eyes filled with angry tears. "Bastard. What does he know about me? So I sleep with a woman. Does he know I also support my dad? Does he care that I have a house payment to make and that I'm still paying off my student loans?"

"He doesn't care. Once he realized you were a lesbian that's all he could see. Everything you did was tainted by it."

"Shit — I mean, most of the time, minute-to-minute, I forget I'm gay. I mean, I'm just not thinking about it all the time. Like I don't think about the fact that I'm blond either. I just am. Okay — every payday when I saw the taxes I paid because I got Geena's health insurance through Alpha I thought about it because it made me mad, it's so unfair. Damn — her insurance, too. I'll need to find a place where I can insure her. After COBRA runs out I wouldn't want her to be stuck with the crappy university health insurance."

"Tell me about it." Geena and Clay worked at different colleges, in different state-regulated systems, but the benefits were all the same for part-time instructors. It was probably just as well that she'd never added Clay to her benefits as her domestic partner. It would have saved them some money, but Clay was intellectually opposed to unnecessarily registering with any kind of government agency, and they couldn't get the coverage unless they registered as domestic partners.

"There was a really gay-friendly company in West Hollywood that wanted me, but that commute is horrible. It's two hours each way on the four-oh-five. Geena might be able to change colleges — there's UCLA and Cal State Long Beach, though it would be a step down to leave the U.C. system for Cal State. Not when she's so close to tenure. Oh." Tori stopped abruptly. "No offense, sorry."

Holly smiled reassuringly. "It's the truth, and Clay knows it. University of California standards are higher and it looks better on a résumé. I went to Irvine because my mother did. Clay went there, too. But he's happy teaching at Fullerton. He knows if he wanted to teach at Irvine then he would have to finally finish the dissertation, but I think he feels it's too late to keep up with the publish or perish requirements. Too many arbitrary academic hoops to jump through."

"Isn't that the truth? Geena went through hell. Writing papers was always easy, until her dissertation, then she just hit a wall. She told me once she felt like she was bleeding every word onto the page and all without knowing if anyone would take it seriously. But she finally finished and got her doctorate. She hates the publish or perish thing, but she loves teaching and research."

"Clay really loves the teaching. He's very devoted to his students — lots of office hours, molding young minds, and all that." The Irish coffee was chasing away the chill.

"Yeah, that's what Geena gets off on. I just wouldn't want to uproot her, not for a job."

"You'll find something ideal. You're too good not to." Holly tried to be reassuring. "I don't know if it would help but I'd be glad to give you a reference."

Tori visibly tried to calm herself. "Thanks. I may need it. I just don't want to move. I don't want to be that far from my dad. I like to stop by a couple of times a week, just to check on him."

"You shouldn't have to live someplace special to be treated like everyone else," Holly said.

Tori blinked. "That's very enlightened. If only everyone thought the way you do."

Holly shrugged. She'd never really thought about what gay people had to put up with it, but she was sympathetic. It had always seemed to her that the rights of gay people were restricted only because of other people's religious convictions. That wasn't supposed to the way things worked in this country. "It just seems fair."

There was a bustle at the front door and Geena hurried in. "Oh, baby, I'm so sorry . . ."

Tori began to cry in earnest, angry and hurt tears. Holly turned her gaze away from their embrace because it was an intimate thing, Geena's arm wrapped firmly around

Tori's waist, Tori's forehead pressed into Geena's shoulder, as if they were meant to fit exactly like that.

She stood up to go, both because she wanted to give them privacy and because it was time to weather both the traffic and the storm to reach her aunt's.

Geena was wiping Tori's tears away with her thumbs. "We'll be fine, you know that."

Tori took a deep breath. "I'm not crying over it anymore. Bastard. And Sue! I can't believe she didn't stand up for me, either. Just Holly." She sniffed.

Geena gave Holly a taut smile. "Thank you for driving her home. I left as soon as I could."

"You can't exactly walk out on a class," Holly acknowledged. "It was no problem. But I have to get going."

"Have lunch with me tomorrow," Tori said suddenly. "We can talk job-hunting strategies. And I won't be depressed at having nothing to do. One o'clock at Tish's. It's near Culver and Walnut."

"Okay," Holly said. "Let me give you my number so you can call if something comes up." She had not given any thought to what she would do with her tomorrows.

She tucked Tori's phone number in her pocket and took her leave. Running through the rain to the car, she realized she could literally do anything she wanted until she found a new job. Anything at all. She would have to ask Clay for some ideas.

The 405 was a parking lot, so Holly decided to traipse up Harbor Boulevard all the way to Garden Grove, where Aunt Zinnia had lived for at least the last thirty years. National Public Radio didn't hold her interest, and flipping radio channels just bounced her from commercial to commercial. She dug out cassette tapes as she drove, dismissing one after another as just not quite right for her mood. It was going to be a boring drive.

She was so distracted she didn't merge out of a right-turn-only lane in time and was forced to go around the block to resume her northward journey. It seemed like fate when she noticed the books-and-music store just up ahead. She got rained on yet again, but the store was steaming warm. She left a half-hour later with two new cassettes, a replacement copy of *The Mathematical Tourist* — the binding on her old one had finally disintegrated past saving — and a decaf coffee concoction so thick with cream it was like drinking a hot milkshake. Loaded with refined sugar, she noted to herself. Deeee-licious. Burger, alcohol, refined sugar, quitting her job. The list of chaos was getting longer by the minute.

She slipped the Gypsy Kings cassette into the player and turned it up as loud as the Taurus's tinny speakers could manage. Spanish guitar virtuosity combined with unstoppable rhythm had her slapping the steering wheel as she drove.

She could not remember being so energized and happy in a very long while. She turned her mind to searching out a memory of previous highs like this one and had to go back much further than she had imagined. Six years ago? Yes, six. They'd been lovers by then for about two years. It had been Clay's idea to join an eco-tour of Death Valley and the surrounding wilderness.

They had been backpacking for two days in a group of eight, plus the guide, leaving the valley floor finally for the red-dirt foothills that yielded eventually to the Sierra Nevada mountains. Toward dusk their guide called a halt and she had dropped where she stood, not quite ready to tackle opening out the small tent that she and Clay shared. She was enjoying the trip, but she ached, every inch of her, and she felt like a soft, city girl. Which is what she was. But she was trying to become more, and Clay was committed to helping her.

Clay looked as if he could have hiked another fifty miles. Even the guide, Kevin, looked more tired than Clay did. Clay ambled up the hill for a little bit, and called down that the view of the valley floor was even better.

"We made good time, people," Kevin announced. "We're a good two hours beyond where we usually get to on the second day, so I brought us around through this pass because of the view. It's very important tonight for you to check for and treat any walking blisters — there's plenty of antibiotic ointment. We'll get to water early tomorrow, so don't hoard it tonight. Dehydration is a serious threat."

Holly wearily unzipped her pack and wished that Clay would come back. He was shouldering their water and she was thirsty. Suddenly the guide hollered at someone, "Look out!" Then a cry of pain had them all exclaiming and turning.

The rattlesnake smashed into a tree not far from where Holly sat. Kevin was staring at his stomach in stunned surprise, then slowly he lifted his shirt to confront the two puncture wounds.

"Oh, my God!" Jerri tended to hysteria, but Holly didn't begrudge her, not when she was feeling faint herself. The echo of the crack as the thrown snake smashed into the tree was louder than the pounding of her heart. Jerri was gasping out, "I'm so sorry, I didn't see it on the boulder — he stepped right in the way." The last to her husband, who clutched her close to him.

Clay came running from the hilltop and was urging Kevin to stay calm. Another man grabbed the guide's battery-powered CB radio and followed Kevin's instructions. In minutes they were patched through to air search and rescue. Kevin began to shiver, but he managed to tell Clay how to administer the anti-venom and they all waited for the welcome thrum of a helicopter.

Only it didn't come. They took turns signaling with a mirror into the sun, and the rescue teams still couldn't find them. They weren't where they were supposed to be. In spite of the anti-venom, Kevin had quickly slipped into unconsciousness without telling them the name of the pass they were in.

"It's just a matter of time until they find us," Holly tried to tell Jerri. "They have to expand the radius of the search, that's all. When the sun goes down we can build a fire."

"Does anyone have matches?" Clay asked the question heavily, as if he feared the answer.

Kevin had an emergency supply of them, even though

fires were illegal in this part of the wilderness, for reasonable fear of forest fires. The wind began to rise.

The sun went down and Kevin grew more feverish. "It's just a matter of time," Holly kept telling herself. But how much time, and would it be soon enough for Kevin?

Their signal torches all went out in the wind in spite of the tinder-like condition of the scrub. Jerri's husband was reporting in to the frustrated pilot that he still could not hear any sounds of a helicopter. A second helicopter was on its way from Edwards Air Force Base, but the time was slipping away. They had two cell phones among them, but they received no signal, and wouldn't have been much help anyway.

The stars came out, with a sudden sharpness that was unknown nearer to civilization. There were so many of them, including the North Star, Polaris, glittering magnificently. It was of no help — they had a compass and knowing where north was wasn't enough. They needed to know where true west was. What they really needed, Holly thought, was a mariner's sextant. A couple of readings, a little calculation, and they would know their longitude and latitude. Until the advent of radar, it was how all travelers knew where they were.

She felt far away, suddenly, and her mind was digging through all her geometry texts, every article she could remember. The angle — it was the angle, doubled, that would tell them where any given star was with respect to the horizon. And you could find the angle through multiple reflections of overlapping star and horizon.

"Is there another mirror?" She startled Clay, who was leaning against her back.

"What do you need a mirror for?"

"Not one, two. I need two mirrors. And Jerri." She scrambled to her feet, putting the shallow sound of Kevin's breathing out of her mind. She needed to focus.

Jerri was on the trip to stargaze — astronomy was her hobby. She had a complete guide to the stars in her pack.

"Holly, what *are* you talking about?"

"A sextant — we can make one of our own."

Jerri, who had been miserably silent for the last while, spoke up excitedly. "Yes, oh yes, that would work. I'll need a flashlight to read the star map." They had been sparing the batteries so they would have signals when they finally did hear the helicopters.

Jerri's pocket telescope worked for one of the arms, and a pen for the other. Working quickly with first aid tape, Holly bound the mirrors to the arms and then set the arms to form a wedge that was about an eighth of a circle. She would have to be more precise about the angle later, when it was crucial. Using the eyebrow pencil that Jerri sheepishly produced, she drew an X across each mirror to pinpoint their centers. The star reflecting the horizon reflecting the star reflecting the horizon — when that happened in the center of each mirror, the resulting angle between the mirrors, doubled, provided longitude and latitude. But it would only be as accurate as her approximation of the angle. It had worked for Thomas Godfrey 300 years ago and it would work for her.

"Are you sure you know what you're doing?" Clay was whispering. "You're getting everyone's hopes up."

"We'll have to go to the top of the hill. We need a good bit of horizon for the horizon glass. The more readings we can take, the more likely they can triangulate." The parts of a sextant were coming back to her as her mind rescued more and more of what she had read.

"When did you learn this?"

Abruptly, she was afraid to tell him. She was certain she knew how to figure out where they were, but she wasn't sure he would believe her. "Seventh grade," she admitted. "It was in a geometry book I got at the library."

"You were never even tested on the material? What if you're wrong? You could send them the wrong way."

"I know. But I don't think I'm wrong."

"But what if you are? I know you have this gift for numbers, but navigation is hardly the same thing."

"It *is* the same thing," Holly answered. Her voice shook with certainty. "The very same thing. I can do this."

"Based on something you read when you were what, twelve?"

"Eleven. It was just before my mother died. I remember it," she insisted. She turned her back on him to start the hike up the hill.

Jerri's husband came with them, bringing the radio. Jerri picked a star and Holly used the telescope to focus on the horizon, then adjusted the pen arm until the reflection of the horizon and the reflection of the star crossed in the mirrors. Jerri's husband radioed in the name of the star and Holly's estimate of the angle the two arms formed.

After a few readings to the pilot they were patched onward to a very excited radar officer at Edwards who knew exactly what they were trying to do. He radioed back when a reading seemed to fall outside of the circle he was marking on his map, and they would take another.

And then they heard the distant *throp-throp* and it seemed like only minutes before they were exultantly slipping and sliding down the hillside toward their camp, now illuminated by the searchlight of the waiting helicopter.

A paramedic was already trying to help Kevin. The co-pilot beamed at the three of them. "Who's the lady with the sextant?"

Holly held it aloft like a victor's trophy. That was the memory she loved, the last time she had felt so sure that she had done the right thing and was thrilled simply to be alive. She shared a spontaneous high-five with the co-pilot and basked in his enthusiastic, "Excellent work!"

Somewhere she still had the note from Kevin thanking her again, for he was certain that she had saved his life. She had kept the makeshift sextant, too, but it had been years since she'd seen it.

She had not thought about that day for a long time. She wasn't sure that she had realized before how dubious Clay had been about her abilities. She had known exactly what she was doing and he hadn't trusted her yet. Today, she was certain, he would have no doubt. She had done the right thing in resigning. It had been a spontaneous but ethical decision, rooted in her values, not just quick action prompted by a special skill she possessed. She had stood up for Tori because her code of morality said she should. And that was something Clay would understand because he had taught her to do so.

From high to low. Holly had to sit for a minute at the curb, clearing her mind for the imminent conversation with her aunt. Conversation between them inevitably led to confrontation, but Holly had, for the last few years, managed to avoid the harsh exchanges that had been so prevalent in her teenage years. She reminded herself that it couldn't have been easy for her aunt to have taken in a child she'd never expected to care for, an eleven-year-old made sullen by grief.

She felt the gentle, familiar tide of that grief, still. Lily Markham had been killed in a laboratory explosion while working on a research project on alternative energy sources. Holly had vivid memories of her vivacious mother, but they had softened with time and love. No amount of concentration would make the colors bright again. It struck her then that she was the same age her mother had been when she'd been born. Her mother had been a relative rarity twenty-six years ago: a never-married woman with a child. Her mother told her that getting pregnant had been an accident but finding out she was going to have a baby had been one of the happiest moments in her life. She never told Holly who her father was and Holly hadn't been old enough to yearn for that knowledge by the time her mother died.

A live electrical source, supposed by everyone to be disconnected, had sparked, igniting a tank of compressed natural gas. Her mother and six other lab workers were instantly killed in the explosion, and three more people died in the resulting fire. That night, Holly had moved from the only house she remembered living in, but Aunt Zinnia only lived six blocks away. Grandmother Rose had been failing, and although Great-Aunt Daisy was much healthier, she had never learned to drive. Everyone agreed that sooner or later,

Holly would need to be driven somewhere. Aunt Zinnia, a comfortable widow six years older than her dead sister, was the only one who could take her in and give her a relatively normal childhood and adolescence. Within weeks she was transferred from her mother's to her aunt's choice of school and nothing was the same except for the familiar neighborhood.

Aunt Zinnia married Uncle Bernard a year later. He was a silent, withdrawn man who found it easier to work long hours as an accountant than to face his wife's caustic tongue. Holly might have found in him an ally, because misery loves its own company, but he hardly spoke to her. He died almost two years to the day of the wedding. Aunt Zinnia barely grieved. Only now did Holly ask herself why they had married when love seemed so clearly not a part of the equation.

For a long time she thought she was the problem. Uncle Bernard didn't like it when Aunt Zinnia slapped her, that had been evident. But he never spoke up about it. Only once, she remembered, when her aunt had been telling her how clumsy she was, Uncle Bernard said vaguely, "Leave the girl alone, Zinnia."

As she grew older, she was aware that her aunt's harsh discipline had stemmed from an abiding disagreement with her dead sister about what decent women do and don't do. Decent women attend college, but they don't get advanced degrees, and certainly not in something as unfeminine as organic sciences. College, Aunt Zinnia told Holly time and again, was for finding a suitable husband. Barring that, it should provide a useful skill for a woman to fall back on, like teaching or nursing.

Her mother had gone to college but had refused perfectly acceptable suitors, then decided to have a child, on her own. Aunt Zinnia had been determined that Holly would not follow in her mother's footsteps.

The lectures, deprivations, spankings and slaps hadn't, in the end, had much success. Holly pursued a bachelor's degree in mathematics and moved in with Clay when she was nineteen, and decent women didn't do either of those things.

Clay said that Holly wasted a lot of energy maintaining some semblance of an adult relationship with Aunt Zinnia, and he didn't really understand why she kept trying. He had serious differences with his own parents and saw them only at family events, and never with Holly along. She found it harder to walk away from people. She knew she didn't want Aunt Zinnia's acknowledgment that her parenting had been cruel and unfeeling most of the time — she didn't need it. She supposed that she kept up contact because Aunt Zinnia would sometimes, reluctantly, speak of sister Lily, and Holly would feel close to her mother for a few minutes.

Jumping over puddles, she made it to the front porch without soaking her shoes further, but she still shucked them off while she waited for her aunt to answer the door. Muddy feet were not permitted inside.

"Oh," Aunt Zinnia said. "It's you."

And we're off! Holly decided that nothing was going to ruin her good mood. She still had Gypsy Kings music surging through her veins. "It's me. Have I got the day wrong?"

"No, I suppose not. Come in, then."

Not surprised or deterred by Aunt Zinnia's lack of enthusiasm, Holly bounced inside and accepted the offer of a cup of tea. Her aunt dined early and Holly had deliberately timed her arrival for after dinner. A cup of tea meant she would be staying for approximately thirty minutes, which was how long a cup of tea could be expected to divert them.

"Did you get someone to patch the gazebo roof?" It was a safe topic, and her aunt discussed the affair at length, expressing decided views about the shoddiness of the workmanship regardless of the outrageous sum that had been charged.

"It doesn't leak, at least not right now. I'm sure it will next year. Used to be when you wanted something repaired you could call someone named Murphy or Kroger, but now it's nothing but Gonzales and Yee, and most of the time you have to draw a picture to communicate. None of them speak a word of English."

Holly listened to her aunt's casual racism and said nothing. She'd given up on changing her aunt's attitude about two years ago. They'd had much more amicable meetings since. An inner voice posed a disturbing question: You eliminated Aunt Zinnia from your efforts to make the world a better place, but what did you take up in her place? She pondered the question for a few minutes, and unwillingly remembered Jo's comments at lunch. Already it seemed a year since lunchtime. At the time she'd had no idea she would be changing jobs. She could change careers, maybe. Teaching was a noble and rewarding profession. She had a gift; it could have a productive use. She didn't have to use it to build bombs.

Her aunt's tirade was wrapping up and Holly refocused. "Do you think I should become a teacher?"

Aunt Zinnia reacted with suspicion. "Why would you ask that?"

"Because I quit my job today —"

"Whatever for? It paid so well, and you had the pension."

"Yes, but they fired a co-worker for no good reason and I quit in protest."

After a shocked pause, Aunt Zinnia shook her head in dismay. "You never look before you leap, do you? Surely you didn't have to go that far. A good-paying, stable job is a blessing. What does Clay have to say about it?"

"He doesn't know yet. But I expect he'll support me. It was the right thing to do."

"Oh, Holly. What am I going to do with you?"

Holly felt like she was twelve again. "You don't have to do anything with me."

"You're just like your mother. She never thought anything she did would reflect badly on the family, on me. She pursued her own happiness and no matter the cost to anyone else. It was selfish —"

"Please don't," Holly said sharply. "I won't listen."

"You don't know what she was like. How could you? You were just a child." Aunt Zinnia set down her cup and saucer and brushed imaginary lint from her lap. "I don't like that you and Clay live in sin, but at least he agreed

33

with me about that doctorate nonsense. You'd have ended up just like your mother, career-mad and alone. Her only religion was being unconventional."

Holly likewise set her cup down. "I won't listen to you talk about her that way." Did Aunt Zinnia really think that she and Clay had similar views on any topic? The two of them had had completely different reasons for not wanting her to pursue her math degree to its logical conclusion in a doctorate program. She heard Jo whisper, *But wasn't the end result the same?*

"It was unnatural, the way she lived for work. Going to the lab day in and day out. She didn't care where she lived."

"She lived for me, too. I remember that she told me she loved me all the time. I remember that she was beautiful."

"Not that any man would have her. She dated plenty, but turned down all the good ones who wanted to settle down. And then having a baby."

"I do have to be going," Holly said firmly. Her aunt seemed intent on nursing old wounds.

"Of course," Aunt Zinnia said automatically. As they moved toward the door, she added, "Teaching is a good profession for a woman. You can have great success and still be female."

Holly gestured at her curves, perpetually fifteen pounds too lush. "I don't think anyone thinks otherwise."

"You know what I mean. These days — women in jeans at work, wearing such unattractive footwear, no regard for style. They all look like gardeners." Her look dismissed Holly as a member of that group.

Holly squeezed her toes, appreciating her comfortable ankle-high black Reeboks. "I'd rather not have a bad back from high heels."

"If there weren't so many women dressing the way you do people might think ill of you. But it seems like more than half the women I see are just like you."

"What do you mean by ill of me?" Holly was amused by her Aunt's vehement turn of phrase.

"They might think — well, look at you. That you didn't want men to find you attractive."

"I don't — I'm with Clay. I don't care what people think. I know what I am."

"Can't you make a little effort," her aunt wheedled. "Your hair just needs a little highlight —"

"Lord, no. Too much maintenance." She had a sudden thought. Wickedly, she added, "The woman who was fired today, you would have approved of her, though. She always looked very feminine. But it didn't help her keep her job."

"I'm sure they had good cause. There was no reason for you to act so precipitously."

"They fired her because she's a lesbian." She smiled a little at the way the word shook the air in her aunt's chilly foyer.

She lost the smile when she realized her aunt had gone pale. "Are you okay?"

"I'm fine," her aunt said tightly. "They'll think you're one, too. Did you ever stop to think of that?"

She had, for a nanosecond. "I know I'm not, so what does it matter?"

Her aunt said crossly, "You *are* just like her. You just don't care."

"I'm trying not to let other people define me. It's hard work, but I try."

"Just don't socialize with this woman, or her kind. Promise me that much." There was an edge of desperation to her aunt's plea.

"Sorry, no can do. We're having lunch tomorrow."

"Holly, what are you thinking? They recruit — she'll be after you!" Her aunt was well and truly vexed.

In the face of all that ire, Holly merely shrugged. Finally, she had managed to show her aunt she was independent. She felt petty, then, because her aunt was set in her ways, and she had upset her just to prove she could. "I don't believe that's true, and even if it were, they'd have no more success recruiting me than they would you."

Instead of reassured, her aunt looked even more upset. "How dare you suggest something like that?"

"I didn't mean — they say it could be genetic, maybe inherited —"

"You've upset me, you wicked girl!"

Holly froze, and many years of living with it made her quickly step back. In a heartbeat she remembered that her aunt would hardly strike her now, but for a moment she *had* been twelve again, and expecting the sharp blow. "I'm sorry, Aunt, that wasn't my wish."

Aunt Zinnia roughly opened the front door. "I want you to go."

Holly went, and after the door closed, she found her wet shoes in the dark and plodded out to the car.

Well, she thought, that certainly went badly.

It was just six blocks from her aunt's house to the home she'd shared with her mother until the accident. Holly wasn't sure what made her drive by — it was dark and the rain rendered shadows impenetrable. The little house shared a courtyard with three others, but in the dark they looked like one mass of wet faux adobe under Spanish tile roofs. Theirs had been the one on the far right. None of them looked any different.

She saw an indistinct figure moving in what would be the kitchen window of the house next door to theirs. She could not even tell if it was a man or a woman, but then — with the prick of an unrecognizable emotion — she thought it had to be a woman. Maybe the same woman who had lived next door to them, all those years ago. The right height, but more than that she could not discern. Perhaps the same short hair. Another reason Aunt Zinnia had disapproved of Lily. Lily hadn't minded living next door to a black woman.

What had been her name? A car came up behind Holly in the narrow street and she had to move on. What had been their neighbor's name? The harder she thought the more she could only remember thick, sweet hot chocolate, warmth and the sound of voices in companionable conversation.

* * * * *

Drive-thru Chinese, a vegetarian chow mein loaded with broccoli and bok choy, was the answer to the indulgence in red meat. It was too awkward to eat and drive, so she let the rain pelt down as she sat in the parking lot. Belatedly she remembered the new Gypsy Kings, and she turned it up very loud. By the time she finished she had recovered her sense of humor. Aunt Zinnia was a bitter old woman and prone to taking everything the wrong way.

Heading home, she risked taking 22 to I-5, but had to leave the freeway long before she connected back to the 405. Instead, she followed Barranca Parkway past the Marine Corps air station and caught Culver into the heart of Irvine. She made a quick stop at the organic market near campus, soaking her feet for hopefully the last time that day, and drove through the park to the cul de sac they lived on, just off Turtle Rock Drive.

It was a house they were fortunate to have. Clay's father had made the large down payment necessary for an affordable mortgage payment. They also lived simply, so Holly had been paying extra every month to be debt-free all the sooner. Living simply was hard to do in a consumerist society, but they worked at it, Clay especially. He didn't mind wearing mended clothes. She thought guiltily of the mile-high mending stack. That was definitely something she could tackle between jobs.

His stolid Volvo was in the driveway, and Holly had a thrill of excitement, imagining Clay's approval of her decision to support Tori. Normally he was not pleased with her impetuous nature, no more than Aunt Zinnia ever was.

She set the groceries on the counter and smelled incense. Clay was meditating. Quietly, she did the dishes, tidied the living room, started a load of laundry and watered the plants. Just as she was finishing with the last bank of African violets in the deep kitchen window, Clay emerged from his study.

He looked just as he always looked, unconsciously graceful and at peace with himself. Tall and ascetic, he hadn't liked it when she said he had perfected the Tortured Thinker look, but it was true. As a teenager, she had found the brooding eyes devastating and they were still attractive. She didn't like his beard, but it had been a long time since she'd told him so. It grew so thick and fast that shaving was an enormous chore.

"You're later than usual," he said.

"I was visiting with Aunt Zinnia."

"Any luck?"

"Oh no, we had quite an argument. She was upset with me — you'll never guess why."

"You spoke to someone who isn't white." He turned from the refrigerator with a carton of cottage cheese in one hand.

Holly grinned. "Guess again."

"You mentioned environmentalism."

"I'll give you one last guess. It's a hummer." She stowed the watering can under the sink and watched him take a spoon from the cutlery drawer.

"You told her your mother wasn't a self-centered bitch."

She laughed. "No, but we did fight about my mother."

"Then what?" He leaned against the counter and crossed his ankles.

"Are you ready?"

He swallowed and signaled consent with his spoon.

"I quit my job."

His face went still. "What?"

"I quit my job. Ask me why." She could not stop grinning.

Flushing, he asked, "Why?"

"Because they blatantly fired a co-worker because she was gay. They even made up some crap about her being tardy, as if that mattered, but it was really because she was gay. I told them if she went, I would go, too. So . . ." She shrugged one shoulder.

In a flat voice, he said, "You had one of your brainstorms."

The phrase echoed in Holly's head, most of all because she hadn't anticipated it.

When did you send away for the application, he had wanted to know. She replied that it had just seemed like a good idea, and look what it had gotten her, admission to

MIT. You had one of your brainstorms, he said firmly. You gave in to an impulse without thinking it through.

"Yes," she answered. "I suppose I did. It was the right thing to do. It's not right to fire someone because they're gay."

"Did you stop to think at all?"

He was out of patience with her. But . . . but she didn't know what she had done wrong. *It's always something*, Jo seemed to whisper.

She had applied to MIT's masters program because her undergraduate advisor had urged her to do it. But she hadn't thought it through. Clay set out the issues for her, calmly and clearly. What good is a master's degree in something as anti-humanist as mathematics? Math is how they build bombs and waste money on space stations. Math is how they use statistics to pretend homelessness doesn't exist and that everyone who wants a job has one. Math is how five dollars an hour is equated to a living wage. What was the point of a master's degree in that? And a doctorate? MIT just wanted her mind, just wanted to exploit her on the altar of capitalism . . .

His arguments went round and round in her mind.

He walked with her to the mailbox but said nothing, made no gesture. It was her own hand that pulled down the lid, and her own hand that deposited her letter declining the scholarship and degree program MIT had offered. The lid swung shut with a loud clang.

As they had walked back to the student dorm where she lived, he had said something like — no, exactly this: "What kind of job were you planning to get?"

He said it again now. "What kind of job were you planning to get?"

She blinked at him and felt as if she were struggling with a circular reference.

"You made a rash decision and as with all of them, now you have to live with it."

"I was thinking . . ." The skeptical look on his face made her voice trail away.

"You haven't thought about it, have you?" Sighing, he looked so sad. He was thirty-five and she'd known him — or of him — since she was sixteen, ten years and counting. They'd been lovers for the last eight of those years. "What is it, Holly? What would help you slow yourself down so you can consider the consequences of your actions?"

The stubborn thought resurrected itself. "I did the right thing. I had to do it, mostly because I *could* do it."

He didn't say he was at his wit's end, but he looked it. "Do we have to start over? Do you need more coaching on your breathing, your meditation?"

She felt a jolt of anger and knew he would think even less of her if she let it show. She'd been angry too many times today, starting with Jo. "I don't feel like you're hearing me. I did it because it was the right thing to do. I did it because that's what I thought. And I thought that it was what you would do."

"We can't speculate on that. I would never be working there."

Jo's voice again. *But he likes the paycheck just fine.*

How could she have thought he would approve? "I don't want to fight."

"I'm not fighting. I'm trying to help you see what you've done."

"I saw an injustice and did the only thing I could to stand up to it."

"Oh, Holly."

She had failed. Failed.

Thoughts she never let free began to spin in her head, searching for solutions, to find the value of y, or express the pattern of raindrops down a windowpane — something to make sense.

A simple time calculation told her that if she had gone to MIT, she would have a doctorate by now. She would no longer be receiving grades for her daily life from Clay. Funny that today she had also realized she was the same age her mother had been when she'd been born.

She was floating in chaos theory, where the elegance of mathematics can express the unknown and the unimaginable. You could even not know what a thing was, and mathematics could express the not knowing.

She stared at Clay and said, "I was thinking about going into teaching. I think I would be good at it."

"We can't afford for us both to be teachers."

Surprised by Clay's grasp of their finances, when he usually refused to mire himself in details, she answered, "I haven't run the numbers, but it could work."

"You didn't think it through, did you?"

"Do you think everything through?"

"I try, because a sense of equanimity is important in a world so out of balance. Our government is controlled by corporations. Our lives have no real privacy."

She cut him off with, "You hated where I worked. You hated everything about it. Why aren't you happy I'm out of that place?"

"I am, Holly. I'm just disappointed that you fell back into your old habit of not considering consequences before you took action."

Impulsively, she reminded him, "We're together because of that habit."

He looked puzzled, but the memory came into vivid focus for her.

She wanted to know if he thought she'd make a good college student. He had pointed out, in his serious way, that she'd been taking college courses for the past two years. But it was official now that she was eighteen, she told him, and she would be a full-time student next fall. Her aunt's reluctance was the only reason she wasn't already. Clearly startled, he had glanced at the calendar on his desk. She would be an excellent student, he said carefully, if only she could learn to focus her energy. If she applied herself to one thing, had someone to help her concentrate, then yes, she could be an excellent student.

It had been too much to bear. He cared about her future. He was saying how bright she was. She had never heard praise like this before from someone she respected so deeply, or if she had it was so long ago it hardly mattered. She had stopped to see him in his office because she thought the world of him. He was so dedicated to making the world a better place. She had launched herself across his little office, knocking over books and papers in her haste to embrace him, to show him how full he made her heart. Her abandon was the act of a child, but it had taken them to an unexpected corner. Ten minutes later she had no longer been a child, or a virgin.

"I seduced you, in your office, without a thought to the consequences. I don't recall a lot of reluctance on your part."

His puzzlement was genuine. "I don't remember it that way."

"It's not important," she said quickly. But somehow it was.

"This is my fault," he said suddenly. "I forget that everyone has their part to play in the whole. I expect you to change."

She didn't know what he really meant, but it sounded as if he was giving up on her. "I try. Damn it, Clay, why can't you just agree it was the right thing to do? Can't you at least imagine what I felt and tell me what you would have done?"

"But Holly, it's irrelevant. You acted true to your nature, I guess. I shouldn't be disappointed." He had another spoonful of cottage cheese. "It will take months, if not a year, to get your certification to teach. What will you do in the meantime?"

She was going to cry, so she turned her back and busied herself with the sink. "I stopped at the market. There's pesto hummus."

"Did you get apples?"

He didn't appear to notice her choked voice. "No, I didn't know we were out."

It was his sigh that broke a wall Holly didn't know she spent daily energy reinforcing. Quietly, she said, "Clay?"

"Yeah, babe."

"Do you like the way the house is always tidy and clean? Do you like the way I keep the bills paid and our accounts in balance?"

"Of course." His voice was muffled — he was looking for the hummus in the fridge.

"But it doesn't count in the grand scheme of higher

existence, does it?" She turned from the sink and met his gaze as he shut the refrigerator door.

"As we've discussed many times, no, they're necessary evils. Tasks laid on us by an overextended society — paying taxes and interest charges —"

"The only interest we pay is on our mortgage."

He paused, his teaching face in full evidence. Then he arched his eyebrows as if to inquire if she was done interrupting him. "I'm speaking in generalities. These tasks don't make anyone a better person. If anything, they rob us of our essential humanity."

Very quietly, she echoed, "Us?" A thought seared across her mind: *This is all Jo's fault.*

"All of us."

"But you don't do any of those things. You taught me that doing one's own household chores is a way to remain in touch with how much space you take up and how many resources you absorb as you go through life, but you no longer do any. And you haven't written a check in at least five years."

He cocked his head to one side, as if puzzling through an illogical statement.

"I do them all. I'm the one getting robbed of my essential humanity. Is it any wonder I can't seem to get closer to your definition of Nirvana?" Her voice rose. God, she was almost shouting, but she couldn't stop. "It's better for the planet to fix things, but who's the one who finds a place that will actually repair a hedge trimmer? Of course it's better to mend a sweater instead of throwing it away — but when is the last time you threaded a needle? I work hard to help you live simply according to your values, but who does that for me?"

The patient smile — it put her back to the first class she'd ever taken in college.

Aunt Zinnia didn't want her to be there, but short of defying the strong advice of both her high school principal and their minister, she couldn't refuse the educational opportunities that Holly's bright mind deserved. Holly loved the Irvine campus. She was only sixteen, and she was taking a sophomore-level calculus class. To balance the math, she was also taking "Age of Advertising," a social criticism course. She was answering a question — Professor Hammond made her so nervous. He looked at her so intently. His patient smile said she was on the wrong track with her answer, but he would help her find her way. He listened to every word she said and even if her answer was wrong, she felt important to him.

Aunt Zinnia had made her feel twelve again, and now Clay was making her feel sixteen. Why was it Jo's voice that persisted in her head? *But how do you really feel, Holly?*

"I need an answer, Clay. Who does that for me?"

"We all have our role to play, Holly. Everyone has their own part."

Quietly again, finally hearing the edge to her voice, she said, "Are you saying this is my lot in life?"

"Holly, you're getting all mixed up."

He was crossing the room toward her, with that patient smile on his lips. She wasn't sixteen anymore, and that smile, the compassionate criticism in his eyes — they no longer had the same effect.

He put his arms around her. "You made a rash decision, but I do know that when you give yourself a chance to think about your options, you will come up with a good solution. You're very good at that."

His hands were warm on her back. Was this her lot in life? He wanted her, which was uncharacteristic. He preferred the dark of night, after meditation, and with due consideration for her own precautions. Ever since her impetuous fling across his office and into his arms, he had decided when they would make love. His beard burned her throat, as it always did, and she had to dig down, a very long way, to pretend. It usually wasn't so hard.

He mistook her gasp for desire and drew her into the bedroom. Feeling dazed, she turned back the bedclothes and removed all the layers she habitually wore: thick pullover, button-down shirt, jeans, knee socks, her underthings. He neatly folded his own sweatshirt and jeans and set them on the chair. He was in bed before she was, and she slid over to his side because he expected it. She didn't know why she

44

felt so dead. She wanted to tell him she wasn't in the mood, but couldn't begin to explain why. The rustle of the condom packet sliced like a razor on her nerves.

He mistook her gasp again — he couldn't know that it hurt, a little, because she was not aroused. His elbow came down on her wrist and she suddenly felt as if they didn't fit, not the way Tori and Geena had fit. The image of them clinging to each other with unspoken commitment and caring blazed behind her closed lids. She knew Clay would not be inside her much longer. It was getting easier to pretend.

It didn't seem fair, afterward, that he would so easily drop off to sleep. She had too many equations clamoring to be solved.

She cleaned up and then curled on the sofa in her robe until her feet were like ice. She had thought she wanted to be an evolved being, the kind of person that Clay admired. She had thought he would help her get there. *He likes the paycheck just fine.*

This was all Jo's fault. And Jim Felker's. It couldn't be hers.

Bed was warmer, even if she couldn't sleep. She wished desperately for an electric blanket, but they were just one more way that the human animal lost touch with the natural world. She moved closer to Clay, who was always warm, and asked him, in that quiet voice with the edge she had not realized was anger, "So this is my lot in life?" He slept on.

Solve for the simplest answer. God, she was a fool. No one lets you grow up. You just do. She pushed her frozen feet under his legs and occupied her mind with volume equations where the constant was the bulk of her belongings and the variable was the number of boxes she would need.

3

Things did not seem so bleak in the morning. Sometime before dawn the rain stopped and Holly had finally fallen asleep. Clay woke at sunrise, as always, and was well into his yoga routine before Holly padded out of the bedroom. His rigid adherence to yoga had kept him incredibly limber. This morning, after such a bad night, the sight of his lanky but graceful form doing something so routine was comforting. He had always said yoga would help her both physically and mentally, but she never seemed able to find the time.

She made tea and tossed together curried tofu and chopped Boca burgers over leftover rice and carrots for breakfast. He joined her while it was still steaming.

He read the paper while they ate, and Holly thought about her impulse last night to call it quits. Where had that come from? They had eight peaceful and companionable years together. Why would she throw that over? Nothing from last night seemed at all clear.

"We should probably start around four," he said.

She blinked at him.

"Though I suppose leaving work early is now moot. We could leave even earlier — get a jump on the weekend traffic."

They were attending his department chair's wedding in Ventura. She'd completely forgotten. Her Palm Pilot would have reminded her later this morning.

"I'm having lunch with Tori from work, but we could leave after that."

He arched his eyebrows. "Why the lunch?"

"Moral support. To discuss our job prospects." She shrugged.

"Were you friendly with this woman?"

"Not particularly," Holly admitted. "She kept her private life pretty private. Which is why firing her for being gay was just so wrong. I told you about Diane, and no one ever did anything about it. Tori supports her father, too."

"I didn't think they had families."

Dumbfounded, Holly could only stare. "Of course they do. Where do you think gay people come from?"

"I hadn't given it much thought."

"Tori is close to her father." Unlike you, she might have added. "She visits him frequently and supports him. I assume from this that she is close to him."

"I had no idea you were such an expert."

"I'm not — but I'm not stupid either."

His gaze grew sharp. "Are you calling me stupid?"

"No, but that was, well, a stupid thing to say." She refused to back down.

"Look, I believe that discrimination is wrong. Period. You know that. But that doesn't mean that homosexuality is normal, either. Just like sado-masochism isn't normal. It doesn't occur in any animals except humans, which means it's a learned behavior."

"What does sado-masochism have to do with homosexuality?"

"Now who is being naïve?"

Holly tried to think of Tori in chains and Geena wielding a whip and shook her head, smiling. "I don't think it's me. I'd be as surprised to learn Tori and Geena were into that as I would if it were ... your parents. They just don't seem the type. Besides, sado-masochism is not an exclusively homosexual behavior. And you have said yourself that consensual acts between adults are nobody's business."

"No one looks like their sex life."

"I suppose that's true. But I still think you're wrong." She was abruptly unsettled by the idea of how Tori and Geena made love ... who kissed whom first ... She shook it away. "And as you said, it doesn't make discrimination against gays right. Did you know that Tori has to pay taxes on the insurance she gets to cover Geena? That just doesn't seem fair. Because they can't get married."

"Why would they want to get married? I know we're going to a wedding tonight, but I've never understood them. Why would anyone invite government intrusion into their private affairs?"

"Just because you don't understand why someone wants something doesn't mean they shouldn't want it." Holly cleared her dishes, not meaning to make them clatter so loudly. "Now that I think about it, I know I read somewhere that female elephants masturbate each other."

"You're going to have to cite your source on that one." Clay finished his tea, looking as if he would laugh. He ran one hand over his short, dark hair. He always looked carelessly yet attractively groomed.

"Sorry, professor, I don't have my notes." Holly tried to sound lighthearted, but she was shaking way down in the pit of her stomach. "I just remember thinking at the time that an elephant's trunk was a lot more flexible than I had ever realized."

She recalled that she had bought strawberries the day before. She could use a diverting pick-me-up. She offered him some as well.

"In January?" He shook his head somewhat sadly.

All she had wanted was a taste of summer. It seemed like it had been raining for months. It had been a long time since she had lapsed — at least in what she had brought home. Clay didn't know about the burger, the alcohol and all the sugar she had devoured yesterday. He would no doubt say they explained her erratic behavior, especially the craving for strawberries. Strawberries in January, as she ought to have remembered, was just another way to lose track of the turning of seasons. She would never be closer to the natural world — the only world that really mattered — if she continued to make her body believe it was summer in January.

It's summer in Australia, an inner voice whispered seductively. It had to be Jo's voice. Who else could it belong to?

"I'll see you back here around three, then?"

She nodded, and he left her to the empty house and her now wooden strawberries.

"Thank you so much for meeting me today." Tori had pulled into the parking lot of the little Italian restaurant just as Holly had gotten out of her car.

"I'm just glad it's not raining," Holly said as they walked toward the building in the chilly air. A handpainted sign read, "Tish's Kitchen." The sky had gone a watery blue with tinges of gray.

"It seemed like a good omen to me. Geena has to teach today and I was too depressed to think clearly. I was really glad to have something to look forward to. Otherwise I'd be in my pajamas eating ice cream right now, and probably watching reruns of *The Avengers.*"

"Doesn't that sound decadent? Perhaps I shall try that on Monday." Clay would disapprove. Screw Clay, she thought abruptly. Jo could not even begin to know the damage she had wrought, and Holly would never tell her. She did not want to seem like a weathervane, blowing whichever way anyone's advice pushed her. She could think for herself. She ignored the "hah!" that seemed to come from deep inside her.

Solve for the simplest answer, she told herself. This... unsettled feeling — it was not Jo's fault.

"Fortunately, this place is full of comfort food. I've known the owner for years." Tori pushed the heavy door open and led the way inside.

"I've probably driven by here a million times, but I never noticed it," Holly observed. Tish's was homey and cheerful, with an open fire separating the bar from the small dining room. They chose a booth where they could see the fire. Muted Italian ballads added to the relaxing ambiance.

"Comfort food" was an understatement, Holly realized as she perused the menu. "Gnocchi in an alfredo sauce," she pointed out to Tori. "Could anything be more comforting?"

"And more deadly to the arteries? I'll split it with you," she added with a laugh.

"That's a deal. Can we also split the spinach salad?"

"Sounds great. A little virtue, a little sin, it all makes life worth living. You're a vegetarian, aren't you?"

"Most of the time," Holly said. "Political and health reasons. My formative years were spent in a home where beef was the nightly entrée, and I occasionally lapse. Shows what my willpower is worth."

"Life's too short for every bit of food we eat to be viewed as some sort of medicine. I eat salmon because I love it, not for the supposed cancer-fighting fish oil. Sometimes, a salmon is just a salmon. With herbed butter."

Holly laughed. "And wrapped in puff pastry?"

"There ya go. Now you're talking." Tori was grinning. She turned her wide smile to the woman who approached their table with notebook in hand. "Hey, Tish. What's shaking?"

Tish slid into the booth next to Tori with a sigh. "Both busboys called in sick plus one server and Friday afternoons are my busiest time of the whole week. TGIF. I'll age a year before midnight." Tish looked to be in her mid-forties, and her thick black hair was streaked with silver.

"I'm unemployed. I could clear tables for you."

"Unemployed? When the hell did that happen?"

"Yesterday. I ran smack into a homophobe with the authority to fire my queer little ass."

"That sucks. You going to sue?"

"I don't know. I'll probably never get satisfaction. Geena was reading up on it last night, and unless I can show some sort of pattern on this guy's part I don't have much more than he said/she said."

"You've got me," Holly interjected. "Though I suppose he could just claim I misunderstood."

"This is Holly," Tori said to Tish. "She's straight, but she quit in protest. Isn't that amazing?"

"You did a good thing," Tish said to Holly.

Unused to her sexuality being in question, Holly shrugged to hide her sudden discomfort. "I'll admit that my boyfriend and aunt thought I acted . . . precipitously. But I don't."

"That's what matters," Tish said sagely. "They're not looking in your mirror every morning. What can I get you?"

They ordered and Tish heaved herself back to her feet. "If you're serious, doll, I could put you to work."

"Geena's taking me out tonight, but my body is yours until four."

"Promises, promises — if only I had time for that," Tish said over her shoulder.

"Tish and I go way back," Tori explained. "She's sort of like a big sister. Took me under her wing when I was coming out."

"I didn't know lesbians had mentors." Holly couldn't help smiling.

Tori spluttered into her water. "I never thought of it that way. Tish, uh, showed me the ropes. Because I was clueless about certain things."

"I think I understand." Holly decided that pretending

she understood all the nuances was the safest course of action. She felt flustered and foolish and didn't want it to show.

"Are you sure you're straight?" Tori was grinning too broadly for it to be anything but a joke.

"Same man, eight years — it does add up that way."

"If you ever change your mind, I know several single women — nice women, mind you. Good mate material."

More seriously than she intended, Holly asked, "Does it happen that way? Do people really just change their mind?"

Tori's air of teasing faded. "You're right, of course. If you hang out much with me you will get teased about being straight, which I suppose is not fair, because I don't think I'd appreciate having anyone suggest that I could change my sexuality on a whim."

"I wasn't offended," Holly said quickly.

Tori was nodding and looking relieved. "Well, no one assumes that heterosexuality is a phase."

"I hadn't thought of that."

"But if you ever want to know something, just ask," Tori said seriously. "I'll be happy to help you out."

Holly snickered.

Tori flushed. "Uh, okay, that didn't come out the way I meant it to. What I meant was, just because I was discreet at work doesn't mean I'm naturally shy about being a lesbian. I'm not. Don't think you'll ruffle my feathers if you want to ask something. In fact, most of the gay people I know consider themselves ambassadors to the straight world. Our job is to patiently educate and therefore eliminate fear and hatred." Tori ended with one hand on her heart and the other in the split-fingered Vulcan greeting.

Holly laughed again and decided she liked Tori. It was too bad that the corporate culture at Alpha had prevented them from forming a friendship. "My Aunt Zinnia, who is old and has always been disagreeable, believes that the only way gay people can increase their numbers is through recruitment."

"Blech." Tori's upper lip curled. "I hate that one. I'm sure she also thinks we stalk children. Yuck."

Their lunches arrived with extra plates and they quickly

divvied up the gnocchi and salad. Holly ate every bit of spinach in its balsamic vinaigrette by way of compensation for the delectable potato dumplings and the heavy cream and cheese sauce. "Tish serves wonderful food," she admitted to Tori.

To her surprise, Tori abruptly frowned. "Yeah, but she has this thing about letting anybody in."

A shadow fell over Holly's plate and the next thing she knew a long-limbed brunette was sliding into the booth next to her, not so gently using her hips to bump Holly farther in to make room. "Hey, Tori. How's tricks?"

"Murphy."

In the prolonged silence that followed, Holly was aware that Murphy was studying her, but Holly looked anywhere but at the woman. Tori was obviously not pleased to see her and Holly didn't want to interfere.

"Still holding a grudge? I don't know why."

Tori sipped her coffee, then resumed eating the last of her gnocchi.

"Who's this?"

Holly looked Murphy in the eye, at first because she found the woman's tone overly familiar, and then because Murphy's hand was on her knee. She did not like being pawed by men and saw no reason not to resent it just as much from a woman. "Remove your hand."

The hand retreated, but Murphy winked.

"Leave, Murph," Tori snapped. "I mean it."

"Your new squeeze. Did you finally leave Geena? I'd almost respect you if you have."

"Do the right thing, for once, and just go."

Murphy turned in the booth toward Holly, leaning toward her with an air of shared intimacy. "She was crazy about me once." She made a leisurely examination of her right hand, flexing and curling her fingers and examining her cuticles. "Make that twice."

Tori flushed and turned her head away.

"Whereas you obviously disliked and disrespected her," Holly observed, as congenially as if they were discussing the weather. She had always hated conflict, but apparently she was getting over that. "Otherwise you would never go out of your way to embarrass her in front of a friend in this manner. Or is this a schoolyard thing, where you punch the one you love?"

For just a moment Murphy looked nonplussed, then her mocking smile returned. "The mouse that roared, I see. Catch you later, T." She slid out of the booth with a graceful push and went back the way she had come.

"I am so sorry about that, Holly."

"It's no big deal," Holly answered, though she was miffed. Mouse that roared, indeed.

"Geena and I called it quits once, about three years ago. I was miserable and let Murphy too close one night —"

"You don't have to explain. I'm not judging you. I just didn't know lesbians could be boors."

"I just didn't want you to think I'm something I'm not."

Remembering Clay's comment that no one looked like their sex life, Holly tried to put Tori back at ease. "It isn't really any of my business, is it? To each her own. I sincerely believe that."

"I know you do." Tori hesitated, then said slowly, "Alpha rewarded people who worked hard, and we both worked pretty damned hard. I think if we'd spent a little more time away from our desks, we might have been friends, you know what I mean?"

"Yes, I do. I was thinking that myself, just a few minutes ago."

Tori was still choosing her words with care. "And part of my feeling is that we have some values in common, impressions I have of the kind of person you are and you must have of me. Like I said, I just don't want you to think I'm something I'm not. Murphy was such a mistake. I knew it at the time, but I was so unhappy. She taught me something about myself I didn't know, but that wasn't worth the trouble she's been since." Tori flushed. "Geena knows it happened. I told her everything Murphy —" She broke off, but her color continued to rise. "Anyway . . ."

Eager to turn the subject away from sex, Holly asked, "What did you fight about, if you don't mind my asking."

"Money. Long and short of it." Tori grabbed at the subject as if it were a lifeline. "I made more of it than she did at the time, and we were both pigheaded about it. She would always make a point of telling me when something she bought me had come from *her* money. I always said that we were a couple and what was mine was hers. But then I would decide to do something extravagant and excuse it by saying it was with *my* money. We had a knockdown drag out about buying a new car. I wanted to spend more than she did and acted like my higher salary ought to be the tiebreaker. Things were said that we both resented."

"But you patched it up."

"Yeah." Tori's color was back to normal and she scooped up her last spoonful of gnocchi and sauce. She swallowed quickly and added, "After I was with Murphy I realized that I had been playing house with Geena. Pretending to commitment. We lived together and slept together and said that we loved each other, but except for my body I'd never really given her anything I valued. Not my absolute trust, and not my future. I had to stop being so self-reliant and lean on her some if I was going to really let Geena into my life. And vice versa."

Every word struck a chord in Holly, and she was aware, again, of how distant she had felt from Clay yesterday. His failure to leave his perspective for even a moment in order to empathize with her decision had left her faith in his judgment badly shaken. "Did she feel the same way?"

Tori nodded. "She did, and since I think that of the two of us she's far wiser, I knew I was on the right track. We pool all our money now, and we have to decide together on something major. We started planning our retirement — discussing really long-term issues. Where we want to live in another ten years, if we want to have kids. All those things. We'd avoided them before." She shook her head with a self-deprecating sigh. "Damn Murphy anyway. She's such an arrogant shit because she's good in bed, and it was, well, an eye-opening night for me. But it didn't matter. As soon as my head cleared I wanted Geena. I wanted it to be Geena loving me like that because I wanted her with me forever."

"I understand," Holly murmured. Try as she might, she could not picture herself some thirty years in the future and still enduring lectures about the decisions she made. She could not imagine another fifteen years of hiding her lapses into food that was bad for her, or even five years of doing the household work that Clay found too disruptive to his search for inner peace. She could not, she knew with a heartsick shudder, imagine even another night of digging down deep and pretending. Tori had experienced something with Murphy — and for years with Geena — some physical bond Holly could not fully understand. Eight years with Clay and she had no way of appreciating what a night of pure passion might be like.

It was all seeping away from her, her certainty that she had chosen well, that she was living a good life, that Clay's path was worth her commitment and support.

God, she thought, what am I considering?

She had been fine this morning. That she had calculated it would take seventeen boxes in two carloads to remove her clothing and belongings from Clay's house was irrelevant in the morning light. What exactly had he done to warrant her leaving him?

Jo's voice — or was it her own? *He's done exactly what he's done to make you stay: nothing.*

"Are you okay?"

"Yes," she said automatically. "I was just remembering something I forgot to do."

"I've been jawing your ear off."

"No, I was really interested. Money is a tricky subject." How could she explain that she made very few of the decisions about how they would spend their earnings, that is, when they spent it on anything other than the basics. Her savings account was substantial. She was putting money down on the mortgage over and above the payment to pay it off sooner. That was just common sense when they could afford it. It occurred to her, now that she had to face some sobering realities, that she had not cared at the time that her name wasn't on the title to the house. Fine. Clay's name wasn't on her savings account.

God, she thought again. Is it going to come down to this? Am I this petty? When did I get this angry?

Tish dropped off their check and Tori scooped it up.

"Let me, please. As a thank you for what you did yesterday."

"You don't have —"

"I know. But I want to."

Holly hesitated, then said, "Next time I'll buy."

Tori smiled brightly. "It's a deal."

Tish had lingered after delivering the check. "I really could use the extra hands, sweets, if you were serious."

"I was," Tori said. "You know I'd scrub pots for a week for you."

"In that case, I'll take care of the check." Tish snapped the paper from Tori's hand.

Tori muttered, "Just keep me away from Murphy."

"I did try, but you were deep in your cups at the time."

Tori laughed at that. "Okay, let me rephrase. Keep Murphy away from me unless you want a homicide on the premises."

"She's about ready to leave," Tish said. "I'm sure she has to get her beauty sleep before she goes to Jack's tonight."

"I was thinking about asking Geena if she wanted to dance the night away, since it's the first Friday of the month. But you think Murphy will be there, huh?"

"Yeah, when isn't she? I'm going to work your butt off — you'll deserve a night on the town."

"Jack's is not exactly the Ritz." Tori turned to Holly. "It's the nearest gay bar and on first Fridays they have Ladies' Night. It's pretty much a dive, but it beats fighting traffic all the way to West Hollywood or Laguna Beach. Though the bar where Melissa Etheridge used to play is very nice."

"You should treat yourself to whatever you want," Holly advised. "I have to be in Ventura by eight."

Tori glanced at her watch. "You have to leave by, what, three? You'd better hit the road."

"Fortunately it won't take me long to get ready."

"Yeah, I've always admired your natural look. I take way too long to get ready in the morning."

Holly took in, for the first time with more than a

passing interest, how lovely Tori was. Her eyebrows were gracefully arched, and her eyelids dusted with a delicate mixture of browns and oranges that enhanced her bright brown eyes. Her olive cheeks were smooth and soft and Holly knew they would not burn her throat...

Aghast, she floundered for something to say and came up with, "I'm too lazy."

Tori shrugged and picked up her purse. "It suits you and Geena both. I have flaws to cover. Show me where to put my stuff, Tish."

Holly left with a promise to call soon and drove away with a sensation of escape. When she pulled into her driveway she was glad Clay wasn't there. She turned off the engine and sat for a minute, her head on the steering wheel.

It was too much to take in. She could hardly wrap her mind around the idea that Clay was not the man she had thought he was. Her opinion of him, formed at sixteen, had been based on his persona as a teacher. It had not changed in all the years since, not until yesterday, when her image of him as a man and a partner fragmented like a smashed mirror. That alone made her feel as if she was walking a spit of land between the yawning chasms of past and future.

But there was more, more to bear, more to fear. More — she could not even comprehend. Murphy with Tori, doing something to her that three years later still made Tori blush. Holly could imagine Tori whispering what it was to Geena, asking Geena to do it, too. Their bodies merged in a midnight glow. What was it? Did it matter? Something wonderful, something she, Holly, had never had. And would never have with Clay. Might never have... with a man.

The car seemed suddenly airless and she hurried inside, trying to turn her mind to immediate needs. She needed to change for the wedding, and pack a few edibles for the long drive. It would take more than four hours to go a little over a hundred miles in rush-hour traffic, but not even half that to return home any time after nine.

She showered, the water as hot as she could stand it, shampoo suds cascading down her shoulders and stomach.

She was lost, abruptly, in the feel of her breasts under the slick lather.

A question formed. An equation wanted to be solved.

You could not even know what a thing was, she had thought only yesterday, and mathematics could express it. How to express this? The sensation of skin, the prickle of her nipples and the question — is this how other women feel?

Her fingertips felt alive. She turned off the water at last and toweled her hair. She looked at her body in the mirror, then gently touched her lips, her hips, at last her breasts. Is this how other women feel?

She had no way to solve the equation. The principles of mathematics demanded that an equation be solved by logical reduction, not trial and error. She could not logically approach this question. She could not substitute values when she had no idea of the variables and constants for the equation. It was beyond her mental grasp. But trial and error led to thoughts of Murphy and Tori . . . Tori and Geena.

She felt nauseous and grabbed the sink, striving for some semblance of calm.

The front door opened and closed, and she dug down very, very deep, to pretend. This pretense was far more important than anything she'd had to do before. She smiled at Clay and spoke and watched herself going through the motions of asking after his day and listening to the answer as if she cared.

While he showered she rooted around in the back of her drawer for lingerie she'd bought years ago, thinking it might . . . might change the way she felt when Clay touched her. She'd bought it for herself, but Clay had thought she'd meant to titillate him. He had been disappointed with her.

And like a fool, she railed at herself, *you set aside how you felt.* She wiggled into the cleavage-creating black bra. It fit since she still had not lost those fifteen pounds she'd been perpetually fighting. Black pantyhose, they had to be there somewhere. She carefully struggled into the hose, then put on the black pantsuit made of raw silk, her one item of evening wear. It had served her well for years at faculty parties and family holidays. They went out so rarely she did not need more, even though tonight she wanted more than she needed.

She wished she had something shocking red, with hair to match. She wanted to feel alive. The mouse that roared? Yes, she wanted to roar, mouse or not. Her simple haircut offered no real opportunities for change — it was wash and wear so as not to need a blow dryer. Then she remembered her grandmother's jewelry, the only thing she had of her grandmother's. The rose pendant and earrings. They would suit her mood.

Clay did not approve of jewelry. It distracted from the natural state of the human body, was spawned by consumerist notions of appearance and allowed for the casual flaunting of wealth.

Screw Clay, she thought. Or rather, she admitted, studying herself in the mirror, don't. And she smiled at her reflection. These pieces weren't the same thing as a Rolex — these were family heirlooms. They were her heritage, such as it was. She felt self-assured and attractive, and she liked the feeling.

She watched him come out of the bathroom and felt a surge of the same courage she had found yesterday, facing Jim Felker and his petty bigotry. She could tell him now that she was going to leave him. She almost did. But she would let this idea grow for a little while, to prove it wasn't a mere brainstorm.

The last time — had last night been the last time she'd feel him inside her and count the minutes until it was over?

In life's equation of what mattered, how had she thought her physical relationship with Clay could substitute for the value of love? How had she thought that was worth bearing? How could she discover what would make her happy, at least physically? Trial and error . . . Murphy and Tori . . . Tori and Geena . . .

The equation she could not solve seemed to have women

as constants. And then she understood at least a piece of the puzzle. She was the variable for now. She was the thing that was changing and would change, until she found her own answers.

4

What made it hard, from the moment they got in the car, was that Clay was in a good mood. His semester was shaping up with interested students and he'd been asked to co-teach a graduate seminar under the aegis of the department head.

"I think I might try to get the all-important Ph.D.," he admitted. "I know it's just a piece of paper, about what you can research and not what you truly understand, but not having it is an unfortunate barrier."

"One of those necessary evils that rob you of your essential humanity?" She took advantage of an 18-wheeler's lag in acceleration to cut over a lane. The 405 was, as usual, a parking lot.

He didn't seem to notice the ironic edge to her tone. "Just that. Of course, I'd feel like I could really go for it if your situation were settled." He threw her a charming glance and all at once she remembered the way he had been the first time she had seen him. Profound and compassionate, he had been dedicated to helping his students escape from the relentless message of a consumerist society. His first question for the class, that first day, had been, "So, what did you buy today?" The follow-up had been, "Why did you buy it?"

It seemed ages ago, before he'd given her the presence of mind to accept herself. She amended her thoughts. To accept herself as he saw her. She had never accepted herself as she was. That much was clear. Of course, to accept herself as she was she needed to understand who she was. That equation was too complicated and frightening to approach rationally, so she put it away.

"My situation? Oh, you mean job. I'm going to look into the master's degree I turned down. I haven't kept up on the field, at least not much, and a lot changes in four years in the sciences. There may be opportunities I never foresaw. Certainly, there may be developments I can't follow or understand." It was an unsettling thought.

"So you really are going to do it? What are we going to live on? I don't think my paycheck will cover the mortgage."

"It does, you know," she said softly. She wanted to explain to him that he would have to figure it out from now on. She felt as if she was being a little unfair to him. She knew a part of his future and he had no clue. "And we live so cheaply." She felt a fraud to say "we."

"You could get something part-time, maybe? That wouldn't interfere too much with your studies."

Dumbfounded, she realized he was being supportive. He was actually suggesting a solution that would allow her to pursue her dreams. "Would this all be okay with you?"

"I admit that last night I was taken aback. I meditated on it, and what you said was right. Just because I didn't understand why someone wanted something didn't mean they shouldn't want it. Certainly not when it comes to improving the mind. You want this and if you are careful to avoid the negative applications of what you learn, you should be fine."

She pretended the need to change lanes so she could look away from him. It had been four years since she'd dropped that letter into the mail and said good-bye to this future. Why did he have to be this way all of sudden? Understanding, encouraging even? She had not caved in yesterday, had not admitted that she had made what he declared a mistake. Had he finally realized she had a right to a mind of her own?

Had she misjudged him? Was all of this turmoil of her own making? She'd never been friendly with a lesbian before. Maybe it was just her libido talking — finally. Lesbian sex was foreign, forbidden, exotic. It was Murphy and her hands, and imagining them on Tori's body. A fantasy, but nothing more. Maybe that was all there was to it. Yes, that could be all. She would plug that notion into a formula and see if she could live by it.

"Am I being presumptuous?" His sudden question made her look back at him.

"About what?"

"You said the degree you turned down. That was at MIT. That's a long way from here."

"I — I wasn't considering colleges yet. I was going to step back and look at the field and try to measure what ground I would have to make up."

His nod was approving. "That's a good plan."

She felt even more like a liar. He had obliquely asked if her plans meant she would consider moving. She had as much as said no. But she was going to move. Wasn't she? Where had her anger gone?

It was well after sunset when they finally reached the Ventura Highway and turned north for the last time. The wedding was at one of the private estates that lined the cliffs from Oxnard to Santa Barbara. The two faculty who were marrying had had to move up the date because of a parent's illness, and had taken a Friday evening at the elegant location instead of settling for another site. On a clear day the Channel Islands were plainly visible and the drive was soothing and beautiful. Tonight the ocean was silent and distant and a light drizzle had begun when they reached Glendale. Clay seemed to have dozed off. Holly was glad of his silence, but not the dark.

The dark was a palette and her mind filled it with images and fantasies. The dark made it too easy. Raindrops wandered down the windshield, becoming prisms in the lights of oncoming vehicles. Each flare of light was a moment from the past that she examined as if she was cleaning out her mental attic. Keep this memory, throw that one away.

Keep the part of Clay she could still respect. He was right about a lot of things — about pesticides, and testing cosmetics on animals. She remembered the first lecture that first day in class, when he had explained what ought to have been self-evident. A simple thing: for the price of lunch at McDonald's, a person could buy tortillas, rice and beans and feed not just themselves, but four other people as well. So why not do that? Tuning out the relentless pace of modern life, which encouraged the belief that there wasn't time to make your own sandwich, was ultimately rewarding to both body and spirit.

But she had to ask herself, When was the last time Clay had made himself a meal. *Why would he, you idiot? He has you.*

Oh, but he was right about the public love affair with technology. Much of what he'd said had come true. Technology wasn't helping people transfer work to machines, it was making people and machines interconnected. Look how reliant she was on her Palm Pilot. Clay hated it, but it helped her manage her time. Sure, she could live without it, probably ought to.

Or not. Was he right about everything? Everyone probably would be better off disconnecting themselves from machines and living off the land. Of course if everyone tried it millions would starve. But he was wrong about strawberries in January. And electric blankets. And what he implied was her lot in life.

She'd been so proud when he'd organized a campus protest against invasion of privacy through the routine disclosure of medical records from the school medical center. As a result, the policy for the entire state system had been changed. He'd loved the signs she'd made, the food she'd brought to the all-night vigil. *But did he make anything himself?*

She wanted this to be Jo's fault. She needed it to be Jo's fault. She did not want to be twenty-six going on sixteen, still a child and discovering that her hero was just a man, as flawed as any, no worse than most.

Clay helped decipher the map when they turned off the highway. It was hard to shake away the last image she'd painted against the darkness, that of Geena holding Tori.

She found a parking space in the congested, narrow street outside the gates of the house and wished the rain would stop. She waited while Clay shrugged into his suit jacket, then they went up the wide marble steps together. The massive bulk of the house was lost in the night, but festive lights drew them to the front door. As soon as the door opened Holly was washed over by lively music from a small baroque ensemble. It was bright and warm inside. The darkness, with its forbidden pictures, receded.

They mingled and Holly chatted with people she knew from faculty parties, then followed the musical cues when it was time for the ceremony. It was simple and heartfelt and she liked it. She knew how Clay felt about weddings, but there was something deeply human about the proclaiming of commitment and loyalty in front of family and friends. Someday she wanted to do that. Maybe without the lilac-hued roses and long white gown and seven attendants, none of which was her style. But the declaration — yes, she would love to feel that way about someone.

And there it was, she thought. *You're still looking*, she acknowledged to herself. She could not envision making such a declaration with Clay. Maybe she wasn't angry any longer, but their relationship was definitely over. If they weren't moving toward a point when they gave each other their futures then what exactly were they doing? Playing house, as Tori had said?

Vows were exchanged and followed by a kiss. Holly tried to imagine herself as a bride, but she didn't fit in this picture. She had to fit somewhere, she thought.

They followed the bride and groom to the reception hall when the rituals were concluded. The quiet contemplation during the ceremony had given her an insight she wanted to think more about, but a new band was striking up a lively swing number, making it hard to think.

Clay took her elbow for a moment and she had to consciously resist the urge to pull it out of his grasp.

"Holly, you are looking wonderful. You've lost weight." Winnie Maltin was the dean's wife, and she had always been friendly. The dean was on the other side of the hall, in a cluster of faculty.

"No, I'm just not wearing all my usual layers. It is a party, after all." She felt gratified for having made an effort.

Winnie regarded Clay. "You look the picture of health, as always."

Clay flashed his charming smile. "As do you." After all the years, however, Holly could tell he was already finding the socializing tedious. It was superficial, he had so often complained, and the ability to talk comfortably with people at parties should have no bearing on how a person was evaluated.

"That necklace is beautiful," Winnie continued, turning back to Holly. "I don't think I've seen you wear it before. Certainly not the earrings."

"They were my grandmother's. Her name was Rose. She left them to my mother. I've had them since she died."

"What delicate work. American Beauty roses, aren't they? There's a greenhouse at the rear of the house and they have some beautiful roses in there. George and I were looking at them earlier. You should stroll through it."

Colleagues drew Clay away and Holly chatted with Winnie for a while. The dean stopped to say a few words, then went on his way. Winnie excused herself shortly thereafter, and Holly was abruptly alone and far from where Clay was putting his hands in his pockets and looking disapproving.

What a drip. The thought was unbidden and she knew then that it had to be over. She sipped her sparkling wine with a silent toast to her own future.

After a moment she became aware of a man next to her. She glanced up and he smiled congenially. "How do you know George?"

"I'm a friend of a Fullerton professor," she answered. "And you?"

"Stan Barquette," He held out his hand and Holly shook it, hoping her reluctance didn't show. "I know George from way back. He's a man to consult when you need to make a decision. After a talk with him, I decided to run for the Assembly in district thirty-three."

"Whereabouts is that?"

He launched into a pat speech about his district, its concerns, the needs of his future constituents and how the current representative was headed the wrong way. "He's a good man," he concluded, "and I don't take anything away from his intentions. But it's time for different ideas."

Holly merely nodded politely. Like Clay, she had few illusions about politics and politicians. In response to Stan's polite question she said, "At the moment I'm considering if I'll go into teaching as well."

"Really? Well, we can certainly use all the teachers we can get. Do you have kids? Do you like working with them?"

"No, and I don't know."

"Teaching is a rewarding field, whatever level you decide to teach. Grade-school teachers are the most badly needed."

Suspicious that his assumption was that as a woman she would be most interested in teaching young children, she replied, "I've read that. However, I'm not sure many grade schools have much use for a conceptual mathematician."

It would have been comical if it hadn't proven Aunt Zinnia right. Like something in a cartoon, curtains came down in his eyes and he took a nervous half-step away,

68

feigning a need for one of the napkins on the nearby buffet. Men want decent women, she could hear Aunt Zinnia say, and they'll never be convinced that a woman who is smarter than they are isn't outsmarting them in other ways — ways that decent women wouldn't consider.

To give the devil his due, Clay had never reacted that way to her brain. But — *oh, shut up, Jo* — he had successfully stopped her from furthering her academic success. Was it because he couldn't handle the idea of having a relationship with someone who was smarter than he was, or at least appeared to be?

You don't know how smart you are, she reminded herself. Mathematics could have gone light-years ahead of you while you ran actuarial data. You've never stretched yourself, just rested on what was easiest. Don't go thinking that anyone will be eager to have you. Jo is not right about everything.

Stan had begun to realize he was having a conversation mostly with himself and he ambled away to pursue other networking opportunities.

"How do you know the bride and groom?"

The beautifully modulated voice in her ear startled her and she nearly spilled her wine. She turned to find that the voice matched the speaker, and she was momentarily tongue-tied, but the curvaceous blue-eyed blonde smiled as if she was used to giving people a moment to pull themselves together. "I'm . . . a friend of a Fullerton professor. How about you?"

"I'm here with a friend of a friend. Window dressing. I don't mind."

Puzzled, but not really caring, Holly asked, "Do you live in Ventura?"

She felt slightly dazzled by the smile she received. "No, I have the obligatory rat-infested apartment in Hollywood so I can write the folks back home in Clearfield, Iowa, that I live there."

"I'm starting to think you look familiar."

"I did a shampoo commercial and a beer billboard." She laughed and then tossed her head so her long blonde hair drifted through the air like spun gold. "Does this look familiar?"

Holly had to swallow hard. "I don't watch television so it must be the billboard. That must be a terribly hard business to break into."

"It is. I'm Galina Gerrard, by the way." She held out her hand.

"Holly Markham." It was a good thing that was all she had to say because the touch of Galina's fingertips sent surprising tremors up her arm. She told herself that she had never been impressed by looks over actions. How could she possibly be tongue-tied, just because Galina was gorgeous?

Galina didn't let go, not right away. Her smile dimmed slightly, but there was new warmth in her eyes.

Holly finally took her hand back and said the first thing that came into her head. "People in Iowa name their daughters Galina?"

"No," Galina said, her eyes sparkling. "Galina is a better name for an actress than Ruby Sue."

She ought to have been in a panic. She ought to have done something to get herself to safety. She was falling, drowning, and all she could think was that she did not want to move.

"Oh shit," the actress said suddenly. "Please say you'll be around for a while. I have to go shmooze with the guy I came with. He's winking at me." She looked torn.

"Go take care of business," Holly advised, not wanting her to go and desperately afraid of why.

"I'll look for you in a little bit."

She nodded. Had she just made an assignation? What was she doing?

Yet she knew exactly what she was doing. She was watching Galina walk away in her skin-tight blue silk dress and imagining ... wondering ...

She escaped to the greenhouse, leaving the wine and party noise. She needed to be clearheaded. But she didn't want to solve for the simplest answer, or think about the variables that would help her explore the chaos she could feel swelling inside her. For a perilous moment she had

70

envisioned herself in a wedding ceremony, and the groom wore a blue silk dress.

The greenhouse was quiet and dimly lit, heavy with the scent of roses and rich soil. She noticed a profusion of lily-of-the-valley set into a nearby alcove, and she thought of her mother. And wished, as she had not wished in a long time, that her mother hadn't died, because she needed to talk to someone she trusted. How could she be so confused? She'd had female friends before, and never felt this way.

She went to her knees to inhale the delicate fragrance of the nearest bloom and tried to clear her mind. Could she forget this if she meditated? It had never worked for her the way it did for Clay. Her mind would wander and she always found herself worrying about incomplete chores.

It was several minutes before she realized she wasn't alone in the long, plant-crowded room. On the other side of a wall of hanging plants she heard whispered voices. She thought about clearing her throat, then a low cry sent her crouching farther down. It was a woman who cried out and her eager moan pounded in Holly's ears.

Was this what women sounded like? She had never made those sounds, never groaned in what sounded like pain but could only be pleasure. She could hear an echoing moan from the man, then it was drowned out by the woman's fervent, whispered pleas.

The thrumming in her ears twined with the woman's voice, and when the stifled, urgent groans subsided she played it all again in her head. She had never made those sounds, never heard them before, but now it was so easy to hear Tori with Murphy, with Geena. To consider, to wonder, what it would feel like to have no choice but to make those noises, to be so aroused and fulfilled that there was no choice but to moan with proof of it.

When she surfaced from her reverie she was alone, feeling ill and dizzy. It would be cold outside. That would help.

She stood in the drizzle for longer than even her simple hairstyle could take, but she couldn't make herself go back inside.

"What the heck are you doing out here?"

71

Galina — Ruby Sue, Holly thought. Anyone named Ruby Sue could not be dangerous. But she was, and so beautiful, so vivacious. Her silk dress was getting wet.

"Trying not to be seen."

"Oh. Shall I leave?"

Holly shook her head and felt weak. "There was — I was in the greenhouse and then this man and woman came in and before I could tell them they weren't alone they were —"

"Really?" Ruby's eyes seemed to have a light of their own. "Let's go peek."

"They're gone," Holly admitted. She wanted two things at once — to go and to stay.

"Who was it?"

"I don't know. Some woman in a black dress, that's as much as I saw or wanted to see."

"Let's go make sure. Folks in Clearfield told me that Hollywood parties were just orgies, and I've never yet seen anything the least bit juicy. It's been kind of disappointing." Galina seized Holly's hand and pulled her toward the greenhouse door.

Holly went with her. She felt weak, desperate, wondering how to solve her equation. How do women feel? How would she feel? She could hardly hear Galina's rapid-fire questions over the thrumming in her ears.

"Here? Or over there?"

She pointed.

"Oh, I see." Ruby disappeared around the wall of hanging plants. "From here you can't see either door. During the day the windows would give you away, but at night, in the dark . . ."

Holly turned the corner into the little alcove created by the plants and benches. There was also a small armchair and an unlit reading lamp. She told herself to make a joke and to get the hell out of there. She was too close to Galina, who had perched on the arm of the chair.

"Where were they? Over here?" Galina pointed to the dimmest corner.

Holly nodded. "I didn't see much. I was right around there, but on my knees to smell the lily-of-the-valley."

"This is kind of professional curiosity." Galina looked at her through long, silky lashes. "I mean, let's face it. This sort of thing doesn't happen all that often. At least not in my circle of acquaintances. Certainly never in Clearfield. I want to be an actress, and sex in semi-public places happens all the time on television and in movies. Just seeing someplace where it did, and putting myself into that woman's position — was it just a quickie for some couple who likes to take some chances? Perhaps it was old lovers who felt the old passion when they ran into each other. Or did they meet tonight and feel the urge to do something dangerous?"

"I don't know." Questions like this had never occurred to her, not until tonight.

Galina rose gracefully from the chair and leaned against the wall where the woman had been. She ran her hands over her stomach and closed her eyes for a moment. "Of course you don't. But we can imagine, can't we? Perhaps it was strangers in the night," she murmured more softly. "Yes, it's quite private here."

She was all mystery and silk, and her dress clung provocatively where rain had dampened it. Holly wanted to back away, but now Galina had her hand, was pulling her into the corner, turning her so her back was against that same wall.

"Can you imagine it," Galina whispered. "Two people see each other, want each other, and do something about it? I'm tired of bony waifs in my bed. I saw you and realized how long it's been since I've had a woman who was soft, and curving..."

Galina's hand slipped around Holly's hip. There was no air. "I'm not..." she tried to say, but she wasn't at all sure she had actually spoken.

"And I've always had this fantasy of doing something just like this."

Dangerous, seductive... Galina was leaning into her now, her breasts shocking Holly's into responsive tightening. Her hands ran up Holly's arms until she cupped Holly's face and then the world paused. The music stopped, the rain stopped. Her heart stopped.

All for a kiss of fervent desire, for the eager meeting of their mouths. Her mouth opened, she pulled Galina's arms around her. She kissed her. And moaned, low in her throat.

The world began again, and her heart pounded behind her eyes. She thought she might faint because the kiss was perfect and it would be easier if everything could just end here. Because the next moment would bring all the rest of it, the new questions, the self-doubt — the fear. Her moan became a whimper and even terrified she continued that kiss, aware of the heat of Galina's body and that it had been so long since she had felt warm.

"Oh yeah," Galina murmured, when their mouths finally parted.

What could she do? She had never been so frightened of herself, of another person, not ever. Unproven truths were all she had to defend herself. She strangled out, "I'm straight."

Galina came in for another kiss. Holly rocked on her feet, surged against Galina, wanting to feel . . . words decent women didn't use surged up in her mind, and she wanted to use them all, to tell Galina what she wanted to touch, where she wanted to be stroked. Truth had become merely a theory, a theory expressed by a false equation. She said it again, because of the fear and because Tori had said it and Tori would know, wouldn't she?

"I'm straight," she said again.

Galina took a wobbly step backward, leaving Holly to shiver with the return of what she had never known was perpetual cold. "Do you really think so?"

"I — I must be."

"Why?"

Holly could only shake her head and then turn her face away, hiding the tears that spilled down her cheeks.

Galina leaned into her again, her body taut and urgent. "I don't fuck straight women."

Fuck. The word pierced Holly and she could hear the final rending of her life from its anchors. She shook her head because it was the only part of her body that would obey her. Shook her head while her arms reached for the heat again.

Galina stepped back, then reached into the little bag that dangled from her shoulder. She extracted a white rectangle and held it up to the dim light.

"My phone number is on the back of this one," she said. "Call me when you're not straight anymore."

Holly wanted to take the card, feeling weak for wanting it so badly, the card . . . the fuck. Decent women . . . Was she not decent anymore? She could not make her arms move now, nor did she react when Galina stepped toward her one last time to slip the card down until it was tucked into her bra.

"I'm not a bitch, you know." Galina's matter-of-fact tone brought a deeper flush to Holly's face. "I'm just honest."

Holly pushed past her and escaped into the cold night. The rain was falling harder, but she didn't feel the chill. All she felt, as if it had been dipped in acid, was Galina's card burning her skin.

The rain was one type of cure for the heat that suffused her when she thought about what she wanted — how she wanted it. The darkness brought images again, and there were new equations wanting solutions. She had had female friends before and never felt this way — or so she had told herself not a half-hour ago. But the past didn't support that statement. Female friends? There was only Jo. She'd already been enthralled by Clay when she had met Jo. She'd had friends in the neighborhood and at school when her mother was alive, but Aunt Zinnia had put her in a different school, a Lutheran school that was more rigid. Aunt Zinnia had insisted that Holly put her studies first, and her life had been regimented. There had been no adolescent friends, neither girls nor boys. Holly had even understood why her aunt kept her away from boys — that was her job. But she had never wondered why the girls, too.

There was something . . . something her aunt knew that she did not. Something that had made her refuse every invitation Holly had received for sleepovers and weekend trips. Something that had made her willing to use Holly's love of learning as a substitute for friendships, even though her aunt would later oppose Holly's desire to further her education. Decent women did not go to college to learn, they went to find husbands. Decent women didn't study mathematics, didn't push themselves into a field where men excelled. Decent women remembered they were women.

Decent women did not fuck other women.

They didn't want to fuck other women, they didn't want to go back inside and beg another woman for her mouth, her hands, her body.

Once she started to laugh she found she couldn't stop. But it was unbelievably funny. Two days ago she'd gotten up at the usual time, done all the usual things, and never suspected that it was all fabrication, founded on nothing more than adolescent worship and a desire to live a good, useful life. How could these things have hidden such a truth from her?

There was something she did not know and she had no idea how to ease the ache of ignorance. She had never been confronted by a problem she could not solve. She had only allowed Clay to stop her looking for harder problems. She seemed besieged by coincidence, which, given her understanding of statistics, was even funnier. She knew if two people at a party for twenty-three discovered they had the same birthday, they would exclaim over the coincidence, but she knew there was better than even odds of it happening.

But what were the odds a straight woman would defend a gay woman's right to keep her job and wake up the next day . . . changed?

She was cold. So cold. Drops of rain streamed down her face, merging and separating. Finally, she understood their dance was random.

Part 2:
Marble

Doubtless it will seem strange to many that the hand unaided by sight can feel action, sentiment, beauty in the cold marble...

— Helen Keller, 1903

Reyna, Now

"Holly," the woman in her arms whispered back. "I'm Holly."

Reyna tasted the name on Holly's mouth as she kissed her again, falling deeper into painful urgency. Holly clung to her for a moment after the kiss, shaking her head as if dizzy. Reyna could not remember ever having this profound an effect on a woman. It had surely gone to her head and overwhelmed her good sense.

Holly gestured at someone, a sketchy good-bye, then they were moving toward the door. After a brief delay to reclaim her jacket and helmet, they stepped into the cool, moon-drenched parking lot.

The pulse of the music inside the club faded to a dull rhythm. Holly stood irresolute, unfocused.

"This way," Reyna said. "There's someplace we can go about four blocks from here."

Holly nodded and her voice seemed far away. "I'll come back for my car — later." Then her gaze returned from some distant point and caught Reyna all over again, nakedly desirous.

Reyna dropped her jacket and helmet next to a parked car so she could capture Holly's face in her hands. How could anyone be expected to give up this delight? Each kiss seemed to reach deeper, seemed to uncover yet more layers of need and longing in both of them. Was this what it was like to have a woman melt in your arms? There had been so many, and none had felt like this.

Her hands left Holly's face to grip her shoulders, then sweep again over the hot silk that clung to Holly's breasts. Holly trembled, murmured, "Yes."

Only when the car alarm went off did Reyna realize how hard she was moving against Holly, how eagerly they were wrapped around each other, rocking toward their need. Holly jumped at the onslaught of noise and pulled away. Reyna caught her hand and with a gasping laugh, said, "We should probably get out of here."

Holly was ready to run, Reyna realized, so she held tight to her hand until they were some distance from the blaring vehicle. "There's no need to be afraid of me."

Holly turned, her face pale and strained in the moon-light. "I've never done this before."

"I have," Reyna said, meaning it as a joke, though it was also the truth. Holly's expression clouded. Her gaze fell to Holly's breasts, taking in their rapid rise and fall and the hardened nipples that made her mouth ache.

Holly shook her head, but whatever she meant by that was lost in her breathless, "Kiss me."

5

Reyna, Seven Years Ago

Reyna Putnam scraped the last of the strawberry yogurt from the bottom of the container. It had been cool and refreshing after the muggy unpleasantness of the uncharacteristically hot Berkeley day. She tickled Kimberly's ear as she rose from the deck chair. "You want a beer?"

Kim didn't open her eyes. Drowsily, she said, "Sure. I feel so guilty just sitting here, doing nothing. I've got two papers due and about a thousand pages to read before the weekend."

"Me, too," Reyna acknowledged. "But we can't study every minute. It's too hot." As she crossed the deck of the little apartment they shared she could see the heat rippling off the Campanile. It seemed to be wilting.

The kitchen windows were shuttered against the heat. Blinking in the dim light, she didn't notice the man seated at the kitchen table. Only when she had two beers in hand did the refrigerator light reveal his presence. The door swung shut and they were in darkness again.

"What do you want?" She spoke harshly; he had frightened her. Had they left the front door unlocked? No matter — a locked door wouldn't stand in his way.

"Is that a nice way to talk to the man who pays for your education?"

It was always that way with her father, always about what he paid for and her lack of gratitude. She could not be grateful for what she did not want.

"Let's not revisit that." Reyna put the beers down and turned on the kitchen light but did not sit. She felt braver on her feet. She was beyond his reach, she reminded herself. He had no leverage, not even money. He only supported her while she was in college because it looked good to do so, taking responsibility for the child he'd fathered out of wedlock. He could always withdraw his support. She'd never asked for it and wouldn't complain if it ended. But his enemies might notice. That he was too ambitious to willingly supply his enemies with fodder was his concern, not hers.

As if by way of an answer, he pulled a piece of paper from a slender file, smoothed it on the table, then pushed it toward her.

She picked it up warily. A medical report from the UCLA Medical Center. Her mother's name swam up off the page, entangled with a phrase she only knew from her study of Flannery O'Connor's life. It frightened her to see it paired with her mother's name. *Lupus erythematosus*.

The paper fell from her numb fingers, coming to a rest on the table between them.

She wanted him to stop talking. She was his daughter, after all, and she had known how his mind worked since she was sixteen. Words were unnecessary.

"Her medical insurance is poor, and after the expenses

82

of her breast cancer treatment — still in remission, thankfully — she's almost at her lifetime maximum. My people can be slow or quick with checks. There can be a professional with her twenty-four hours a day, or just checking in by phone."

"I'll take care of her. I'll leave school if I have to."

"I don't doubt that you would. I've always admired your ability to work hard." He was smiling when he ought to have realized he had lost. There was obviously something she did not yet know. He would tell her when it suited him.

She smoothed the medical report on the table and pushed it back toward him. It was bravado in the face of his smile, a smile of victory.

"Immunosuppressive drug regimens can cost eighty-five dollars a day. I'm sure you can do the math. Her insurance will be exhausted in seven months. Without further complications."

She could do the math. Having no idea where she would find thirty-one thousand dollars a year, she nevertheless said firmly, "We'll manage." He kept smiling.

Her life had been of his design, even before he had acknowledged that she was his daughter. Her mother was strong in beauty but frail in spirit, and had always taken the path of least resistance. What Grip Putnam wanted from her he got. Reyna couldn't blame her mother for being true to her nature. He wanted them to move, they did. He wanted discretion, then she was silent.

Then, when Reyna was eight, that had all changed. Grip's son and wife had died in an automobile accident and he'd claimed Reyna as his own. In his first autobiography, written two years into the phenomenal success of his syndicated radio program, he'd said that the tragedy had taught him how important family was, and he knew then that financial support was not enough. His out-of-wedlock daughter deserved everything he would have given the son from his marriage.

He wanted Reyna's last name to be his, and it happened. She was enrolled at an exclusive private school, provided with tutors whenever her grades faltered below perfect, and lavished with language and riding lessons and a closet full of designer clothes. She learned to carry herself like a daughter of the Putnam lineage, a great-granddaughter of a U.S. senator, the granddaughter of a California congressman, the daughter of a conservative analyst who could tip his supporters' positions in almost any direction he pleased. She was not allowed to forget that she could some day be the daughter of a president. Grip Putnam had aspirations and the cool, careful logic required to fulfill them.

She had been sixteen when she'd first rebelled at clothing selected by a media consultant, and wanted to choose her own classes and her own books and movies. Sixteen, before she had realized that her entire life was scripted, right down to the friends she was allowed to make. When she told him she wanted more freedom, she reasoned with him that he could hardly expect less from her. They had the same strength of will. He would not allow anyone to control him — neither would she.

He told her freedom had a price. She proved to him she could adjust to public school, and without a look backward returned the car she'd received on her birthday. She thought he would eventually relent, not wanting his daughter to be seen flipping burgers after school.

Instead, he upped the ante and taught her that the rules for the wealthy and powerful really were different. To her mother's credit, she had never hinted that her sudden firing from an administrative job she'd held for several years might have been arranged to put financial pressure on both of them. Her mother had stoically looked for a new job for four months and kept her calm when she'd discovered the tires on the car slashed a second time. Then the car had simply disappeared — two days after the insurance lapsed. Reyna had had to help her hysterical mother into bed, and she had been badly frightened when she answered the phone.

Her father had asked if she was tired of freedom yet. He even managed to make it sound as if his call was a coincidence.

She was his daughter, and her mind worked like his. In

ten seconds she tallied the coincidences to his account and she'd said yes, she was tired of freedom. Like him, she knew how to wait.

At sixteen, her youth and her mother's frailty had worked to his advantage. At twenty-three, standing in her kitchen, it was a piece of paper that trapped her. For years she would not forgive herself for her instinctive reaction — a reaction that made her completely his daughter, as hateful and selfish as he was. *Mother, how could you do this to me?*

He was still talking, but she didn't have to listen to know what he was saying. Her transcript had appeared from the file. He glanced down as if to confirm something, but she knew he had no need to refresh his memory. "Your journalism degree is finished. You will be getting a double master's — political science and governmental affairs, just as I did. Journalism won't do you any good later on."

He put the transcript back and pulled out a photograph in its place. "You'll also be living alone. Scandalous liaisons are a barrier, too. You'll thank me, later, when the press puts its microscope on you."

God, Kimberly. The photograph was of the two of them walking on campus. She had suspected him of hiring someone to keep an eye on her, but the confirmation of it made her skin crawl.

Kimberly's future was nothing to him. She had so many strikes against her — lesbian, middle-class, black, female and liberal. In her father's world, only straight wealthy white male conservatives had any power. And few of them had more than he did at this point.

"She's a nice-looking piece, but my daughter is not a biological error." He exchanged the photograph for a neatly typed list of names that he set down on the table and pushed toward her as he had the medical report. Surnames that read like a political *Who's Who* tied her stomach in knots. "This is a list of acceptable escorts. A few are even the same color she is, if that is what you have a penchant for. But you won't marry one of them. We'll choose someone suitable."

He must have been planning this moment for years, she

thought, waiting to have some hold on her, some way to make her into his asset instead of a political liability he couldn't control.

"No," Reyna said steadily. "This isn't going to work."

Grip Putnam's voice found its way into millions of homes. He delivered the truth as the sober voice of conservatism. In her small kitchen, his authoritative rumble was overwhelming. "Do you know what lupus does to the immune system? Fevers, weakness, weight loss, anemia, enlargement of the spleen are the most common effects. Skin rashes, heart, joint and kidney disease are also possibilities. A mild form feels like arthritis — everywhere in the body. Though lupus is rare in someone her age, it's not unheard of. But at her age, it can be quickly fatal. Given proper treatment, it can be survived for years, perhaps indefinitely."

The coldness of his voice was more brutal than the words. A part of her grieved for her mother, but that part was weak, and he used weakness. "You loved her enough to go to bed with her. I was the result. How can you use her against me this way?"

Kimberly was suddenly in the doorway. "What's going on?" She moved quickly to Reyna's side. "What does he want?"

Her father's gaze never left her. Kim simply did not exist to him. "This discussion is between you and me. The details are private." He rose. "We'll meet again in one week. You will have made the necessary changes to your life."

Reyna let Kimberly put her arm around her waist. She thought she might faint. She stared at her father, hating him as she felt her future drain past reclaiming.

The last thing he said on that hot afternoon when he smashed her future to tiny bits was, "Her kidneys are being retested today. The first tests weren't promising. I'm told the procedure is painful, but she did manage to get to the appointment on her own."

* * * * *

Two years later, after an exhausting course load, she left U.C. Berkeley with a double master's in political science and governmental affairs. From there she successfully completed a two-year doctorate program at Georgetown's school of government. Her dissertation was "The War on Conservative Values: The Silencing of Conservative Public Opinion Through Polling Practice and Media Reporting." She wrote it while she learned the ropes at her first post-education job as a research associate for the Putnam Institute. Grip Putnam needed an heir apparent and now, Reyna knew, he thought he had one.

"How was her day?" Reyna's whispered question brought the drowsy nurse to her feet. Jean — this one was Jean. There had been so many in the six-plus years since that hot afternoon in her kitchen.

"Fine. She wasn't very hungry at dinner, but she did manage some broth and a slice of that wonderful bread Mr. Putnam sends. She ate better at lunch."

The flutter of her mother's eyelashes answered Reyna's next question before she could ask it.

"I'll leave you to it," Jean said, heading quickly to her bedroom.

"Hi, honey," her mother said in a voice grown reedy with unrelenting pain. Reyna patted the back of one blue-veined hand as gently as if she was touching a hatched chick. Anything harder could hurt more than it comforted.

"Hi yourself. What's Jean reading to you?" She listened with interest to the reply, but her mind was still turning over a possibility, a chance for relief from a situation that had long been intolerable.

"I saw you on television last night. You're such a striking couple."

Reyna sat down in the comfortable chair the nurse had vacated. "The movie wasn't very good." But the publicity had been fine, meeting with Jake's and her father's exacting standards. There were rumors of wedding bells between the house of Graham and the house of Putnam. Rumors were all they were. Jake knew she was seen with him only because she was compelled to do so, though he didn't know the means. "I got home really late and I've been dragging all day." Exhausted or not, she would find the energy it took to go out tonight, if she could also find the courage. She had laid the groundwork, now all she had to do was go through with it.

"What was it about?"

Reyna described the paper-thin plot of the big-budget action thriller. The premiere had been well-staged, and afterward her father had granted an interview with the Christian Broadcasting Network, which allowed him to voice his opinion that more Hollywood studios could follow this film's example. The protagonist prayed to Christ for strength, and that was a step in the right direction for faith-phobic Hollywood. Compared to other films of its type, there was minimal violence, sex and foul language. Reyna also thought it had minimal plot, minimal acting and minimal meaningful dialogue, but no one asked her opinion. She'd just been a poised and silent female on undeclared congressional candidate Jake Graham's arm.

She knew as she talked that her mother was deep in a fantasy about Reyna being settled down, taken care of — in other words, married, an estate that she had never enjoyed. Gretchen Langston had been a beautiful woman until lupus had seemed to fold her in on herself over the past six years. Every day her skin seemed more translucent, her eyes darker with pain.

Reyna cooperated and Grip took good care of them. Her mother did not know — or did not want to know — the price Reyna paid. Any resistance on her part led to worrisome complications and delays in medical reimbursements and appointments. They were always resolved happily, but some symptoms of lupus were directly worsened by stress, and her mother had a low threshold for anxiety.

But tonight, if Reyna had the courage, she could find

something to take the edge off her perpetual headache and channel the frustration and anger that was her daily life. She lived on the rim of a black hole, but tonight she might find something honest and clean.

Her mother was getting drowsy. Reyna knew that Jean would be back with the syringe that would give her some pain-free hours of rest. Jean was part of a rotation of live-in nurses who were with her mother at all times, skilled in pain-relieving massage, homeopathic cooking and rapid response to the seizures that were a growing concern as the disorder progressed. They also made sure Gretchen had her various hospital outpatient treatments, though Reyna tried to go along whenever her schedule allowed.

None of the doctors were using the phrase "final stages" for the related kidney disease, but Reyna did not think they were far off. Dialysis was effective, and as a private paying patient there was never any question of her having the treatments when she needed them. Her mother was able to stay in the little house she loved, near the University of California at Irvine. Reyna was able to drop in for lunch or in the evening for a while, seeing her mother almost every day, since the Putnam Institute, where Reyna was steadily being groomed to be her father's right-hand "man," was only a few miles away. Unlike in other politically successful families, Grip was determined there would be no question of his child's capabilities.

When her mother appeared to have nodded off, Reyna headed to the room the nurses took turns staying in. She knocked and went in when Jean called permission.

Jean was just buttoning her pajama top. Reyna averted her eyes from the curve of Jean's breasts, awash with the memory of Kimberly's similar shape and deep color, how they had tasted, how they had hardened in her mouth . . .

Jean was looking at her expectantly and Reyna struggled to find words. "She's asleep."

"She really did have a good day. The joint pain is less — I think the new tea is helping."

"That's good news. Well, you know how to reach me."

Jean nodded. Reyna was only minutes away, in the condo that the Institute had secured for her. Minutes away if that was where Reyna spent the night.

She had other plans, and she was desperate enough to try.

Kimberly had not believed Reyna would move out, hadn't believed it until Reyna did. Kim had not wanted to participate in a lie, would not let their relationship be made clandestine and unclean, and Reyna did not blame her one bit for her anger. Reyna had heard from her twice in the six years since: once an invitation to her commitment ceremony, which her father's administrative assistant declined, and the second time an announcement of the opening of a new law firm with her partner, specializing in employee and labor relations. The administrative assistant sent flowers.

The years at Berkeley to finish the double master's had been grueling. Georgetown had been no easier, but at least the distance from home had made Reyna feel less under her father's thumb. She had told herself there was a way out if only she could think of one. Being on the other side of the country from him had made it easier to believe she would some day find a way out of the cage he had made for her.

Every month she received a report on the expenses for her mother's treatments. Her father said it was just "FYI" but she knew it was meant to remind her that she could never manage on her own. Her mother had access to the best doctors and care, and without an insurance company to bicker about cost, the hospitals and treatment centers charged the highest possible fees. The total expended in the last six years made her mother uninsurable for any expenses related to the lupus. When Reyna had researched public assistance she'd discovered that her mother would have to lose all her assets first. She could claim her mother as her own dependent but as long as she had assets or income, they would disqualify her mother from assistance. A public program would not pay for a Jean to provide 24-hour- a-day companionship and watchful care.

The first few years she'd told herself everything would change when she finished her education. She'd consented to the changes he'd demanded because her mother's illness frightened her, and because the education he would pay for would bring her independence when she graduated. Then she would be able to secure a good-paying job with insurance, she told herself, and she would be able to tell him to go to hell. She hadn't understood then about pre-existing condition waiting periods. To cover her mother she'd have to be able to pay all of the expenses on her own for a year. She couldn't have known that by the time she left Georgetown, her mother's kidney disease would escalate. She could have found a six-figure job some place other than her father's institute, she knew, but it wouldn't be enough, even before taxes. By the time she saved enough money to make it for a year paying the bills, the bills had doubled in size. Her father's bottomless checkbook was there for her mother. She could have careful, life-extending care and keep her home and dignity. In the larger scheme of things, all that largesse came at such a small price to Reyna. What was a dream or two in exchange for her mother's comfort, peace of mind, and additional years of life?

So she worked at the Putnam Institute and conducted research for conservative causes, thinking all the while that it was only for a few more years. Every time she thought specifically about time she was wracked with guilt. Looking forward to an escape could only mean one thing: she wanted her mother to hurry up and die. She didn't want that, she knew it in her heart. But sometimes at night, sometimes when she felt so alone and the black hole seemed about to swallow her . . . sometimes, she would think about its being only a matter of a few more years and she would feel . . . relieved. Comforted. And then . . . she would wish she knew exactly when she would be free because it would be easier to bear, knowing.

It was just another reason to hate herself — asking God to give her an exact date for her mother's death.

Her days were busy with meetings, conferences, poring over research data and writing position papers, all for causes she loathed. She played the part of her father's hostess when she had to, including photo opportunities. But she accepted the situation, and knew that she had it easy. She really could be trying to manage on her own, trying to earn a living while taking her mother to almost daily medical appointments and all the while sinking into debt that would ultimately take everything. It could be worse, she told herself. When her mind was occupied, it was possible to rationalize her role in press releases with titles like "Study Shows Man-Boy Molestation on the Rise."

In the past six years since that afternoon when her father had claimed her future for his own purposes, there had been one interlude, one brief affair while she was at Georgetown, when she had felt alive. Margeaux. They had wanted the same thing — sex and discretion. It had been three glorious months until a visit from her father ended the illusion of freedom. Private detectives had discerned the affair almost immediately, but he had needed time to arrange things to his satisfaction before ordering her to end it. She refused, not yet believing he would do what he said he would do. He warned her, but she still refused. She and Margeaux were not in love, but she hadn't wanted to believe he was that ruthless.

A few days later Reyna discovered her mother had had a seizure — and no nurse had been with her. Her father claimed it was just an oversight, but Reyna no longer believed in coincidences where he was concerned. Again, yes, she was tired of freedom.

When she'd met Margeaux for the last time, Margeaux had said it was for the best. Her grades were too low to maintain the program, and she'd just received notice she was being academically suspended. Her family had sacrificed a lot for a Georgetown law degree, but Margeaux would finish at an upstate New York college, closer to home. It was more affordable. Her father had just been laid off, too, and, well, she had to accept the realities of her situation.

They'd gone back to Margeaux's apartment and Reyna had not known it would be the last time she'd feel a woman moving against her, under her, on top of her. She had relived that night hundreds of times in the years since because it, and Kimberly, was all she had to treasure. A few months later a letter from Margeaux revealed that her father had been miraculously rehired and she had received an unexpected scholarship at her new school. Shortly after that, during a seemingly casual visit, her father had mentioned that her "little friend" seemed so much better off in her new locale.

When you did what Grip Putnam wanted, everything was fine.

She was not doing what he wanted, not tonight. She couldn't stand it anymore. At a meeting earlier in the day, discussing public relations opportunities to improve the image of the National Rifle Association, she'd found herself listening with interest to the rules for obtaining a handgun in California. Her sense of horror had made her feel faint. Regarding herself in the bathroom mirror a few minutes later she realized something was going to break, and badly. She was caught in a fabulously gilded cage that swung at her father's whim over the black hole of his designs. Without a taste of freedom she would do something unspeakable, either to her father, who deserved it, or to her mother, who did not.

Though she usually drove with one eye focused on her rear-view mirror, looking for the private detectives she knew were always lurking, tonight she didn't care. They would follow her to a place where she'd gone many times — the university's Friday all-night art film marathon. Bergman's faith trilogy was on the marquee, leading off with *Through a Glass, Darkly*.

She bought a ticket and a box of Raisinets, just as she always did. Her black jeans and Armani leather jacket allowed her to be just another dark-haired woman in the theater. She waited for the movie to start, then, under cover of the dim light of the cinematic Nordic night, she slipped out the rear exit. From the alley she walked to the next block and up the stairs to the apartment over the motorcycle repair shop.

"I was beginning to wonder if you were coming tonight." Tank Peña eased his bulk onto the tiny landing, leading the way down to the shop's rear door. "I finished her yesterday and she purrs like a kitten."

Tank had found the motorcycle for her, refurbished it and then registered it in his own name, though she would be the only rider. It was a minor informational fraud, Reyna had rationalized. He chattered about the idiosyncrasies of Yamaha bikes and 750 cc's, but Reyna only saw the silver name melded into the black body: *Virago*.

Tonight, it fit.

Borrowed leather gloves and a black helmet transformed her from a research and media specialist for conservative causes to unrestrained biker chick. It felt wonderful.

She realized Tank was waiting for some acknowledgment. "She's beautiful," she said belatedly, but with feeling. The engine purred so cool and clean she didn't even have to raise her voice. Kim had taught her to ride. Her father had never noticed her driver's license also allowed her to ride motorcycles, or he would have surely told her to give it up. The link between bike and dyke was too close.

Cash had been all Tony needed to fix Reyna up with something — he just wanted to see another beautiful bike on the road. He hadn't asked many questions. He was still enough of an anarchist to like the secrecy and the tax-free income. She had plenty of money of her own. The Institute or her father paid for almost all her expenses. Her after-tax income was embarrassing, and yet it couldn't begin to cover the medical bills that mounted up with each dialysis treatment and trip to the ICU. What she had saved up so far would get them about eight months before there was nothing left. But she kept saving and investing because sooner or later, money would mean independence.

She withdrew hundreds of dollars in cash a month but spent little of it. The rest was squirreled away in her apartment for things she wanted to buy with no way for her father to find out — like a motorcycle, or a motel room for a few hours.

She parted from Tank with a wave. With the thrill that only a completely forbidden activity could bring, she headed for the open road, feeling for the first time in years that eyes were not on her every move.

For the next thirty minutes, just riding was enough. She almost felt like she could take the bike back and it would be enough to dance around the black hole and know she wouldn't fall in. She could smile tomorrow, cooperate, listen to clients who described gays as pedophiles, lesbians as man-haters, feminists as Nazis, the NAACP as radicals, amen, world without end. She could help them write their speeches, twist research to suit their arguments, find new ways to present hate disguised as morality. It was what the Putnam Institute did, and she was good at it, a real chip off the old block.

It was from an outraged male client that she had learned about the monthly ladies' night at the nearest gay bar. Wasn't it outrageous that women who ought to be ashamed of themselves would parade around as if they had a right, dance to that disgusting music, cruise for perverted sex, and so close to where they lived? Reyna's heightened perception had detected the undercurrent of salacious arousal at the idea. Coping with her own revulsion, she had almost missed what the information could mean to her.

She cycled a cloverleaf to head west on the 405, leaning hard into the turn as the wind billowed her jacket open. The air was like ice but it made her feel even more alive. Orange County was the conservative center of California politics, and some neighborhoods were little better than restricted communities. The Putnam Institute was located in the county's political heart, Irvine, and nestled deep in Bonita Canyon, a few miles from the University of California at Irvine.

She left it all behind, whipped past the John Wayne Airport, then a short jaunt north to the border zone between Costa Mesa and Santa Ana. The bike didn't want to slow down, but she followed the route she had memorized. Another generic L.A. boulevard gave way to a still busy strip where restaurants were only now beginning to close their doors. At the far end she turned into a parking lot choked with cars.

She cruised slowly past the front door to Jack's. A small sign indeed proclaimed it Ladies' Night. Even over the vibration of the bike she could feel the bumping pulse of the music inside. She eased into a spot between the nose of a Subaru SUV and the wall of the club. With the engine off the music was even more pronounced. Above that she heard the babble of women's voices.

It hurt to be so close and not be part of it. She kept her helmet on until she was inside, then checked it, the gloves and her jacket with a pouty, bored blonde. The ten-dollar bill she tithed to the doorkeeper trembled in her shaking hand.

She stepped inside and let Madonna carry her to the dance floor where it was dark and no one cared that she was dancing alone.

She never learned the woman's name. She didn't have to know. It was better that way. What she didn't know her father would never learn. It was just for tonight, just for an hour, maybe two.

Her teeth felt sharp on Reyna's throat. From a mutual recognition on the dance floor they had moved to the outdoor patio, which was screened from the outside world by thick shrubs, and dark enough to ignore what other couples were doing. She heard a gasp nearby, knew what it meant and wanted to feel that gasp herself, to take and be taken. She moaned and unbuttoned her blouse, eager to be naked, to be skin to skin with this stranger. She was a woman and that was all that mattered.

"We're going to get tossed if you show any more skin," the woman murmured. "But if you want to show it, we could get more involved in my pickup — it's parked outside."

In her father's world it was sordid, but how could it be to her? She had to hide, lie, disguise herself to be here, and her father's world drove her to those extremities. That she could find any kind of bliss, no matter how short-lived, under these circumstances was a matter of solace. If this was all there could be, she would survive on it. The mattress that occupied the entire bed of the pickup was meant for just this purpose, as were the thick curtains that darkened the windows of the enclosing shell. Privacy, anonymity — it was what she had come there for, and it felt like salvation.

The kisses were as penetrating as the fingers inside her, stealing her breath, stopping her cries, holding yesses between their mouths. She filled her hands with hair and skin, with breasts and thighs. They coiled around each other, trading places but always entwined, moving together toward having enough.

Longing and denial made her feel as if she'd never tasted a woman before, the salt of her, the wet, welcoming slick. How could anyone give this up? God had given her the capacity to love this, to share this intimate act with another woman. Wouldn't turning her back on it be hubris? Who was she to deny how God had made her?

Afterward she wanted only air, to breathe with happiness and savor feeling like a woman. Her companion seemed content to do the same for a few minutes.

"Jesus," the woman finally said. "You just about put me to sleep. Good lord."

The thigh pillow under Reyna's cheek moved and reluctantly Reyna sat up, nearly bumping her head on the roof. Fingertips brushing her breast took her by surprise, but the hot swell of desire felt wonderful as it flushed her skin.

"Let me say thank you," the woman murmured, and Reyna let her.

She walked the bike into Tank's garage, then slipped the key under his door. Across the street, down the alley, to her car — she walked slowly as if Bergman had wearied her. She shook her hair around her face to hide what felt like a glow of peace.

6

Seventeen boxes and two carloads — Holly had gotten it right. The motel room was stuffed with sagging, bulging cartons, leaving her only the bed to rest on. Stretched out, she had no choice but to think.

Clay had not taken it well. She could even see it from his point of view. He could easily explain it to a friend with, "She flipped out. One day she quit her job and two days later she packed up and left. I have no idea why."

When she'd come in out of the rain, the party had been winding down and Clay drove them home. He didn't appear to notice that she was soaking wet. As she shivered in the car, she considered that she was lucky that their lives weren't complicated by children or entangled financial affairs. Remembering what Tori said about realizing she'd never given her future to Geena, Holly knew the same was true of her and Clay. She'd never asked herself where they would end up together. They had worked hard to keep everything the same from day to day, as if tomorrows would never come and neither of them would ever change.

She took a warm shower when they got home and was relieved that Clay had already fallen asleep. She dozed off, finally, but only for a few hours. She had left Galina's card to dry on the table next to the bed. In the morning she tucked it back into her bra and tried to forget what it represented. Work clothes were the order of the day. She made him breakfast for the last time and then went to the garage for boxes.

"What's up?" Clay was frowning into the refrigerator, obviously not caring for its contents.

"I'm leaving."

"Where to?" He closed the door and looked up. She did not flinch from meeting and holding his gaze.

Calmly, carefully, "I'm leaving."

Abruptly, he looked like a balloon with all the air out. "You've had another one of your brainstorms," he accused.

She wanted to be gentle, but she also felt a tide rising inside that pushed her to this moment. "Call it that if you like. I realized in the last few days that we share the same space but hardly connect, and not even physically."

He was shaking his head. He always shook his head while she was talking. She jotted that onto her mental list of Why I'm Leaving Clay Today. "Are you giving in to socialization about romantic ideals? No one can live up to those images. Most of the world doesn't equate love with passion, or expect them to arrive at the same time. It's only expected in modernized countries, where a massive marketing machine keeps these ideas prominent in our psyches. So we'll buy roses, and chocolate and greeting cards —"

"I don't want roses and chocolate, Clay. Christ." It was cruel, but she would never get through otherwise. "I want an orgasm."

He flushed and she had to look away.

More carefully, she went on, "At a very basic level, we're

99

not sexually compatible. I don't think I — I don't think you can give me what I want, and I will never agree that what I want is somehow wrong."

Harshly, he said, "What is it you want?"

"Passion would be good — oh, stop looking like that. I'm as much to blame as you. I never told you that I didn't — that it wasn't working for me. I admired you, and I wanted to be there for you. And I was. You were the worst house-keeper I'd ever seen, so I cleaned for you. You never ate because you never shopped, so I did that too. You believed that growing our own vegetables was a good thing, so I did it. Whatever you expressed as lacking in your life, I tried to fill the void." She wiped away a tear — it was just tension. "I worked at a job you hated so you could take a sabbatical, and I stayed at that job because we needed the money for the mortgage."

"I — I didn't realize you felt it all such a sacrifice."

"I didn't, not until recently. Then I had to ask myself, for all I gave up, for all the work, how did you balance it out? You were able to take on more classes, but you stopped your private studies. You're pompous about what a simple life is and judgmental about everyone else who doesn't have Holly the acolyte to make living a simple life so very easy. I've enabled all the worst things about you. I made you lazy."

"So you're doing this for me." He said it flatly and she could tell he wasn't going to listen to much more.

"No. For me. And I'm praying that in a year you'll also be in a better place. We've become so stale —"

His voice was sharp and bitter. "Because I don't cuddle, or go down on you, or what?"

"That's not it —" It was, partly.

"I never asked you to do that to me —"

"I know. Maybe you should have." There had been a time, she knew it, that she would have done anything to please him. But she had never thought it would, and it appeared she had been right about that. Abruptly she thought, *I'm not the only one with a problem here.*

He shuddered. "We're not animals."

"I can't remember the last time you laughed," she

added softly. "I can't remember the last time you hugged me for no reason at all. I understand if you don't see that as a problem, but I do and I have to . . ." She floundered. "I need light. I need heat."

"And this all came to you out of the blue?"

She had not foreseen this crossroad, and certainly not how hard it was to remain silent. She could tell him more, and be rational about it, probably. She could explain that she found his ideology contradictory, and his assumptions to be without merit on many issues.

But she was angry now, and wanted to hammer at him that she was a human being, with a body, that he might have touched her, kissed her, told her that he loved the way her skin felt — God, anything. Any small thing that showed a moment of affection on his part. He was the one without any essential humanity.

She was silent because she didn't want to say any of those things. She was the one who had refused to see his flaws for eight years. The only person she could fix here was herself.

She left the kitchen for the living room and began removing books from the shelves. When he followed her she said calmly, "I don't want to quibble about what belongs to whom. I'm taking my books and clothes, of course. My music and the food I know you won't eat. That's all." She blew dust off her Bertrand Russell texts and set them in the next box. "I can show you an accounting, if you like, of the household money. I'm not taking any of it. But I am keeping my savings account. It's roughly equal to the extra I paid down on the mortgage, which is in your name, along with the house. You come out ahead if you count appreciation in. I just want this to be clean."

His voice was chilly. "Where will you be if I need to reach you?"

"I don't know where I'm going," she admitted.

"Typical of you." From chill to acid.

She sighed, held back the anger and said mildly, "Yes, of course, I'm wrong as usual. But in a few hours you won't have me underfoot, needing a constant grade. I should think you'd be relieved."

"I was only trying to help you."

"To be like you, and that's what I'm trying to tell you, Clay. I don't want to be like you. Not anymore. I grew up, all at once."

"Fine." He stalked to the kitchen.

Holly paused in her work to write Tori's phone number down for him. She didn't want him calling Jo before she had a chance to tell her — Jesus, to tell her she'd been right. About everything. And thank her for caring enough to risk their friendship with truth.

She carried the paper into the kitchen. "Leave a message for me with Tori. I'll let her know you might have to call."

"Tori? I thought —" His gaze was all over her suddenly, speculative and furious. "Is that what this is really about? Because everything you've said so far is bullshit."

She turned back to the living room and he grabbed her arm. "Don't, Clay!"

"It's about this dyke — she's got you in a sweat and now you think you are one. That's why you quit your job. There's nothing wrong with me, you just want —"

"Stop it!" She shook her arm free. She was blushing furiously but he wasn't right, at least not about why she quit. "What I might want or not want from a lover has nothing to do with the fact that what I don't want is you!"

He thought he had her in a debate now. He surged in to take the advantage. "What will you do after her? When you no longer want to be queer?"

"And you call yourself a liberal," she snapped. He was towering over her now and she tried to hold back her panic; she had never seen him physically angry before. "Leave me alone!"

"At least I'm normal!"

She retreated, he followed. "Just leave me alone!"

"Who would have thought that that angry, bitter woman was right about something," he said insidiously. "She was actually right."

She stopped retreating. "Aunt Zinnia? What's that supposed to mean?"

"Ask her yourself."

She felt the blood draining out of her face. Last night, standing in the rain, she had felt there was something she hadn't known. "Tell me," she said intensely.

He took his revenge by laughing. Then he had slammed into his study and though later she would smell incense, she hadn't had to face him again, not even when she had come back for the second carload.

So you're holed up in a cheap motel, she told herself, going over the scene with Clay as if it will change something. Not exactly a good plan — okay, Clay was right about that. But she could not have managed another day. When dams burst, floods are inevitable.

She didn't look at the bedside table. Would not look. But she knew Galina's card was there. "Call me when you're not straight anymore," she had said.

Was she not straight anymore? What did that mean?

Dinner, she had to go out to get something to eat. She was, in fact, ravenous. Yes, dinner was a diversion she badly needed.

It was only convenience that took her to Tish's. It was close and she wanted comfort food. She needed to call Tori, she remembered, to warn her that Clay might leave a message. There was a pay phone outside the restaurant. Yes, convenience was the only reason she was there.

All the while she knew the truth — she was still walking the spit of land between the chasms of past and future. She even knew she was tottering toward the future at last. But she could pretend that coincidence and circumstance were at work. Even knowing that true coincidence was rare, she lied to herself, for the moment.

The restaurant was mostly populated by women and the sight of them made her suddenly afraid. They would all think — they would all assume something she wasn't. At least not yet. When will you be, she wondered. What's the rite of passage? When will you not be straight anymore?

She would get the food to go. Tish recognized her, though, and called out, "Tori, your friend's here."

Tori had on an apron and bright yellow gloves. "Heya, Holly. Liked the food, didn't you? I told you so. I'm still slaving away. It's the cold and flu season."

"You're a good dishwasher," Tish admitted fondly.

"For this I went to college?" She turned back to Holly. "I think I'm going to go the whole route and become an actuary. What do you think?"

"I think that's an excellent idea."

"Geena is behind me one hundred —" She stopped. "What's wrong?"

"It's just tension," Holly said. She fumbled in her pocket for a tissue, even though she knew she didn't have any. It was just tension. And she was here for convenience, not for the warm shoulder Tori offered as she drew her into the kitchen and away from prying eyes.

It was a flood and her incoherent account told Tori only a little bit about why. She didn't want Tori to know the whole truth.

"This is all my fault," Tori said after a while. "You fought because you quit and you quit because of me."

"No," Holly mumbled. "I quit because it was the right thing to do. I didn't know he'd be an ass about it. I didn't expect that." She raised her head at last from Tori's shoulder. Tori smelled like oregano and disinfectant. There was something charming about the combination.

"You can stay with us." Tori's offer was heartfelt. "Until you find a place."

She shook her head. "No, but thank you. It's nice to know I have a safety net of some kind. I'm just looking for something simple and cheap until I decide what to do."

"Hey, I have a friend with an illegal mother-in-law rental. You don't tell the county and the rent is really reasonable. Great little cottage for one in the back yard. One big room downstairs, a complete kitchen, and a single room upstairs. I think it would suit you just fine."

It sounded ideal. Wary of leaping before she looked, though, Holly said, "I'd love to take a look at it."

"Her name's Flo — you'll die when you talk to her. She's got a dreamy English accent. Gets me every time." Tori found a pen and pencil and scribbled furiously. "Here's her number. But I'm leaving here in about an hour. Why don't you have a bite to eat and I'll call her and maybe we can go see it. The previous tenant moved out this week and I don't think she's had time to clean and paint it, though."

How could she have not known that Tori was such a nice person? How could she not know whatever it was that Clay said her aunt knew? She was ignorant, for all her brains, that much was clear.

Tish served her dinner at the dark end of the bar to spare her being single in the dining room with a blotchy, tear-streaked face. She had an enormous plate of noodles, broccoli and roasted garlic tossed with olive oil and Parmesan cheese. By the end of it she felt better, not so much teetering toward her future as perhaps allowing herself to fall because it was the only way to move on.

She had agreed to a slice of a very decadent-looking chocolate cheesecake when a voice in her ear murmured, "Well, if it isn't the mouse that roared."

Two things happened at once. She said, "Leave me alone," and she felt a clenching, tight and hard, deep in her abdomen — muscles moving she did not know she had.

Murphy leaned on the bar. In spite of the winter temperatures, she wore a sleeveless muscle shirt with her jeans, and obviously nothing under it.

Holly thought, "Save me," and hoped Tori got the message. But she hadn't told Tori about not being straight anymore.

"Now I've been told that Tori is still with Geena and you're just a friend. That you have a boyfriend."

Holly said nothing because her mouth was watering, and the sheer magnitude of her physical reaction to Murphy's long, lean body had taken her completely by surprise. She was nothing like Galina. What do I like, Holly wondered, now that I'm not straight anymore?

"But I do always wonder," Murphy went on nonchalantly, "how a straight woman can be friends with a dyke, hang out in a eatery run by a dyke, with dykes at most of the tables and, deep down, not be there because she's curious."

Murphy shifted her weight and Holly wanted to close her eyes. But Murphy would know why — it would be to shut out the clear view she had of Murphy's taut nipples, pushing hard against the shirt, straining. Her mouth wouldn't stop watering and she had to swallow.

Murphy's voice was smooth and intimate. "I know women who have scruples about straight women. But I'm not one of them. I don't care where a woman has been or where she's going next. When I'm with a woman I've got one goal — finding out what she likes, even if she doesn't know herself, and getting her there."

Holly's sweater hid the gooseflesh that prickled her arms and back, and she was glad she'd put on all the extra layers. What could Murphy want with her? She wasn't Tori. It had to be just for the conquest. The clenching muscles were now in her thighs, and her hips ached from the effort to keep them still.

"Get lost, Murphy."

Tori, thank God, at last.

"Can't blame a girl for trying, can you?"

"Yes, you can," Tori snapped.

Thankfully, Murphy and her nipples left Holly's periphral vision.

"I'm sorry about her," Tori said as she slid onto the barstool next to Holly. "She's only bugging you because of me . . ."

Holly couldn't say anything, not yet, but she could feel Tori's gaze on her as intently as Clay's had been earlier. The blush started at the top of her head and ended in a knot of heat between her legs.

"Oh . . ." It was all Tori said for a while.

Tish brought the cheesecake but Holly couldn't eat it, not then. Finally, she sipped some water and felt like she could breathe.

"Everything is happening all at once, isn't it?" Tori's voice was kind.

Holly blinked back yet more tears and nodded. "Yeah. It started . . . sort of yesterday at lunch." She laughed, not happily. "What a difference a day makes."

"Wow. Most women I know, well, it always seems gradual to them. Like the truth sneaks up. That's how it was for me. For Geena."

106

"It feels like I've been struck by lightning."

"Stay away from Murphy," Tori said seriously. "I understand how appealing she can be — and physically you'd have no regrets, but —"

"I know," Holly said quickly. "I know. I just, I've spent my entire adult life trying to be in control. Clay was always so quick to point out when I wasn't. And this is . . ." She swallowed hard. "I can't control this. Five minutes more and I'd have been wherever Murphy wanted me." She twisted her fingers around each other, unable to say that she would have been begging, pleading, aching for things she could not even name. "I feel like I'm going from one addiction to another."

"And it doesn't feel good. Oh hon, I know. Let's get the cheesecake in a box and go see Flo's place. At least take care of the shelter, food and clothing. Then you can focus on the rest."

Holly let Tori do the driving and most of the talking. She'd gone from Aunt Zinnia's domination to Clay's, and if anything was going to be better she had to take control of herself. Maybe she would be sexually satisfied with Murphy, but if she wasn't careful she would go on making the same mistakes. Maybe she'd like the fire better than the frying pan, but either way she got cooked.

Flo did have a dreamy accent. It was the first thing Holly thought and she gave Tori a glance of pure betrayal. They should have waited, how was she supposed to withstand such a thing?

If anything, Tori was fighting a smile.

All Flo said was, "It's a pleasure to meet you."

Holly kept her hands in her pockets, though she felt she was being rude. Shaking hands with Galina had led to a lot of trouble. She thought about Galina's card. Was she not straight anymore?

The cottage was built for one. A breakfast table, sofa and one chair would finish the downstairs, and upstairs there was room for a bed and perhaps a desk. The upper floor smelled strongly of the beige paint that had been recently applied.

"It's students who most want it, but I'm tired of the

bother and the mates who come round at all hours. My last tenant was an older woman. She's moved to be nearer her daughter." Flo was perhaps in her mid-forties, with soft features to match her lyrical voice.

Holly was paying attention, or at least she was trying to. "I don't have a job at the moment, but I've saved up quite a lot of money. I don't even have furniture, so I could get exactly what fits. This is what I'm looking for."

They came to terms quickly and Tori gave a happy bounce. "I knew it was a good idea. I feel totally less guilty."

"You picked the last one very nicely," Flo admitted. "I should pay you a fee."

"Pay me in scones," Tori suggested brightly. "With clotted cream and strawberry jam."

"Bring Geena tomorrow for supper and we'll be quits. We'll do chips and eggs, too, just like my mum used to make home in Chester." Flo had led them inside her back door and was putting the lease papers out on the table. Not to be a complete idiot, Holly read them, found them agreeable, and signed on the dotted line.

There were footsteps overhead, then on the stairs. A woman a few years younger than Holly burst into the kitchen. "Oh, sorry, babe. I thought you were done."

"Just about. There's nothing on telly tonight. I just checked."

The younger woman dropped a careless kiss onto Flo's lips. "Then we'll have to think of something else to do."

"This is Holly," Flo said, after she had shared a contemplative smile with her lover. "She's renting the cottage."

"That's great. Nancy," she said, holding out her hand.

Holly had no choice. Nancy had a strong, warm grip. Holly had not known her arms could feel such a range of tingling sensations.

"You have anything against beige?"

Holly shook her head and took her hand back.

"Good. I'll be finished with the downstairs tomorrow."

"Will I be able to move in on Monday?"

"Yeah, though it'll still smell. Cold weather and paint, it takes forever for it to really cure out." Nancy shrugged. She had broad shoulders. "I do commercial painting by day so I can do artistic painting by night."

"Oh, so that's what you do with your nights," Tori quipped.

"Painting of one kind or another." They all laughed. Holly joined in though she was thoroughly unsettled by the idea of Nancy's sharp edges merging with Flo's soft curves.

It seemed that all she could think about was sex. Sex and Galina's card. Flo's mouth. Nancy's hands. Murphy's nipples. Tori's eyes. Galina's kisses. Was she not straight anymore?

It was easy to settle into a house so small, and a visit to a used furniture store had completed the effort. She gave herself a few days to settle in — there could never be enough bookcases, she quickly concluded — and tried hard not to think about anything but mathematics.

She surrounded herself with library books and rapidly realized she needed a computer. More technology — Clay would not understand. But she could find out about degree programs and requirements for colleges everywhere more quickly on the Internet than through the mail. She could join the Academy of Mathematicians and start reading the journal online. There was so much she could do, and so easily, that when she asked herself if it all somehow robbed her of her essential humanity, the answer was no.

So she took the plunge into technology with a cute little laptop that had a built-in modem. She pored over the guide for beginners, made lots of mistakes, and came close to heaving it out the window at least four times. When she finally began navigating around the World Wide Web she wished for a printer. Technology *was* addictive. She bought a small color inkjet the next day and stopped to worry if she was damaging her essential humanity. She shrugged it off — even the Amish were selling quilts online. If the Amish could square their consciences with some technology, then who was she to worry?

She found out that she could automatically synch her

Palm Pilot to her laptop, sharing the addresses and appointments on both. It was so, well, cool. Clay was nuts. There was so much to learn that it was easy to not think about other things . . . Galina, Tori and Geena, Tori and Murphy. She saw Flo coming home from work and Nancy meeting her at the door with an eagerness that surpassed Clay's at his most passionate. As she walked the narrow driveway to the street one evening she glimpsed Flo unbuttoning Nancy's shirt while they were in the kitchen. It had been hours before she stopped seeing the image of Nancy's hungry, trembling expression behind her closed lids.

She tried not to think about Clay, because thinking about him made her think about Galina's card and then all the rest. Sometimes at night she would shiver under the sheets and ask herself what it would have hurt to go with Murphy, to learn everything about what she liked. What held her back?

It was her common sense, a quality that neither Clay nor Aunt Zinnia had ever thought she'd possessed in any sufficient quantity. Well, she did have it. She knew she needed to start off in this new life with some semblance of control. But at night she didn't feel in control and her hands brought only torment.

Two weeks passed in a numbed blur, with mornings that were over before she'd finished one cup of coffee and evenings that dragged endlessly. She joined the mathematicians' society and read online journals until her eyes felt raw and her brain spun with puzzles and proofs, new and old. Theories and ideas were waiting to be tested in the ever-broadening, free-flowing exchange. The love of a good riddle discussed in the local brewery after classes had made way for Internet message boards devoted to single equations and new ideas added all the time. The humor and joy of it caught her all over again, just as it had when she was a girl. How could she have thought anything could substitute for something she loved?

She spent six hours alone happily absorbing the discussion around a sound-wave proposal. Was it possible for two drums to be sound-wave identical but shaped differently? Yes, was the answer. The suggested equation for building two different/identical drums speculated that nearly infinite arrangements were possible. So far, two eight-sided drums had been designed based on the formula, one sort of L-shaped and the other closer to a Z. Clicking ever forward through the messages, she read that the two drums had been tested and compared by microwave in a sound lab.

Scientists were thrilled. They now had a mathematical formula they could use to predict sound-wave results in any given material — say, steel — regardless of how it was formed. In a solid block or a thin wheel, it no longer mattered. X amount of steel in Y configurations should result in Z kinds of wave forms. If your business was testing train wheels for cracks, you could now use a microwave sound test instead of the less reliable hammer method. A reading outside the predicted result could indicate a crack much earlier than even an experienced railroad worker's ear could. Forget steel — the manufacturers of silicon chips were euphoric. They now had a method of testing their computer microchips that didn't damage the delicate silicon components.

God, she loved math.

She read, she slept, she read, she dreamed, she read, and she wondered how she could find her way back into the field. There was so much she had to catch up on. She'd lost so much time. Could she make a career of it? At twenty-six, with a birthday rapidly approaching, she was old to be taking up a master's and doctorate program. Perhaps she should aim lower, get a teaching credential and employ what she knew. Jo was right — girls needed role models in math. But she didn't have any coursework in teaching. How could she get a credential?

Self-doubt came easy when you were lonely, she realized, and she went for long walks to vanquish what she called the Echo of Clay. She still felt poised between the past and future.

So. If her work future was stalled by her lack of confidence, she would focus instead on her personal affairs. She had let them slide, refusing to look at Galina's card, tucked into the edge of the bathroom mirror. She'd buried her head in math to avoid the messy questions that went unanswered. She was not straight anymore, but she wasn't a lesbian — at least she didn't feel like one. She didn't know if it was possible to be a theoretical lesbian, or "all but sex" lesbian. How to go from theory to practice? Sitting in her little cottage day in and night out was not an answer.

And there were darker questions, from her past. Perhaps that was the best place to begin. The past was finite, it could be explored, summarized and redressed. Her future needed a past.

On a Friday night two weeks after her last visit, she pulled up to the curb outside her aunt's house. She was not expected.

Winter had taken a break, and though there had been a brief rainfall the night before, the twilight sky was illuminated by early stars.

She was nervous about the confrontation, but laughed to herself when she accepted that even with two mirrors, the horizon and a familiar star to navigate by, she still wouldn't know where she was. She hadn't known for most of her life.

She needed clarity for this conversation and so she would approach it with the most rational methodology she could. There was a secret, and Clay knew what it was. He'd said her aunt had been right about something, implied that her aunt had known all along that Holly was a lesbian. She remembered, too, her aunt's furious reaction to Holly's jibe about homosexuality running in families.

There was a secret and she had already reduced it to two possible answers. Neither of them made sense, but that did not deter her. They didn't make sense because the equation was incomplete. So she had to ask for more information to fill in the constants and variables that had been hidden from her. If she could stay calm, she might find what she needed.

"It's you," Aunt Zinnia said when she opened the door.

"It's me. I know I didn't call, but I need to talk to you about something."

"Come in, then."

Aunt Zinnia did not make tea. They perched on the sitting room chairs and Holly asked her carefully constructed question. "Why weren't there any pictures of my mother for me to keep?"

Aunt Zinnia didn't answer immediately. She studied her hands, then finally said, "You know she and I had disagreements."

"Yes, but you might have let me have a few. For myself. Since she was my mother."

"You are probably right. At the time, I thought it was for the best. There weren't very many in the house, and they were all recent."

Holly asked her follow-up question. "What did you think I'd see in them?"

Aunt Zinnia shrugged. Her diffidence was feigned, Holly knew. Aunt Zinnia had a reason for everything she did, right or wrong.

Paul Erdős, the beloved mathematician and champion puzzle creator and solver, proposed that a person could answer a question by throwing as many darts as necessary in the general direction of a target. The pattern of hits over properly constructed objects on the target would indicate where the solution lay. She had two possible solutions: The secret Clay had alluded to concerned either Aunt Zinnia or her mother.

Now she had at least one hit within the range — Aunt Zinnia had refused to say what the photographs might have told her. It ought to have been an easy answer. For that one answer, she felt more certain that the secret was about her mother.

All the thinking of the past two weeks had led her to acceptance. She did not know if homosexuality ran in families, but all she needed to know was that Aunt Zinnia thought so.

"Did you think that if I had pictures of her, I'd be like her?"

The shrug was more abrupt. Hit two.

"You went to great pains to tell me she wasn't a decent woman. Too pushy, too smart, too independent. Was there anything else? That made her not decent?" She could accept the answer. It wasn't such a shock after all. If her mother had been a lesbian that was just the way it was. Her mother had loved her and nothing changed that. But knowing would help her emerge from the shadow the past cast on her own future.

Aunt Zinnia was just staring at her. "I don't know why you are asking all these questions."

"Because I am trying to make sense of it. You were so afraid I'd be like her. You even told Clay something about it. He wouldn't tell me what it was but said I should ask you. So I'm asking."

"I have no idea what either of you are talking about."

"A secret. About me."

"I don't have any secrets."

The lie was monumental and Holly was sure she was right. She had a readable pattern over the target. "My mother was a lesbian, wasn't she? And you've been afraid all along that I would become one, too."

Aunt Zinnia's lips thinned as she paled. "I want you to go."

"You completely cut me off from my friends when I moved here. You wouldn't let me make friends with girls, no sleepovers, no chances for experimenting — you were scared I would realize I was gay. How did you know I was?"

"I didn't know —" Aunt Zinnia's mouth snapped shut.

"But you wondered. Because my mother was."

Her aunt's face was working with the effort to hold back, but the words escaped anyway. "She was raising you to be one, too. When she died in such a stupid accident I could only think that God had given me a chance to save you. She was going to *tell* you. Because she didn't want you to feel it was wrong if you had the same perverted tendencies —"

"She never thought of it as perverted," Holly said tightly. "She would never have said that. She loved me and loved herself. I have to reach so far back to find my memories of her, but they're there, and these past few

114

weeks they've been all I have to remind me what it's like to love who you are. She made me feel that way, while you and Clay worked overtime to make me think I was flawed and needed constant correction and improvement."

"I don't want to talk about it anymore." She looked suddenly exhausted.

"Just tell me I'm right." Holly stood up, and refused to feel pity for her aunt's obvious distress. She watched the knotted hands twisting in her aunt's lap and hardened her heart. She may be old, but she knows the truth. *She owes me the truth.*

"I won't."

Holly turned on her heel and left. She was practically certain she had the equation filled out correctly. How would she bridge the gap between practically and absolutely? Without certainty, she could not search for an answer to the second secret — the bigger secret, apparently. If her mother had been a lesbian, then where had Holly come from? Aunt Zinnia probably knew the answer to that as well, but getting more out of her would be difficult, if not impossible.

As she had after her last visit to her aunt's, she drove past the house where she had lived until her mother's death. It wasn't raining this time, so she got out of the car and tried to open all the memories. She recalled vividly the day her mother had died, and random events earlier than that. A picnic, a good grade, a neighbor who dropped in sometimes. Disassociated recollections were easy to recall but hard to make sense of. Harder still to realistically know how old she had been at any of those times because it's not uppermost in a child's mind.

Her mother had been going to tell her she was gay because she wanted Holly to be aware of possibilities. Had something tipped her mother off? Holly couldn't remember any special friend that she had been overly fond of. Was it her love of comfortable clothes — her aversion to make-up and stiletto heels? Why was she the last person to figure it out? It was far more probable that her mother had simply wanted Holly to know the truth, and live with an example of being open and proud about who you are. If so, it was a gift she had needed, because no one else had bothered to teach it to her.

She watched the house and hoped for one of her brainstorms, but nothing happened. She was about to go when a sedan went by her and turned into the driveway the four houses shared. It carefully pulled into the carport of the house that stood next to theirs.

She hadn't been able to remember their neighbor's name last week. It was dark, but she was sure it was a woman getting out of the car and opening her trunk. Holly took a couple of steps closer, telling herself that the slender, erect carriage, the rapid, sure movements were just a superficial resemblance. It was unlikely after all this time that it was the same woman.

The woman turned on the porch light once she was inside. When she came back for the rest of the groceries the light shone across her features. The same short-cropped hair — not as black — shaped the same regal head. Her dark face was angle on angle, and Holly almost felt as if her brain was tearing open some previously hidden area. Memory surged. She knew when this assured and happy woman laughed that it would roll over her ears like deep peals from church bells. She had laughed easily.

Her name was Audra Keenan. Audra. Audie.

She could hear her mother saying it now, with a note of affection that was . . . more than neighborly.

The slamming of the trunk shook Holly out of her shock. She stepped forward quickly, wanting to catch Audra before she went inside.

Audra spun to face her, then froze. "Sweet Jesus!" The bag of groceries slid slowly to the ground. "Sweet Jesus," she said again. "Lily?"

Holly was pierced by the poignancy of it, by the wonder of learning how much she looked like her mother. Her mother had been considered lovely, and now she knew she looked like her. She could only shake her head.

"No, no, of course not," Audra murmured. "Holly, you have to be Holly."

The sound of her name triggered another wave of memory that left Holly faint. Old, old memories, long-buried and discarded by a child, flared into overwhelming vibrant color. Audra was there, with her mother, and they were laughing, shoulder-to-shoulder. "Audie," she murmured.

"I lost track of you when you graduated from high school. I lost track of you . . ." The same firm voice, not as calm as she remembered.

"No, I lost track of you. I forgot you —"

"I didn't exist. You didn't belong to me. She took you." Tears sparkled in the dim light.

"Audie," Holly said again. The dizziness was receding.

"Come in, child, please. It's cold out."

She helped Audra pick up the fallen groceries while her heart seemed dance in her chest. She had only hoped to find answers. She had not expected — dreamed — she would find another mother.

PI Talking Points: SSM
Draft 4

- Evidence is overwhelming that few gay couples are stable, and those that are expect and agree to outside sexual contacts. So when gay people talk about marriage they mean something different than what ~~folks~~ the rest of us usually mean.
- The ~~aggressors~~ activists here are not ordinary people, who are doing their best to live according to ages-old, time-tested morality and family ~~values~~ definition, but those who are trying to harness the power of the law to force acceptance of their agenda.
- Same-sex relations are ~~an affront to~~ a negation of the ties that bind, which are the continuation of kinships through the procreation of children.
- Homosexuals feel guilty about ~~what they are~~ their lifestyle choices and seek the support of society to relieve their guilt. Legal marriage is just one step on ~~their~~ the gay activist's agenda.

7

"Whose side are you on?"

The question upset Reyna more than she could show. She doused her anger and repeated, "Your arguments won't be taken seriously if you don't appear to understand that freedom of speech is available even to those with whom you disagree."

The man across the conference table from her had been frowning for the last two minutes. "Do you think I wanted my daughter watching two lesbians getting married on her favorite comedy program?"

"Our poll results suggest that most parents would say your first and best remedy is to turn off the TV, and talk to your daughter about why you did it. Parental censorship is okay, but government censorship — that's not acceptable."

Danforth Jackson Hobson IV had an expressive sigh. It played well on television and was no less impressive in person. He was disappointed that she did not see the obvious and was clearly saddened for the state of her immortal soul. "It's an abomination to God, an offense to our Lord. That's the difference between us and them. The homosexual agenda has to be stopped. Your father and I have been waging this war for two decades. We can't afford to lose. He understands. Do you?"

The question didn't fluster her, but his intense scrutiny was threatening to. "My job is to help you reach the people who aren't listening. They don't want to listen to hate and intolerance and they think that's what you're about. Look at the poll numbers." She jabbed at the summary of their most recent telephone bank results. "One hint that *your* agenda includes limiting fundamental Constitutional rights for *anybody*, not just homosexuals, and the number of people who say they agree with the American Values for Family agenda drops from sixty-eight percent to thirty-three percent."

He was still regarding her with sympathetic sadness. Apparently, her misguided sentiments were obvious. Her father would understand that her dogged attempts to soften this man's attitudes toward homosexuality came from her own history. Grip didn't care whether she failed or succeeded, as long as the strong partnership — and the seemingly endless flow of funds — between Hobson's antigay-antifeminist-antichoice organization and his political machine wasn't jeopardized. To Hobson, conservatism was a way of life. To her father it was a means to an end. As much as she hated Hobson and the words she wrote on his behalf, she at least understood that he was acting on convictions rooted in his understanding of a holy book. Her father had no convictions except those that bought, bolstered and stockpiled power.

"It happens right here," she pointed out. "Question: Do you think that celebrities in prime time have an obligation to model good values for young viewers? Answer: Sixty-eight percent yes. Question: Should television programs be limited in the topics they can discuss during prime time? Answer: Thirty-three percent yes. Question: Should television programs be limited in the kinds of lifestyles they portray in prime time? Answer: Thirty-three percent yes."

"I am aware of those numbers. Those people don't realize the insidious dangers of television, which continues to surprise me. Our message is not getting through."

"And it won't if you continue to highlight that limits on freedom of speech and expression are your highest priorities." Reyna felt the sting of bile in her throat. "You would be better off downplaying that aspect of your energies and instead making allies with those people who do support your —" She almost said *moderate* but caught herself in time. "Your views that they share most strongly."

"You want me to lie."

"It's not a lie, it's —"

"Spin, I know." He sat back and Reyna realized his focus had left her personally and returned to the more general issues of AVF positioning and fundraising. Her job was to help him improve both. "Gays Are Scary" was a tried and true fundraising message. "But I was one of the people who objected vigorously to the way the attorney general downplayed his righteous views to appeal to the middle. I must admit, however, he has been able to do some good work for our side since."

What Hobson would never accept, Reyna knew, was that the United States would never be what he dreamed of. There would never be a state religion, never be a universally held conservative ideology. Democracy would not become theocracy, not directly. They might think the careful plotting of her father's political career would eventually put him in the White House. But even then the rabid Far Right would not have the fearless Christian leader they prayed for. Grip Putnam would set them aside, once used, and then do whatever it took to keep the power to himself and his trusted lieutenants. Hobson was trusted, but not with power. Never that.

She realized that the tic below her left eye had started to shiver. She rubbed her face to make it stop. She needed to end the meeting. She could only stomach being in the same room with Hobson and his convictions for so long. "Okay, we've agreed to these draft changes on same-sex marriage. I'll have them done ASAP and fax them to your assistant. But we've got a long way to go on free speech. Let me try again." *Let me show you how to win people over with soft words that hide your real goals.* "Then we can meet to discuss the draft. It will be more productive." *Let me help hide the monster that you are.*

Hobson agreed and eventually left for his meeting with her father. It preceded a Putnam Institute cocktail party honoring husband and wife University of California at Irvine professors who had completed an extensive archeologically-based history of the life of Jesus. She would be required to play her father's hostess for at least an hour, and to make small talk with people she loathed. People who believed, at their very core, that homosexuals were only acceptable two ways: converted to heterosexuality or removed from society through jail or death.

She felt the tremor in her lip as she hurried down the cold, echoing corridor to her office. She needed to be alone.

She locked her office door and went into the only place where she was guaranteed privacy — the bathroom. She locked that door, too, and turned on the faucet so her angry moans would not be overheard by the "security" equipment in her office.

The black hole was bad, worse than yesterday. It had barely been a week since her last foray to Jack's — only a week since an explosive sexual encounter with yet another anonymous lesbian.

She huddled on the cold tile floor and knew the seals were coming off the cavern where she kept her rage and frustration. Temptation danced in her heart, as it always did. Jack's was not the only outlet. She could go as far as West Hollywood. WeHo was too risky, she answered the thought. She had to stay at the party. Her father would want to talk about it afterward. She could not go anywhere. Not tonight. It was only three weeks until the next Ladies'

Night at Jack's. There had to be a way to stand the longing until then.

She was suddenly still. She fantasized soft hair and her fingers easing between spreading thighs and the taste of it in her mouth. She could not go anywhere tonight. If he found out she'd devised a way to elude the private detectives he would stop it forever. She could not bear to lose the only thing that saved her sanity.

She knew how he would do it. He knew she hated him and therefore used no subtlety. He'd put it very simply. "You will get rid of the motorcycle, stop any contact with other lesbians, or the nurse goes. This is for your own good." Maybe he'd threaten the medication, too. Either way her mother's quality of life would plummet.

The black hole was bad. Worse than it had been in a while.

Bad because she could not stop her mind from turning the logical corner. She was a prisoner to her father's designs and her mother was the hostage. If he ended his support she would die months, if not years sooner.

Perhaps it would be for the best. Reyna could not stop the thought and she bit down on her lip with a moan of despair. What kind of person have you become, she asked herself. What kind of daughter balances her own happiness against her mother's very life?

I'm the kind of daughter he made me, she thought bitterly. He plays with her life and now I think I can, too.

You can't go anywhere tonight.

She moaned again and heard the new edge to it. She wanted to feel a woman against her. She wanted to hear her laugh or cry, to share a hot day or a walk in the rain, to lie down and lose themselves for hours. But these things — conversations, dates, movies, the idea of a shared life — were out of the question. All she could sneak into her existence was sex, and she could not jeopardize that lifeline. To have at least the renewal of physical contact required no repeats, no names, no wondering about the woman she was with that night — what she might do for a living, what she might like for breakfast. Just raw, needy, to-the-point sex. Until . . . she choked on the inevitable. Until her mother died and her father lost his only hold on her. It could be seven more years. A good daughter would hope for seven more years, for seventy more years of life for her mother.

She got to her hands and knees, then used the sink to leverage herself to her feet. She reached for the light switch. Her face in the mirror was ghastly white and her eyes were as lifeless as ice. It was what the black hole did to her. She could not go anywhere tonight.

"Reyna, darling, I'm so glad you're here." Her father's hand was cool on her back. He said in a low tone, "I was hoping you would change."

"I didn't have time," she muttered. Her cocktail dress was hanging in the closet in her office. She could not bring herself to put it on. Not tonight.

"Come meet the guests of honor," he said jovially. She could tell he was displeased.

She expressed her pleasure at meeting the two professors and listened with a fixed smile to their compliments about her father's conservative zeal and the work of the Putnam Institute. She nodded and prayed that whatever expression was on her face could be mistaken for pride. Her father's phenomenal radio success had financed the foundation of the Putnam Institute, and millions and millions of dollars from conservative groups seeking Grip's guidance and the research prowess of PI's vaunted staff had built the campus where Reyna spent her working life. The money created the power, and she was a prisoner to it. Her father saw to it that she had little time to herself.

"You're the author of the talking points on prayer in public schools, aren't you?" The woman was speaking to her alone, now. Her husband had been lured away by Grip to meet a new arrival.

Reyna nodded and wished to be elsewhere. "I had a lot of help," she said, trying to spread the blame around.

Professor Atchison smoothed her red suit. "I'm sure that's just false modesty. You made several brilliant points."

Reyna gave her the smile that hid how much the comment grieved her. "It's all in the service," she said brightly.

The professor regarded her seriously. "There's adequate and there is brilliant. I know the difference and use each precisely as I mean it."

"I don't take compliments well," Reyna answered. What was the woman's first name? She'd forgotten in the space of a minute.

"That's not surprising," the other woman said drily. "Women are conditioned that way. I spent three hours choosing this suit and two hours on this ridiculous hair style." She waved an elegant hand, heavy with a diamond wedding ring, at the twist of smooth brown hair that graced the nape of her neck. "Tell me I look wonderful."

Taken aback, Reyna dutifully said, "You look wonderful."

"Oh, it was nothing," the professor replied, then her mouth widened in a grin. "See? I even know I've been conditioned to negate compliments and I do it anyway."

"It's hard to overcome your programming." She sought a way to escape the conversation.

"You, Eleanor Roosevelt and I all agree on that."

The pairing of her name with Eleanor Roosevelt's set off alarm bells in Reyna's mind. She hoped that none of that showed as she studied the other woman — lord, what *was* her name?

"Irene, honey, there's someone I want you to meet." The other professor — Dan, she recalled now — was back at his wife's side.

Irene was consummately poised. She nodded her acquiescence before turning back to Reyna. "I lent my copy of the talking points to a student and keep forgetting to ask for another. Perhaps we could find one before the evening is over?"

"Certainly," Reyna said automatically. The alarm bells were louder, but there was nothing on which to base her fear. Unless there was a deeply suppressed but predatory gleam in Irene's eyes, or a shared nuance of restraint. Eleanor Roosevelt had had a long-term lesbian relationship, and although most people thought of her only as a First Lady, Reyna always thought of her as journalist Lorena Hickok's lover. Lorena had been the first woman to cover the White House for the Associated Press, and Reyna had long admired her. No, Reyna cautioned herself, no, it's all you. Irene didn't mean anything by it. You're the one craving what you know you can't have — not tonight.

The party became a blur. She let herself be pulled into a what-if conversation with other staffers about elections and polling results. Normally she eschewed them as unproductive, but tonight she had an extra glass of wine and talked politics. Anything was better than the images that spun wildly through her head of a room pulsating with music and women who moved against her. She could almost hear the music, the moaning, and she made herself talk about seats that might be won and districts reclaimed, issues carried, as if any of that mattered a damn when she lived such a monumental lie —

"I was wondering if we could find a copy of those talking points."

The cool voice cut into Reyna's schizophrenic hold on her fantasies and the conversation. She nodded. "Sure, I'll print you one if there aren't any in my files."

She led the way from the reception hall through to the marbled floors of the main lobby, then along through the security door to the rear elevators. Her office was on the fifth floor, the same floor as her father's suite of offices, but at the opposite end with the other senior research analysts. The only light was supplied from the main hallway, but she knew her way around after all the years of late nights.

She swiped her access card when they reached her door. The other buildings of the Institute campus gleamed white in the night. Sometimes the serenity of the setting, with only canyon and trees in the distance, soothed her. But not tonight. "If you'll hold it open for me I can probably find a copy without having to phone in the after-hours code for the lights. It's a pain."

Irene stood silhouetted in the doorway and Reyna registered the pleasing shape but only peripherally. She was hungering for a lesbian, not just any female body. Her vision blurred for a moment, because it was easy to pretend that Irene was a lover, waiting for her to leave work behind, eager for the moment when they would be alone and together.

"I can't find a copy — I'll need the lights," she explained. She punched the eight-digit key combination into her phone, got it wrong, tried again. Finally, the office lights came on. She blinked at Irene, who did not look in the least disconcerted by the abrupt fluorescent glare. "They're too bright at first, aren't they?"

Irene let the door swing shut. "But it's energy-efficient."

There was no argument to be made to that, so Reyna went back to searching her file cabinet for a copy of the document Irene wanted. She knew the research coordinator had copies in her files, but they were locked — everything was always locked.

"No luck. I'll print you one."

"Or maybe you could e-mail it to me."

"That would work," Reyna said carefully. They could have settled that downstairs.

Irene wrote her university e-mail address on the back of one of Reyna's business cards and pocketed a second one. She left the address on Reyna's desk, then looked up suddenly into Reyna's face.

The alarm bells were back, clanging against Reyna's already fragile nerves. Was it her or was it Irene? She didn't want Irene, for all her charm and poise. Could it be Irene?

A flash, a crack in the perfect picture of a married university professor — gone before she was sure she'd seen it. Recognition, even, not of the longing, but of the way they were both fighting it.

There was something there, Reyna knew, because they

walked back to the party in the kind of silence that holds a secret, and parted once they arrived. She was able to make a departure before she gave in to the temptation of another glass of wine. Home, she would go home.

She went to the Friday night movies instead. She had turned toward home, but then caught sight of the tan sedan that had followed her out of the parking lot. Bastards, she thought, sit in the cold near the theater, then. No reason for her to be the only one who was miserable.

She was in marginal luck — it was Mel Brooks night and for a while she found the energy to laugh and the nagging headache faded. Maybe she could just go for a ride, let the wind blow away some of the pain. She knew she could never get all the way to WeHo and back before the end of the final movie, when she would be missed by the private detective out front. But a quick, fast bike ride — that had appeal.

She went up the dark aisle and was saved by a flash of light from the movie that illuminated the back rows of the theater and the man sitting there who carefully did not look at her. She went to the restroom and then back to her seat, fighting tears. When the movie was over she left, not lingering for the last feature. Her breath in the cold air misted her sight, but her ears clearly heard the measured steps of the detective. Tonight was not a new face, but they all looked the same, weary retired cops to whom she was a tedious assignment. She often wondered what their instructions were. Report anything suspicious? Any deviation from the normal schedule? Any time she talks to a woman?

She whirled suddenly. "I'm going home."

She had startled him. A flicker of chagrin crossed the weathered, lined face. "That makes it easy for me."

"I don't really care." She headed for her car, sorry she had broken her promise to herself to ignore the detectives.

His voice followed her. "I'm a big Mel Brooks fan, so thanks. Next week is mother-daughter flicks — maybe you could take in a regular movie at the cineplex, for my sake."

She didn't intend to respond, but the words escaped before she could literally bite down on her tongue. "I can't wait for mother-daughter films. And fuck you."

Good move, she told herself, as she squealed away from the curb. Now you've got one of them mad at you.

She drove sedately homeward, hating the headlights in her rear-view mirror. She parked in her assigned space and trailed upstairs, feeling tired, depressed and empty, and knowing it was never any different.

It wasn't until she slipped her cell phone into the charging cradle that she remembered she'd turned it off in the theater. She switched it on and went to check her messages, even though she wouldn't do anything about them until morning. Her cell phone rang even as she listened to the message from the nurse — damn it, damn it — left over three hours ago. She grabbed the cell phone off the cradle.

"Her condition is improving, but you should come right away," the nurse — it sounded like Jean — said urgently. "They were able to remove the tube about an hour ago. She's asking for you."

"I'm on my way. I went to the movies," she said irrelevantly. She flipped the phone closed and raced out the front door and down the stairs to the parking garage, all while still repeating to herself, "I went to the movies."

She hated herself with every stoplight, cursed herself and any progeny she might ever have for her selfishness. Only today she hadn't been able to stop herself wondering when this might happen. Rationally, she knew that fate didn't work this way. She had almost been wishing her mother's suffering — and your own, she reminded herself harshly, as if they could possibly be equal — would soon be at an end. But that was not the reason her mother had had a severe seizure. She would never believe that God worked that way.

Maybe, she prayed, she hoped, maybe it wasn't too bad. Jean had said her condition was improving. She pushed the light at Commons and then squealed up to the parking lot of the University Medical Center. If the detective was following her it was at a distance because she seemed all

alone as she ran across the asphalt to the main doors.
Maybe this seizure was just like the last one, severe but
short-lived. Maybe, she prayed, she hoped, this isn't it. She
didn't want it to be, truly she didn't, she had never meant
it. And she still ran, knowing the quick route through the
staff entrance and on to the less-used rear elevators.
Seventh floor, rheumatology, no, what was she thinking?
That was arthritis and joint pain. Not dermatology, that was
skin rashes and they had no night staffing. The internists
were on three, the neurologists on six — intensive care. She
needed to be on the fourth floor. She ran down the stairs.

"Reyna!" Jean's voice called her to the left when she
emerged from the stairwell. She felt dizzy and her mouth
was dry.

"I was at the movies," she said and then she was very
quiet because the swirling voices in her head — reminding
her of where she had wanted to be, what she might have
been doing when this happened — were threatening to
drown out the calming effect of Jean's words.

"She's stabilized, and her vitals are recovering. They
think it was the anti-malarial regimen she began — it
doesn't work for everybody. Dr. Basu was here a few
minutes ago and he was really pleased with her turnaround.
She's been awake for about thirty minutes."

"I was at the movies," Reyna offered, aware at the same
time that she was disconnected from what was happening.

Jean put her arm around her shoulders. "Coffee first.
My lord, you're shivering. She's fine. Come on, let's get
some coffee. You don't want her to see you like this."

It was too sugary and needed milk, but Reyna felt
better halfway down the cup. Jean had been right. Her
mother's condition would hardly be helped by seeing Reyna
in a panic. Jean reappeared from the secret recesses of the
hospital, where she had worked from time to time, with a
cheese sandwich. Reyna made herself eat it, wondering if it
was tasteless because she was so numb or because it was
hospital food.

"Your color's back, that's better," Jean commented.

"Thank you. I'm not even your patient."

"You're welcome. I bet all you've had since dinner was popcorn."

"I skipped dinner. Had some hors d'oeuvres and wine around seven. And Raisinets." She met Jean's gaze for the first time. "Bad night to go to the movies."

"Don't think that way," Jean said firmly. "Your mother worries about you. Worries that you work too hard, that you don't get much fun. Tell her where you were — she'll be happier for it, I promise you."

She nodded, knowing that Jean's understanding of her mother no doubt surpassed her own. She got to her feet and felt steadier. "If I haven't thanked you lately for the wonderful care and support you give my mother, let me rectify that — thank you."

Jean's smile further warmed her eyes. "Your mother makes it easy to care. Go on in now."

"Do I look okay?" She put a nervous hand to her hair, suddenly aware that she'd been in the same clothes for nearly twenty-four hours.

"You're fine," Jean assured her.

The respiration monitor greeted her with its steady pulse. She tiptoed to the edge of the bed, taking in the signs of the removal of the breathing tube and the adhesive that clung to one reddened cheek. Her mother appeared to be dozing, but it wouldn't last for long. Painkillers were required for deeper, sustained sleep.

She sank down in the chair that was never close enough to the bed and still managed to gently lay her head near her mother's feet. She was so tired.

It was about three o'clock in the morning, the witching hour, she mused. Utterly drained, she prayed to the compassionate god she believed in for what she needed most: strength to bear whatever she must if it gave her mother the will to endure. What were her petty problems compared to her mother's daily agonies? So she had to associate with people who — if they really knew her — wanted her dead or invisible or brainwashed. Big deal. It was nothing compared to the pain that ebbed and flowed with every breath her mother took. She was lucky to have one outlet, to be able to find a few hours of relief and escape. Her mother's only escape was drug-induced oblivion.

"Reyna?"

She sat up. "I'm here, Mom."

"I'm glad." Her voice was quite hoarse, a byproduct of the tube that had been in her throat.

"I was at the movies, you know, the Friday all-nighter."

"What did you see? Was it fun?"

Reyna swallowed hard. After what her mother had been through tonight, she could still concern herself with Reyna's life. "Mel Brooks movies. He has his moments."

"All by yourself?"

"I couldn't find anyone to go with me," she answered, omitting that she hadn't asked.

"What about Jake?"

"Jake's a dork." It was out before she could stop it, she was that depleted.

Incredibly, her mother laughed, then was shocked into silence as joints all over her body responded with needles of pain. After two deep breaths, she said, "Like Jimmy Peters?"

"Just like." Jimmy Peters was the high-school pest who wouldn't stop coming around no matter what Reyna said. What a fun year it had been, though, that short year of freedom. She remembered that her mother had seemed more friend than anything else. They had only grown apart when she left for college. If she'd stayed home, not run off to Berkeley for more freedom, she might have noticed her mother's butterfly rashes that had first attracted the attention of doctors. She could have been there for support during the lengthy and troublesome diagnosis.

"You're too good for these political puppets. Dr. Basu is very nice. He's single."

Reyna got up to offer water and hopefully change the subject. "I wish they hadn't had to put the tube in."

"Me, too." Her mother sipped carefully from the straw.

There was a long silence and Reyna wanted to take her mother's hand, but it would hurt more than it comforted.

"Honey?"

"What can I get you, Mom?"

"Nothing." She turned her head slightly toward Reyna, who was struck anew by dark shadows under her mother's eyes. "It's just that — sweetie, I want you to be happy. Whatever makes you happy, that's what I want for you. I wasn't always this wise, but the pain — sometimes the clarity of thought is amazing. I used to just want you married, as if that would somehow make up for the fact that I wasn't when you were born."

"You know I don't care about that."

"Neither do I, not anymore. I made my choices. They became your realities, but you're so strong. Honey, I just want you to be happy. Otherwise what was it all for, all the feeding when you spit out the strained peas, and making you wear a sweater when it was cold? I wanted the best for you then, and I do now. I want to see you smiling again." Her voice grew so weak Reyna had to stoop to hear it. "Before I go. "

"Don't talk that way." All the blinking in the world wouldn't hold back the tears.

"I'm not planning on going anywhere." Her mother sighed. "I'll cost your father a fortune, to be sure."

"He can afford it," Reyna said shortly. She mopped her eyes with her sleeve.

"Use the tissues, dear."

She dutifully pulled one from the box on the bedside table. "I will try harder to be happy."

"No more dorks. Go looking for a prince."

"I don't want a prince, Mom." She wanted to say more — the truth she had never shared. She had been planning to tell her mother about Kimberly at the next break, all those years ago, but by then Kimberly had been rendered moot. It had been hard enough to pretend that leaving her beloved journalism behind for political science and governmental affairs was the happiest decision of her life. "Princes have problems."

"So do we all." Her mother's eyes closed. In the half-dark Reyna could see the familiar outline of her mother's profile. The beauty that had smoothed so much of her path in life was now stretched to the point of breaking.

"Do you want to sleep?"

"Yes. I told Jean to hold back until I'd seen you. I just wanted to say — to say what I said."

"I love you, Mom. Don't go dying on me, okay?"

"I'll do my best."

The kiss she pressed to her mother's roughened cheek was as light as she could make it, and she hoped the gesture had not brought any pain with it. She was so self-absorbed, to be craving the hard pleasure of another woman when even the lightest caress caused her mother discomfort.

Jean promised to keep her informed and Reyna wandered wearily toward the parking garage. Not exactly a false alarm, because the seizure had been serious enough to require forced respiration. But not the horror she had expected, either. She would have to have a long talk with Dr. Basu about the antimalarial regimen, though. He had been so hopeful about it.

She was driving again, intending to go home, but instead went deeper into the canyon, past the Institute, winding around familiar switchbacks to the vista that of course had always been known as Lover's Leap. The tires crunched on the gravel as she pulled off the road and coasted to a stop.

She was so numb from her internal coldness that the biting winter air on the cliff edge seemed warming. She let the wind chill her ears and nose while her mind continued to spin. "I was at the movies," she said into the wind, but that was not where she had wanted to be. What if the seizure had been fatal, and her mother had wanted her for a few last words, but no one could find her because she was busy taking whatever she could get from any woman who would have her for a few brief hours? Her mother could have been dying while she spread herself out on yet another motel bed, holding back only her name while she took pleasure, and took as much as she could.

Self-absorbed, greedy, no impulse control — okay, she thought bitterly. Your father is a bastard. You didn't want this life. You're doing this because of Mom, and it's not your fault, it's not her fault. It's his fault to have put a price on her life. But so what?

You want a relationship, you big fucking whiner? You

don't get one. Not everyone gets one. You're not dying by inches, you're not abused, you don't wonder where your kids will get their next meal. It could be so much worse and all you do is complain. When you at least get to have sex, you complain that it's not enough. Tough. When was the last time your mother got to lose herself in purely physical pleasure instead of pain?

But, the answering voice in her head reminded her, but . . . you're losing your soul doing this work, helping these people. You're helping them hurt not just you, but others as well. And that's a price you pay, not your father. It's not his conscience that is making you suffer.

Headlights swept over her suddenly, startling her out of her fugue. She turned to look at the approaching car and remembered, then, that she was never alone.

The tan sedan pulled alongside her own car, then the man inside got out.

"Miss Putnam."

"Can't I be alone ever?"

"Is there something I can help you with?"

She realized then that she was standing very close to the edge and that the detective had most likely misinterpreted her reason for being here. "I'm not planning on jumping."

He nodded. "Is your mother okay?"

"That's no concern of yours."

He nodded again. In the starlight he was silver-haired, and his face was carved with lines that did not suggest habitual mirth. "I've overstepped. Please accept my apologies," he added dryly. "The name is Ivar, Marc Ivar, if you want to report me."

She spread her hands in a nullifying gesture and turned her back on him.

He lit a cigarette and made no move to depart. It irritated her immensely.

"May I be alone, please?"

"I'll head around the corner, but you know I can't leave. Not until you get to church Sunday morning. That's me — Friday night to Sunday morning. And Wednesdays."

"I can hardly get up to no good in the House of the

Lord," she said sarcastically. Attendance at her father's congregational church, a moderate denomination, was mandatory. She used the time to clear her head, and tried to take only the good that came from the pulpit. The god she believed in was a source of strength and wisdom, never punishment or hate. If she ever had a choice, she would look for a church that uplifted her spirit without turning off her mind.

"I wouldn't know. I just have my orders, just like the guy who picks up again on Mondays when you leave work."

She caught herself before she screamed at him to leave, then slowly turned to face him. "Why are you telling me this?"

"What?" He made no attempt to appear confused. She stared until he finally shrugged. "Me and my big mouth. Consider it a gift."

"A gift or a trap? You tell me I'm not watched from Sunday at ten until Monday after work — why would I believe you?"

"You probably shouldn't." The laconic smile was back.

She stalked to her car and had to fuss with the lock. The car was fairly new, recently delivered from the leasing company. Just when she got used to a Buick they brought a Ford. Or was this a Lincoln? She didn't care. Her dignified exit was ruined by dropping her keys.

He finished his cigarette and ground it underfoot. "Think of me as a safe escort."

She wanted to say "Fuck you" again but didn't. She did spin out on the gravel and hoped even a small piece caught him. They were parasites, all of them. She didn't know what Ivar's game was, but she wasn't playing.

The condo was cold and unwelcoming, as always, decorated by a firm hired by Grip's administrative assistant. She rarely spent any time anywhere in it except the office and bedroom. It was to the bedroom she went, where she had sheets and blankets that she had chosen. She wrapped herself tight against the chill and cried, mostly because she had been badly frightened by the trip to the hospital and was too tired to stop the tears. Though she had promised herself she would put self-pity behind her, she couldn't help it, not in the cold before dawn and feeling, above all, utterly alone.

8

Audra set the first heavy photo album in front of Holly.
"I knew that Zinnia would destroy them if she had them, so
I took them like a thief in the night. It was after she took
you, but before they cleared out the house." After a pause
to dab her nose with a tissue, she opened to the first
photograph.

It was too much, too fast. Holly looked at the tiny
infant in the photograph and felt no connection. How could
that be her? She had no memory of seeing this picture
before. The child had a frown that seemed to stretch from
head to toe.

"You hated the flashbulb. I think you figured out early
on that cameras meant purple spots in your eyes. You've

always been camera-shy." With a sigh, Audra turned to the next page.

Her mother looked younger than Holly ever remembered. The studio portrait answered all of Holly's questions save one. Facing her mother was Audra, and between them she was nestled as something they shared.

Aunt Zinnia would never have let Holly see this picture. It was too honest and, as was often true of unvarnished honesty, inflammatory. White and black, two women, a baby — a formula that too many people, even twenty-six years later, rejected in every permutation.

But it was the truth of her start in life, a constant she had only lately understood she was missing. She took another tissue from the box Audra had brought near. "You were always a part of me."

"Always." Audra's voice was low and even, though she drew the occasional ragged breath. "I cut the cord."

She looked at Audra, curious about the story of her birth, but there were more pressing needs. "I don't know how —" She had to begin again. "Why don't I remember you very well? Why —" She watched helplessly as Audra wrapped her long arms across her stomach and rocked, letting the tears fall. "I'm sorry . . ."

"My fault, child, all my fault. I had help down the road, but I chose the path. You can't understand, not after all this time."

"Try me," Holly said gently. "Tell me."

"It's not the world you live in. I look back, and my choices don't make any sense." She sighed. "When you were six we were shopping. You were always so serious about things being correct. You sorted your Halloween candy, and laid out doll clothes in functional groups." A laugh broke the tears and Audra seemed to let go of some of the painful past. "When you were four you lined up all your toys in order of height so they could all see your puppet show. You were always exceptional, and we knew it."

She let Audra talk, hearing the occasional soft consonant that spoke of a southern birthplace. The lilt of it seemed familiar to her, just as the erect way Audra carried herself was.

139

"We were shopping, you see, and you were bored while Lily paid the clerk. Up and down, you wanted me to hold you, to carry you, to hang you upside down, up and down. The clerk was a nice woman, I'm sure she meant nothing by it. All she said was that you were wearing out your — and then she had to stop, because you had called Lily Mama." She set her cocoa-washed hand next to Holly's pale one. "You were obviously not my daughter, so she didn't know what noun to use. So she asked you who it was you were climbing all over."

Holly covered Audra's hand with her own. She might not remember specifics but she had an image of her tiny hand, so white against Audra's.

"You said plain as day, and seriously, that I was your mother." Audra cleared her throat. "Two things, it was two things that came to me. First that I loved you so much. We had always told you to call me Audie, so you had never called me anything else. I realized that I wanted it, I wanted you to call me your mother."

She patted Audra's hand and then let it go so she could blow her nose. "And the other thing?"

"Panic. Because the clerk was looking so confused, and Lily — she knew it frightened me. So she acted like you were the one who was confused and we left. But I knew — I was wrong, but those were the times. I was a teacher, and teaching meant everything to me. It is my calling in life, teaching grade school. I was respected and admired, so much more than where I began in life. But being black, one whisper would have been enough. There were still moral turpitude clauses in teaching contracts. There were people running about trying to make it a state law that no gay person could be a public-school teacher."

"I do understand that," Holly said gently. "In some ways it's no better now."

"Oh it is. Never believe that things haven't gotten better," Audra said firmly. "But back then, what I knew was that in another year no one would ever believe you were confused about who I was to you. You would push your mother and me right out of the closet. Now, Lily was ready.

But I wasn't. Not telling you for so long, she did that for me."

"You had your reasons, risks she didn't have."

"Don't be so easy on me." Audra patted her knee and rose. "I'm going to make some tea. Would you like some?"

"I would, thank you." Holly followed her to the kitchen, brimming with dizzy elation.

Words seemed to come easier to Audra as she filled the kettle and set it on the stove. "After that, Lily and I agreed we'd have to be more circumspect around you. Rather, I told her how I felt things had to be, though it broke my heart, and she supported me. So, gradually, I just wasn't there as much, not while you were awake. We found these houses, side by side, and it seemed like a good compromise. Even so, I was amazed at how quickly I lost track of your every word, your every achievement. It hurt." She turned from the cupboard with a box of tea bags and two mugs. Her mouth was trembling again with painful memory.

"It must have." Holly reached for the mugs and set them on the white-flecked Formica-topped table.

Audra slumped into a chair and Holly sat down opposite her. "The years seemed to slip by. You just kept getting older. I — I —" She swallowed hard and tears sprang anew in her eyes. "Sweet Jesus. I watched your tenth birthday party through the fence." She sank her fingers into her short hair and pulled it in self-admonishment. "It was so foolish, wasting all that joy out of fear."

Audra seemed lost in thought and Holly didn't disturb her. When the kettle whistled she poured the boiling water over the tea bags. Audra took her mug absently.

"Aunt Zinnia told me that my mother was going to tell me about herself."

Audra nodded, seeming a long way away. "Yes, that's true. She wouldn't have told your aunt of all people about me. We were going to tell you first. Lily and I, we were growing apart because of my stupidity. Losing track of days, sometimes going a week without connecting seriously. And in those six years times changed. I had not believed that as a black woman I could get another job worth having, even if we moved, but by then I was sure that if I had to, I could get one up north, San Francisco or Oakland, I could have done it. Times had indeed changed. So I told her I wanted to be a family again." She sighed.

"And then the accident."

Audra sipped her tea and seemed to come back to the present. "The accident. That stupid, stupid accident. Do you remember what day of the week it happened?"

"A Thursday. Aunt Zinnia came to get me at swim practice. I remember that she told me Mother was dead and I thought at first I was cold because my suit was wet."

"We were going to tell you about us on Saturday."

That close. She had been that close to the truth. The might-have-been was painful to contemplate. Two more days and she might never have launched herself across Clay's office into his arms, swept off her feet by the merest hint of encouragement and approval. It wasn't fair that her mother had died. She dashed away angry tears like the eleven-year-old she had been, then found a thought outside her own miseries. "Who told you?"

Audra's breath caught. "No one. I wasn't unduly concerned when the two of you didn't come home, but I was grading papers — my lord, grading papers. Later I couldn't remember the last thing I said to her. The next morning I made coffee and started my eggs, then went out to the porch for the paper. The next of kin had been notified, you see, so . . . so . . . her name, her picture . . . right there . . ."

It was Holly's turn to offer her shoulder and she did so without reservation.

After a long while, Audra murmured, "There was no one I could tell. Another price of hiding who I was. I had no friends who knew about Lily." She pushed Holly gently away and drew herself up with dignity. Holly had a sense then of how she might have turned out had Audra been in her life — she would know how to stand tall, how to hold her head up.

"You had to get through it alone?" My God, Holly thought. To suffer the loss of the love of your life and not be able to tell a single soul about the devastation it caused. To watch other people moving around in your lover's home, taking things, throwing things away that had meaning. "It's over," she murmured. "The hiding is over."

The elation was still there, and it grew as more pieces of her past settled into place.

Audra dabbed at her eyes with a fresh tissue. "I apologize. After all these years —"

"Don't apologize. I think I would have gone crazy."

"I almost did. Because there was no way I could see you, to find out if you were handling it okay. Your aunt —" Audra's mouth settled into a firm, unyielding line.

"My aunt was less than ... tender in her parenting," Holly said slowly. This part of the story could wait for another time, one not so fraught with regrets and hesitant joy.

Audra nodded, and her stiff spine seemed almost brittle. "After all this I think I need a drink. Will you join me?"

Holly accepted because of the symbolic nature of it, and watched as Audra moved the books and knickknacks that blocked the front of the liquor cabinet. There was dust on the lock. She realized abruptly that the dust was another dart, another clue. Audra didn't drink casually, and Holly had the vaguest impression that even after all that had transpired in the last hour, it was only now that Audra needed courage, because there was more to tell.

There was the last question, after all, and after offering so much truth, and so easily, Audra had not volunteered the answer. Holly knew she would have to ask, certain that the answer was why Audra needed a drink.

They touched tiny crystal aperitif glasses and sipped. Holly wasn't sure what to call it, but the sweet red wine was very soothing.

She didn't know quite where to begin. With Aunt Zinnia she had planned her questions to triangulate on the truth. She had never expected an Audra to exist, an Audra who had loved her and knew so many answers. Triangulate, she told herself, but most of all do the math. "How long were you and my mother together before I came along?"

Audra gave her drawn look, then briefly closed her eyes. "We met when she guided my class through a field trip to the university's research lab. That was before she went into the private sector. I had never in my life seen someone so happy with who she was and what she was doing. Both of us were single, dating, and not sure why nothing seemed to work out with men. We met and it was like the collision of stars between us. You came along three years later."

Three years. Audra had been there to cut the cord. Had been in her mother's life when the egg that became her was fertilized. It was the last question.

"Three years," Holly echoed. "You know what I'm asking, don't you?"

Audra nodded.

"Can you tell me?"

"She made me promise I wouldn't. A promise I thought I would have no trouble keeping. But she didn't know that we'd be here, like this. And that you would need to know. And that, that *witch* would do what she did." The brief flare of anger seemed to drain her. "I don't know if I have the strength."

Sweet Jesus. Holly could almost hear Audra thinking it. There were a limited number of possibilities to explain her conception. Eliminated was the explanation of an accident as a result of an affair with a man. Eliminated, by Audra's reluctance to discuss it, was the explanation of a planned conception the two women had undertaken together. What was left?

The anguish in Audra's eyes, the promise not to speak of it — Holly drained her glass and steeled herself. She had not known she would have to be this strong.

"I'll tell you, but it won't be easy, child. For either of us."

Holly waited, knowing the answer now, or some of it at least.

"Your mother was vivacious, lovely — you know that."

"I remember that, yes."

"You're very like her. Her hair had red glints in it. Her eyes were lighter gray."

"She had a smile like morning," Holly added. "I remember that most of all."

Audra's tone became clipped and anxious. "After we were together, she was still constantly turning men away,

144

citing lack of time, heavy career demands, anything to put them off. There was one man who persisted. He worked at the same company and found ways to drop into the lab. She finally agreed to go out so she could tell him privately that she wasn't interested. They'd gone to high school together, you see. She thought she knew him."

She wanted to tell Audra to stop, but there was no courage in continuing the silence.

"She was always gentle and kind, but with him she was very firm, she told me later, and even then he wouldn't listen. He kept insisting she'd change her mind if only she'd give him a chance. He'd always wanted her, and he'd even pretended to like Zinnia to be closer to her. When she wouldn't relent, he told her he didn't believe what Zinnia had hinted at. Lily never thought he would do what he did, even as he did it." Audra pressed her tissue across her eyes. Her voice rasped out the agonizing truth. "He did it to fix her. All the time he did it he told her he was making her normal."

Holly's head was spinning. She rested it on her leaden arms crossed on the table. The roaring in her ears finally receded and she realized that Audra hadn't stopped talking.

"— charges, but she'd taken a shower. I had helped her take it, I held her, and I wanted him to pay. But she knew him, and the cops wouldn't care. Just a misunderstanding on a date, that's what they would have said. Most of them would have thought she deserved it, had they found out about me. It was the — it changed my views on capital punishment, because I wanted him to die. Painfully, and all the while screaming no."

It echoed inside her head, Aunt Zinnia's oft-repeated statement about her mother turning away perfectly good suitors. Aunt Zinnia thought her mother had gotten what she deserved, but then condemned her for getting pregnant from it. And would have condemned her if she had had an abortion, and most certainly did condemn her for having the baby. The baby . . . her. Having her.

Audra's hands were shaking, but she wasn't done yet.

I can't, Holly thought, I can't take any more. Not right now. But there was more. Her mother had known him, and so had Aunt Zinnia. She might have known him, too, not knowing he was a rapist — no. Oh no, no, God. She could not stop her mind from solving for the simplest answer.

Audra was just looking at her. Barely above a whisper, she said, "You've figured it all out, haven't you?"

Holly nodded. Realizing how she no longer felt about Clay had been an earthquake, then the desire for women like being struck by lightning. What could this feeling be, then, on top of the others? The thunder of the past rolled over her.

She didn't want to say his name, but found no way to avoid it. "Uncle Bernard."

Audra nodded and reached for the bottle of wine. Holly was flooded with rage. It washed away to emptiness, then she felt as if she burned with molten heat. Her heart pounded, then missed beats. The answer was untenable, unthinkable. Aunt Zinnia had brought the man who had raped and impregnated her mother into their home and made Holly call him Uncle.

What kind of twisted reasoning was that? How had she compelled him? How could she have rationalized it? How had she thought Holly would feel when she knew the truth?

He was dead. She was glad.

Mother, she thought . . . dear Mother.

"She loved you. The moment she found out about you she was joy itself." Audra was perceptively following her thought process. "She felt that she won, in the end, because she had you and all your love, and all that wonder and joy. Nothing else mattered. She never told him about you, but Zinnia knew — she knew. And she did what she did."

When Holly didn't answer, Audra looked up from her study of the wine. "Come to the sofa," she said sharply.

The lights seemed to be flickering out as Audra helped her lie down. Then there was only oblivion.

Even after coffee and eggs the next morning, Holly felt empty. The feel of silverware in her hands was remote.

Shock, she supposed. Even considering why she felt this way was a faraway thing, too.

They looked through the rest of the photo albums together. There were math tests and report cards, all ending abruptly just before her twelfth birthday.

"Thank you," was all Holly could say. "You were right to take them. My aunt would have destroyed them." She could not bring herself to say her aunt's name.

"I want you to have them," Audra urged. "Take them because they were always meant to be yours. I have my memories."

"May I come to see you again?"

"I would love it if you would. I —" Audra stopped, looking lost. "I didn't think I deserved that. We've hardly talked about what's happened to you since she died, and I do so want to know."

"I'm ashamed to tell you," Holly blurted. "I wasted so much." Shamefaced, she told Audra about Clay, and how she had let herself be dominated by him to the point of turning her back on her own spiritual and intellectual growth.

Instead of pity or condemnation, anger flared in Audra's eyes. "That woman actually applauded when you became involved with this man?"

"Well, she wanted us to get married, but other than that, she thought Clay was good for me."

"And he used to be your teacher, and you were how old?"

"I'd just turned eighteen. A few days before." She blushed.

"I'm surprised he waited three days, the creep." Audra's head snapped into its most regal position. Holly easily imagined a room full of intimidated third graders.

"I was the one who initiated the physical side of it," Holly admitted.

"He was the adult, he was the teacher, and he ought to have known better. He should have been censured. How on earth were you supposed to hold your intellectual own against a man that much older and who was trained to penetrate your defenses? He was supposed to seduce your mind to the love of learning, not your body for his own purposes." Her eyes flashed with indignation. "That woman — she sent you out into the world ignorant of your choices, and she did it deliberately. This is on her, too. She was your . . . parent then. You are not to blame for choosing badly, when that was all you knew. You are well out of it. You are young, and you can begin again."

Blinded by Audra's loving conviction, Holly felt as if lead bindings had been eased from her heart. "Thank you for that," she said quietly. "A friend tried to tell me and I just about bit her head off." Jo — she needed to talk to Jo, who had understood more than she had from the beginning.

"Don't let fear rob you of happiness. I chose that path and it's a bad one. You know what *carpe diem* means, of course."

"Yes. My aunt and Clay both tried to teach me never to seize the day."

"Which is why they are where they are. Time for you to move on."

Finally, Holly found someone she could talk to about all the rest. Someone who would understand. "That's been part of the problem. As soon as I realized that Clay was not the man I thought he was —"

"A new age, sensitive intellectual fascist?"

Holly found a laugh somewhere. Audra laughed too, and her ears remembered, yes, like deep church bells. "I'll take your word for it." She looked directly into Audra's eyes, and finally said the words. "I'm a lesbian. The moment he was out of my mind, I knew it."

She was not straight anymore.

They talked for hours more. She left Audra with a promise to return next week with curricula and ideas about her future so Audra could play devil's advocate. She needed someone to explore ideas with, not take orders from, and Audra seemed happy to fulfill that role.

Another mother . . . the thought buoyed her home again. She needed to tell someone this happy news.

She was unlocking the door when Flo called to her. She turned, thrilled by the sight of another lesbian walking toward her. She hoped it would be ages before it happened so often that she took it for granted.

"Nancy's birthday is today and we're throwing together an impromptu soirée for this evening. Can you come? We'll have heaps of snacks and drinks. Just bring yourself."

"I'd love to. What a great idea." A house full of lesbians — oh, happy day. She was exhilarated at the prospect because she was not straight anymore.

"Tori and Geena will be there, too, so you'll have a few familiar faces. Come over when you hear the noise 'round eight or so."

She assured Flo she would be there, promised she would not bring a gift of any kind, and went inside to the bathroom mirror and then the phone.

She pressed the numbers without hesitation and found some semblance of calm maturity, though the little kid inside her was whooping at the top of her lungs that she was not straight anymore. After listening to the greeting, she said, "This is Holly Markham, we met at a wedding a few weeks ago. You gave me a condition, and I've met it, I think. I'd certainly like to discuss it further, if you're interested." She recited her new number and hung up. She looked at Galina's card for a long moment, remembering the way it felt when Galina tucked it into her bra, then she carefully let it fall into the wastebasket. The ball was in Galina's court. If she called, great. In the meantime, she was going to a party tonight.

She made a second call, and Jo seemed relieved to hear her voice. "You've no idea the chain reaction you set off," Holly told her. "I hope you're willing to take some responsibility for it." She was teasing and let it show in her voice.

"I certainly will, especially since you sound pretty happy."

"Are you doing anything right now? I need to buy some party clothes. I know it's the last minute —"

"Actually, I was just thinking about going out this afternoon because I can't grade another paper. I'd love to waste some time with you."

"Meet me in the atrium at South Coast Plaza and bring your fashion sense. I need to upgrade." She laughed. How could she be so happy? If she was still in shock she wanted to stay this way forever.

"I'll be there. Can we go into the mall and get some chocolate somewhere? I need chocolate and I need it quickly."

"I would never come between a woman and her chocolate, you know that." They agreed to meet in an hour, and Holly regarded herself in the tiny bathroom mirror after she had hung up.

She took off the vest, took off the sweater, took off the turtleneck and finally the undershirt. Her jeans went next, and then the long underwear. It wasn't that cold in L.A. It never had been. What had she been hiding under all those layers for?

She rubbed her shoulders, acknowledged the need for a new bra, and told herself the truth. She'd been hiding from desire. She'd been hiding from her body and what her body wanted.

She showered, loving the feeling of her breasts and shoulders and the sensuous delight of slippery shampoo and a thick, rough towel. Her body was waking up — even her knees felt alive. Her feet wriggled in the warm socks and her butt seemed to shiver at the touch of her underwear. Her breasts filled out the super-cleavage bra, and she put on only an old, soft, button-up shirt in a pleasing deep green, and a fresh pair of jeans. What could be more pro-humanist than appreciating the feel of one's own skin?

She had looked at pictures of her mother and found her beautiful. She now stared at herself in the mirror and admitted they looked very much alike, but she had never thought of herself as particularly attractive. But when X equals X, she had to accept the truth. It seemed immodest, but all in all, she wasn't that bad. Regardless, she didn't need to lose fifteen pounds. She was fine the way she was. Just fine.

* * * * *

Jo hugged her and Holly hugged her back. They stayed that way for longer than they ever had before. Holly liked the smell of Jo's shampoo.

"Thanks for forgiving me," Jo whispered in her ear.

"Thanks for saying something. You changed everything," Holly whispered back.

They separated, but still held hands, and regarded each other. Shoppers parted and merged around them. Jo suddenly lit up with the smile of joy that had surprised Holly only two weeks ago. Now Holly knew what it was. She felt the jolt in her pelvis of what might have been and took the initiative.

"What's her name?" Holly could see her own helpless grin reflected in Jo's eyes.

"Sandi. Your turn."

"No name. But there will be. I've only begun looking, you know."

Jo let go of her hands. "We were both idiots, you know. It might have worked out."

"We'd have fought all the time."

"Yeah," Jo acknowledged. "But maybe not."

Holly said more seriously, "I need a good friend right now."

"So do I," Jo said. She took Holly's face in her hands, right there in the mall atrium, and kissed her.

It was sweet and they tried to make it something more, but the moment Holly felt Jo's tongue she snickered, then Jo giggled and their mouths parted.

"I've wanted to do that for a long time," Jo admitted. "It turned out goofy."

"And then some. Shall we go shopping?"

"Tops or bottoms," Jo said with a laugh.

"What?"

"You know, clothes?" Jo was still laughing as she led the way toward the shops.

"I have the feeling I missed a sexual reference," Holly admitted. "Would you care to explain it to me?"

"You were always naïve," Jo commented. She forged into

the nearest women's clothing store and had to shout over the music. "I'll admit that when I was with Rod it wasn't half bad. I read *Cosmo*, you know. Well, I used to. Now I'm more of an *On Our Backs* girl. Top and bottom are positions, you nit."

Holly's face burned. "I know that."

"Tops and bottoms are the people who like those positions in bed, not literally perhaps, but certainly figuratively."

"Oh." Holly smiled serenely at a younger woman who was avidly eavesdropping while she flicked through choices of slacks. "How do I know which I am?"

"How should I know?" Jo held up a pair of navy blue gabardine pants. "These would make my ass look enormous, wouldn't they?"

"How should I know?" Holly stuck her tongue out at Jo.

Jo put the pants back. "You don't have to be either — you don't have to be anything. You wouldn't pass for butch, but you're not really femme either. But you don't have to choose a label of any kind. Some people like them, some don't. Some like leather and whips and toys, and some like candlelight and walks on the beach. Some like all of the above."

"So here's the question." Holly feigned interest in electric green leggings, but she was utterly focused on Jo. "How do you figure it out? Do you just . . . you know . . . sleep around?" She stopped because she was blushing and Jo was laughing at her.

"You sound sixteen, Holls."

"I know. I feel it, too. I feel like a frankin' virgin. I just want to choose wisely, this time."

"Hey, those would look nice."

Holly regarded the deep purple cotton-wool blend slacks she had absently picked up. "You're right. They're my size." She started to turn toward the dressing room, but Jo stopped her.

"That's always been your problem, you know. You find something that might be okay and you stop looking for something better."

Holly thought it over. "I'll try it your way for a while."

* * * * *

New slacks and a new shirt, new undies, new earrings — it all added up to a new attitude. The new undies had been a must after Jo shrieked at the sight of her utilitarian white panties and informed her that even cotton came in shades other than white. They migrated from clothes to chocolate to dinner while Jo gave Holly a crash course in Lesbian 101. Tops and bottoms, that was the easy part. The question of butch and femme was much more complex. The sheer variety of toys, and the casualness with which Jo referred to them all, left Holly feeling prudish. She didn't think she'd ever stop associating *lube* with automobiles, and never in her life had she heard *fist* used as a verb.

"I've saved you months of research. Maybe that's not such a good thing. Research can be very fun. Oo la la." Jo had obviously enjoyed her role of mentor. She ordered a Cobb salad and the server hurried to the next table.

"No, I appreciate it." Holly tore off a slice of steaming bread. "It's a bit overwhelming. I know so little about sex with men to begin with that I don't have any reference point."

"I think you're better off, if you want to know the truth. You won't be thinking in terms of who's the man and who's the woman. The first time I was with a woman, I kept thinking she had to be the man. You know, because I was the woman. As if a man was necessary even though we were both women." She rolled her eyes expressively.

"I know what you mean. I was at a wedding recently, gosh, just a couple of weeks ago. I suddenly pictured myself as the bride, and it was definitely a woman at the altar with me, but I thought of her automatically as the groom."

"You'll get past that, like I did. Just find out what you like, listen to your body —"

"How? I'm . . . I've changed a lot in the last two weeks. But not so much that I can just toddle off to bed with a variety of women for research. I think I'd have to work my way up to that, and I'm not sure I'd ever get there."

"It's not a clinical study, you know."

"I'm aware of that. Okay, so you told me about the U-Haul syndrome. What if I fall in love with the first woman who sleeps with me? How will that be any different than what happened with Clay?"

"Hopefully you'll have an orgasm for the first time in your life." Jo glanced up. "Thanks," she said to the server.

Holly knew she was blushing again, and she waited to speak until after the server had set down their drinks and rapidly departed. "Thank you for informing the restaurant."

"I still can't believe you never have. Are you sure?"

"I think I'd remember."

Jo reached across the table to pat her hand. "I've always considered you one of my closest friends, but lord, there's a lot we never knew about each other."

"That's the truth." As they had browsed, she'd told Jo about Audra and her mother, and Jo had been delighted with the turn of events. But she hadn't told her how she'd been conceived. She thought about telling her now, but that secret was surrounded by too much anger. She wanted just to be happy tonight. "Would you like to come to the party? I don't think they'd mind if I brought a guest."

"Thanks, but no. Sandi is going to call later. She's at one of those sales kick-off conference-type things. She sells insurance and investments — blue diamond club at her company, which is pretty hot. Like her phone calls." Jo lowered her eyes, but her lips had quirked in that mysterious way that told Holly she'd missed something salacious.

"Is it the real thing?"

Jo's smile softened. "I hope so. How do I tell?"

She thought of Tori and Geena. "Give her your future. That's the best I can do on that one."

"I'll think about it." She turned wicked again. "Meanwhile, she's a tiger in bed and that's just fine with me. Rod thought I was a nymphomaniac, but I just needed fingers instead of a —"

"Too much information!" Holly put her hands over her ears. "La, la, la, I can't hear you. La, la — oh." She lowered her hands and thanked the server for her vegetarian quesadillas.

Jo burst out laughing. "Oh yeah, before I forget, after oral sex don't hurry off to brush your teeth."

Holly fought down yet another blush. They talked about a million things at once, promised to get together in a few weeks, if not sooner, split some carrot cake and parted ways where they had begun.

I just want to go on being this happy, Holly told herself as she drove home. For a little while.

She ended the evening with the phone numbers of two of the women at the party and arrangements to meet for coffee. Jo had said that the coffee date was common, giving each woman a chance to come up with a plausible excuse for calling off further contact if the vibe was wrong. Holly would never have thought of that. She'd never dated, so the nuances of it were lost on her so far.

Sleep was deep and complete, and she woke happy. It was all she needed, for a little while.

9

Summonses from her father made Reyna nervous, and even though she was long schooled at hiding all emotions around him, she couldn't stop the tic under her left eye. She was too tired; she'd spent every possible moment she could at the hospital. It had been an exhausting weekend and the work week had been worse. She was behind on several major deliverables.

That was the likely reason he wanted to see her. She was supposed to have seen that packets for the Values and Faith Summit went out on Monday, but they weren't quite ready and it was halfway through Thursday. Part of it wasn't her fault — she'd been abruptly deluged with e-mails from participants wanting to tweak the agenda one way or another.

Paul Johnson, her father's faithful lapdog assistant, told her she needed to wait just a moment. "He's wrapping up a call." He turned his back on her because he was a superior little shit, and always had been. He was one of Danforth's saved souls, a poster child for the Ex-Gay crowd. Most of the time she pitied him, but today she was just too tired.

She suspected that Paul, who knew everything and said nothing, was privy to the reason Reyna required the watchful eyes of private detectives. He'd once had the temerity to tell her he prayed for her. In Reyna's book, Paul's god wasn't doing too good a job looking out for him. He'd been led to forgo his nature and sublimate his desire to sleep with men. Instead of sleeping with them, he slaved for them. Power was its own kind of sex.

"How's Monica?" Her question made him acknowledge her existence again. Saint Monica was the woman who had married a formerly gay man and produced requisite offspring as proof of their conjugal relations. She pitied the children most of all, growing up with a father who hated himself.

"She's fine."

She waited in silence for a few minutes. "How are the kids?"

"They're fine."

She leaned on his desk, thoroughly out of sorts. "Did you see that article in the *Times* on Monday? About the forum at the Episcopal seminary?"

"I did," he said shortly. "The liberal media as usual smearing the word of God."

"All the paper did was report on the forum. It was the forum that did the smearing — rather, the clarifying of the word of God."

"To say that the Bible is anti-family values — I don't know how those so-called scholars keep their collars, or whatever it is they have."

"Seems to me they're just using the mind God gave them. The examples of where the Bible is not a great moral guide for raising and maintaining families were thought-provoking."

"Using their minds to do the devil's work." He smugly stacked two files together and locked them into the cabinet behind him.

"I really thought their point about the most severe attack on the family coming from the economy was well-taken. Families stay together when their incomes are rising, but fall apart in hard times. But I guess that's a hard concept to debate. It's so much easier to blame uppity women, birth control, easy divorce, promiscuity — oh yes, the homosexuals, too."

He refused to look at her so she turned to study the wall hanging that dominated the gateway to her father's office. Her judgment must be badly impaired, she thought, because it was a waste of energy to bait Paul, and even if she did manage to get a rise out of him it would change nothing. She'd have to watch her mouth when she talked to her father.

Paul's phone chirped. "Your father is free now."

"Lucky him." She did not let him see her brace herself to walk through the door.

His office was massive and yet he seemed to dominate it. Even standing casually in front of his meticulously displayed collection of L.A. Dodger memorabilia he could not be ignored. It was his height, but also the way he assumed that center stage was his and his alone.

"Reyna," he boomed congenially. Behind him the Dodger pennants formed a flag in stripes of red, white and blue. All the arrangement needed was an apple pie. "Just the face I wanted to see. Have a drink. We're celebrating."

She just stared at him because it was a first, offering her a drink in his office. Dryly, she said, "To what do I owe this honor?"

"I've been asked to keynote the New York Republican Convention. Not emcee, but keynote. They want my views on the future of conservatism. Six years ago the keynote was by the fellow currently residing in the White House."

She had his eyes, and they were most alike when he was pleased. But some mornings it was disconcerting to see him looking at her from the mirror. "Congratulations," she said automatically.

He had been carefully changing his image from entertainer/commentator to political thinker. He got to play the Washington outsider with his public yet had influence over an enormous number of Congressional issues. A keynote for such a large convention, even mid-term, was proof that his image-enhancing strategy was working. It struck her then that maybe someday she actually would be the daughter of the President or Vice President of the United States. Not if I can help it, she thought. I don't want to be his daughter any longer than I have to be.

When he handed her the drink she set it down without tasting it. She had no idea what was in it and he hadn't asked what she wanted, anyway. "You wanted to see me about something."

"The Values and Faith Summit —"

"The packet is going out in a little bit. Everyone will have it for the weekend to study before they show up on Wednesday."

"Good. I needed some assurance. The summit is critical, you know that. I hope to be leaving it next week with the pledged support of a wide spectrum of Christian leaders. Now with the convention keynote in New York, California is likely. I could be throwing my hat in the ring sooner than we thought."

Reyna did not care. "Paul could have asked me."

"I wasn't sure the summit was a top priority for you."

"It isn't. My mother is."

"Her care is flawless. You can leave it to others." He smiled as if that should put her mind to rest, but she heard the threat.

She looked at him hatefully, though she knew he could read her emotions. "I'm standing here because I love her. I'm here, living by your rules, because I love her. Because she *is* my top priority. How can you not understand that?"

His eyes had narrowed into the slits that made them no longer resemble hers. "I do understand it. I even respect it."

"You mean you use it." Stop, she warned herself. Nothing good ever comes of arguing with him.

"I don't know why it still surprises me that you have to be forced to do everything, even what's good for you."

"I'm old enough to judge what's good for me. Thirty is not so far off." God, she felt so much older than that.

For a large man, he moved quickly. She gave ground as he loomed over her and cursed herself for letting him see she was afraid.

"Good," he said, after a moment of studying her face. "I wanted to make sure of that, too." He sighed heavily. "Why do you make this so hard?"

She'd given him what he wanted: fear and reassurance that she would do anything to help her mother. Great, just great. She was too tired for this, because she said bitterly, "You do understand that I hate you, don't you?"

"I hated my father, until I comprehended his plans for me."

"I do comprehend your plans for me. You and I have a completely different ideology. I don't want any part of yours." Why couldn't he understand that?

"Honey, you'll thank me one day. The good ol' U.S.A. may not be a monarchy, but some valuable intangibles are still hereditary. The Putnam name is a real family value."

"The polls don't even support your positions anymore. If you won't listen to my instincts, then look at the numbers. You'll never get the White House with fringe policies."

"I know that, but I need the money and the support from people who believe heart and soul in those policies."

"Do you? How can you be sure that they don't cost you more than they give? Danforth can mesmerize an audience full of woman-hating, immigrant-hating, gay-hating bigots, but John and Jane Q. Public tune him out. They might respect his right to his positions, but they don't like them. That will rub off on you when you try to claim moderate ground." It had been a long time since she had spoken to him so boldly about his plans. She didn't care if he won or lost, so why was she giving him her best advice? She should save it for his opponent. That was an idea, going to work for the other side, after her mother — God. She derailed her train of thought just in time.

He studied her for a long moment. The piercing regard

in his eyes was like a mirror. "Danforth and I are old allies."

She didn't have much of a hand to play against that. It was so weak she almost said nothing. She was too tired for good judgment. She spoke when she ought to have remained silent. "And I'm your daughter." It had no effect, so she added her only ace. "And I have studied and conducted as much research into conservative policies and American voter opinion as some people twice my age. You know I'm good at what I do. My own ideology doesn't taint the results. Danforth, and those like him, will bring you down. They're already falling and they don't want to see it."

His eyes narrowed, then the phone chirped. "Remind me to put you on my campaign team," he said, as if it was a joke. As he went to the phone, she bit her tongue and tasted blood. Without another word she stalked out past Paul, who gave her a pleased little smirk, and into the long corridor that led to her own office. On the way she saw the admin assistant working on the agenda mailing scurrying to the elevator with a pile of thick FedEx mailers. The Values and Faith Summit — two back-to-back days of hell.

Agenda item one: God hates homosexuals. Two: Conservatives hate homosexuals. Three: Everyone should hate homosexuals. Four: People who don't hate homosexuals are probably homosexuals. Five: How to raise money by hating homosexuals.

It didn't actually say that — she was far more clever than that. She was an expert at taking every proposal for the extermination of gay people and turning it into a righteous policy aimed at strengthening the only kind of family that mattered: the mythical Cleavers who lived in an America with no divorce, no sex outside marriage, and most certainly no homosexuals.

She sat with her head in hands for a few minutes, aware that she was on camera. She didn't know if anyone ever reviewed the security tapes, but her father had referred to their existence several times, just to remind her she was never really free. The black hole was there. She felt like Wile E. Coyote just as he realized he'd run off the cliff. She wanted to fall, to give in to the fury and anguish, but she couldn't afford the energy it would take to come back from the depths. She had to hold it off now. Think, she told herself, think of the music, and the women.

Horribly, unequivocally, she had to admit that it didn't help. A splitting headache came out of nowhere, and she couldn't hold a memory in her head for more than a minute. She'd used fantasy as a numbing agent so often that it no longer worked.

He had no idea that for a moment she had considered how much damage she could do to him with his autographed baseball bat. Did he think she would never snap?

She opened her e-mail in an attempt to refocus. There were fewer today as the summit package had finally been completed, thank goodness. She scanned the list of new items and a message from IAtchison at U.C. Irvine caught her attention. Irene.

It seemed markedly innocent on the surface, a simple thank you for the talking points she'd e-mailed. In a postscript there was a question. She read it three times, then escaped to the privacy of the bathroom.

What did Irene want with her? It seemed just a friendly question on the surface. Was she a basketball fan? If so, would she be interested in a ticket to Sunday night's WNBA game?

It was nothing — she was paranoid. That was all. Just because WNBA games were crawling with lesbians didn't mean Irene was suggesting anything. She was *married*, for God's sake, but then, so was Paul Johnson. This was just her own paranoia talking. But why would Irene ask, when they'd really spoken so little at the reception?

She paced the bathroom, not knowing what to do. If Irene was making some sort of subtle suggestion she could just play obtuse. Of course she would refuse the ticket. But what if Irene then suggested an LPGA tournament? Quoted Gertrude Stein or suggested "Let's be friends"?

She wanted to laugh at the absurdity of it. Irene was not gay, nor was she prowling. How could she know Reyna was a lesbian anyway? She couldn't.

She managed a quick note thanking her for the offer. She did like to watch the WNBA when she got the chance, but her schedule at the moment was difficult, and her mother needed her. It was a light mix of truth and lies. She was very good at that.

Her headache got worse.

"And that's when I decided I'd had enough. Angie like borrowed money from me all the time, and it wasn't as if she had a job. Angie . . ."

Holly decided it was just best to tune it out. She glanced at her watch again, but the nuance was lost on Gayle. Again. Gayle was her second coffee date of the week and it was obvious that Gayle was not over Angie, no matter how much she said she was, because every other sentence was about Angie.

". . . admitted she'd been sleeping around, and I mean all around. Angie was such a slut, you just wouldn't believe it, and it's not like I'm pure as the driven snow or anything, but Angie . . ."

Her first coffee date had been a little bit better, but it had been Candace who began looking at her watch shortly after Holly explained that conceptual mathematicians primarily play games. She'd lost Candace somewhere between dart theory and Ramsay numbers.

"So what do you do?"

Holly missed the question initially, and floundered in her desire to hide the fact that she'd been thinking about other things. "At the moment I'm considering going back to school."

"Really? To study what?"

"Mathematics." Perhaps she ought initially to go easy on the conceptual part.

"Really? You mean stuff like stranger/friend theory — what's that called? I can never remember."

Holly blinked. "The stranger/friend theory side of things. Ramsay numbers."

"That's right, Ramsay numbers. My great-great uncle was Alan Turing. Mind you, I don't like get any of it and I've tried, but I do know that stuff is like hard. I just don't have a head for math. It was the only thing Angie was good at — she could add up how much something cost with tax and ask me to pay for it in the blink of an eye. Angie..."

Well, that was frustrating. She had found someone who actually understood a little bit about the subject dearest to her heart, but that someone was completely and totally fixated on her ex. She had had high hopes for a meeting time of eight-thirty for coffee and dessert. They might have gone to a movie and then on to more private pursuits. Those pursuits might have led to a lovely Saturday morning breakfast and the beginning of something sustained.

The U-Haul Syndrome was sounding like a darned attractive disease, now that she thought about it.

It was just another frustration in a long week of them. It was patently clear that she needed a faculty sponsor at the university of her choice, but she couldn't choose a university unless she had a good idea that she could find a sponsor there. She could send out a battery of letters to department chairs and see what happened, but it might take weeks, months, to stir interest. Her problem was she had nothing to intrigue anybody except for a four-year-old college transcript. Calling herself a conceptual mathematician was — like, you know — overreaching. With another four years of college she might be able to claim the title.

"I'm really sorry, but I have to rush off. I just lost total track of time." Gayle was rising. "This was fun. Maybe we could do again sometime."

"You have my number," Holly said. Gayle smiled happily, but something in her little sigh said that in the romance equation, Holly did not equal Angie. Add the fact that Galina had never returned her phone call. It totaled up to major depression.

She had not been straight for an entire week. Jo would be calling for an update in what she referred to as Holly's Orgasm Quest. After all the years they'd known each other, it was still a surprise to find out that Jo was downright... bawdy.

She longed for chocolate, and that was after just inhaling an enormous hot chocolate with whipped cream and chocolate sprinkles on top. She wrapped her new coat

around her and wondered what she would do over the weekend. All days seemed alike, actually. Only the traffic
congestion clued her in as to what day of the week it really
was.

She was driving home when great big drops began to
pelt the windshield. She hadn't gone so far as to buy a
television, which meant home would be dank and dreary.
She had discovered her maximum daily intake of mathematics journals and message boards was nine hours. With
all the extra time on her hands she'd given meditation
another try, but with no more success. She needed to be
entertained. If that was a character flaw, so be it.

Through the smear of rain she saw the marquee for the
university's Friday night movie marathon. Now that was a
good idea, and she was just in time for the first feature.

She bought an overpriced Hershey bar and a soda and
headed inside. Someone had left a theater schedule on a
seat and she glanced through it.

Tonight was mother-daughter films. As the theater went
dark she was thinking maybe this hadn't been such a good
idea after all.

She made it through Barbara Stanwyck's *Stella Dallas*
without crying, mostly because she'd seen it before in a
class on feminism in film. It was maudlin and manipulative
but Stanwyck gave it everything she had, which was
considerable. Her voice was lovely to listen to. It was easy
to imagine that voice being her mother's.

Having survived the first movie, she decided to stay for
the next one. She hadn't read *The Joy Luck Club*, but she
had read about it. The film was not supposed to be as good
as the book — what film ever was? — but the screenplay was
by the author and had been critically applauded. It was an
intellectual decision to stay.

She was in tears within minutes. Each of the eight
stories unfolded another facet of both the tenacity of
mothers to survive against crushing odds and their relationships with their daughters, who grew up ignorant of their
mothers' histories. They never knew the mothers who had
sacrificed their bodies, their love, their futures, even their
lives, all so that their daughters would never have to face

those choices. It got under her skin, and the grief she'd always carried for her own mother broke free. Behind it came the anger she'd been bottling up since Audra's revelations.

She huddled in her seat, unable to see for the tears, trying desperately not to make any noise. The theater was thankfully sparsely populated, and in short order she used up the only tissue in her pocket. Her hands wiped away an endless stream of scalding tears and at times she could hardly breathe.

"Here," a voice whispered. A slender hand from the row behind her proffered several tissues.

She couldn't voice thanks as she gratefully pressed them to her face. *Get up and leave*, she told herself, but her tears felt so thick that finding up wasn't a certain proposition. She tried to tune out the movie but found herself picturing Audra watching her tenth birthday party through the fence. Such sacrifice, and for what? She felt as if her head would explode. She was so angry with her aunt — she'd called him *uncle*. Her mother had endured such an unspeakable violence and looked on the result with nothing but joy. She ached for her mother, wished she could somehow go back and make it better, but she couldn't because of that stupid, stupid accident. She couldn't say thank you. There was no way to acknowledge what her mother had done, to honor it.

Out of the maelstrom of loss and rage came an answer. She could honor her mother by living a good and happy life. Otherwise, what had any of them accepted substitutes for?

She clung to the lifeline the revelation offered, but her misery didn't abate. She had to leave, tried to stand, but stumbled.

"Let me help." It was the woman who had given her the tissues. "It's okay. Lean on me."

The proud thing to do would have been to refuse assistance and manage on her own, but the simple truth was she couldn't manage on her own. She accepted the bracing arm around her shoulders and did her best to navigate up the side aisle.

Moving helped, and so did the cold, wet paper towels the other woman offered her when they reached the semiprivacy of the cramped women's restroom. Finally, she managed, "I'm so sorry."

"It's okay. I wasn't doing so well myself."

She managed a quick glance at her Samaritan and was relieved to see signs of recent tears on the other woman's cheeks. She looked back at her own reflection. The paper towels had heightened her ruddy face and she felt hot and dizzy. "I shouldn't have come. It's . . . too close right now."

"I know what you mean."

Their gaze locked in the mirror and Holly caught her breath. The moment when they ought to have gathered their individual pain under an air of "all better" stoicism came. It went while they gazed at each other.

She hadn't been able to tell Jo. Or Tori. Not anybody. The words tumbled out of her. "My mother died a long time ago and I just found out that I exist because a friend of the family raped her. And — and the aunt who raised me after she died married the man and I lived under his roof and I never knew . . . what he did. And he's dead and I'm glad." She gulped for air.

The other woman put her hand on Holly's shoulder and squeezed, hard. "It must seem unbearable." At Holly's nod, she went on, "Have you thought about talking to a professional? Just to help you cope?"

She shook her head — it hadn't occurred to her. "I must seem a little crazy, talking to you like this." The hand was warm and soothing.

"No, I didn't mean to imply that. You just seem at the end of your rope." The other woman swallowed hard and took her hand away. "I recognize the feeling." Her translucent skin stained with red again as she blinked back tears. "My mother is entering the final stages of a terminal illness she's been battling for seven years. She's in so much pain and I can't help. I can't . . . all I can do is work. To keep the medical bills paid."

Holly turned from the mirror, looking into the other woman's eyes directly for the first time. They were like the color of melting ice, so light, but they seemed endlessly deep. She felt something ease inside her, then she was abruptly aware of the dark hair and brows that were at odds with eyes so fair. The easing gave way to a confusion of curiosity that surprised her. She tried to push it away. Was that what people meant when they described a mouth as tender? What kind of shoulders were cloaked under the long, supple leather jacket?

She steadied herself with her hands on the counter behind her and felt vulnerable and yet not afraid. Another inch closer and the other woman could wind her arm around Holly's waist, pull her close, kiss her.

She would have stopped imagining it if she hadn't seen the echo of her desire in the other woman's face. And she kept on looking into those striking eyes, reading a ripple of conflicting emotions, from desire to anguish, from disbelief to anticipation. She felt her lower lip tremble.

There was no air, nor did she need any.

The other woman's hands moved as if they would reach, as if they would take, but the moment was shattered by the bustling entrance of two women who shouldered between them in the limited space.

"I'm glad you're feeling better." For just a moment those fathomless eyes came back to Holly's face. Then the other woman turned and left without a backward glance.

Something in Holly went with her. She felt an indefinable loss that defied quantification. There was no simple answer — or if there was she did not want to solve for it.

When Reyna ran headlong into the detective outside the theater's front doors, she lost it. She had just walked away from what? He could have no idea. She still didn't know what had just happened. Something only a fool would pass up. Something she should not have to say no to. A mouth that should know nothing but happiness, a spirit that was battered but not broken, a grace to be needful and show it. Why should she have to run? She had been about to take what was so openly offered, to put her arms around the other woman's waist and to explore the taste of her mouth, the texture of her tongue, her lips. In that electric moment

Reyna had felt the promise that nothing would be held back.

So she lost it. "Get the fuck out of my way! Can't you leave me alone?"

"Miss Putnam —"

"Take your hands off me!" She yanked her elbow from his grasp. Even in her fury, the fantasy in her head didn't stop — she was back in the bathroom, in one of the stalls, taking what was offered. They twined on a bed, giving what was needed, lost in skin and heat and tenderness.

She turned to run, but he grabbed her again.

"Miss Putnam, please wait —"

She swung on him and he parried, then she was hard up against him, her arms trapped between them. She opened her mouth to scream.

"I didn't know if you were okay," he said heavily.

She wrenched herself from his grasp. "You're not paid to care about me."

"You could be my daughter." The laconic air was gone, replaced by unwilling acceptance. "She'd be your age."

"Smart girl to get away from you," she said, meaning to be vicious.

He let it pass. "The other woman, in the theater —"

"I didn't fuck her in the bathroom, if that's what you want to know!"

"Jesus," was all he said.

Reyna's head was spinning with the images her words called up, of the other woman naked against her, legs around her. "If we're all clear on that I'd like to get out of the rain."

"Wait — this isn't easy." Her fury melted abruptly and she realized he was ashen with some emotion so foreign to his features that she couldn't decipher it. "I'm breaking just about all the rules here. But there are rules and there are rules. There are things a father shouldn't do."

She shivered as the cold penetrated her jacket and the heat of her anger dissipated. "What are you talking about?"

"I'm talking about — Can we sit in the car? Getting soaked isn't going to help either of us."

She consented because he expected her to refuse. His car was just down the street and smelled of stale coffee in styrofoam cups.

"What did you mean about my father?"

"Not him. Me."

She waited, wondering if this was some sort of trap.

"My daughter was a lesbian. I've never said that to a soul."

Feeling as cold and remote as marble, she asked, "Why do I care?"

"I have access to your files going back five years. We have directives. We know what we're watching for. With some clients it's drugs, others it's gambling. We get lots of extramarital affairs. With you, we're supposed to report if you do anything remotely noteworthy with another woman. Like tonight. I ought to be writing it up, but there's nothing to tell. You did a good thing."

Through gritted teeth, she said, "I don't need your approval."

All he said was, "The first Friday of every month."

Her heart stopped.

"I don't care where you're going, and I don't care what you do. But you're going to get caught and I have to guess that won't be pleasant for you. Look, I was a cop for thirty-five years. You don't survive the job without learning to judge people. I guess your old man doesn't want a queer for a daughter and he's got some way of making you mind. I used to think the way he does. I tried to get my daughter cured."

She registered, finally, the significance of the past tense in reference to his daughter. "Where did she go?"

"Someplace called Hope and Healing. She was nineteen, and I made her go. She was a good kid —"

She let him recover and she wondered why he was telling her.

"She wanted to please me, and I was so ashamed. So she went. She came back two months later just skin and bones and so unhappy, but she said she was cured. She dated some boys for a while, then she had a relapse, and I felt like she had to go to the support group. She didn't want to go, and I didn't know why she didn't want to."

Reyna knew. She knew enough about the pattern of ex-gay support groups to guess.

"She finally told me it was like being an alcoholic and at every AA meeting everyone talks about wanting a drink. But more than that, about how much they want it, how the drink would feel going down their throat. Or that they'd had a drink and every little thing that had happened when they'd had it, every detail."

Reyna waved one hand in a weak gesture of understanding. She spoke for him, probably more explicitly than he would have. "They talked about lesbian sex, wanting it, having it, getting off on other people's weakness. She was hit on by everyone, including the group leaders. And somehow this was supposed to help her not want it."

She'd read the stories in the gay press and been tasked to formulate effective rebuttals, to keep people believing there was a cure. Some gay men reported that the support groups were a reliable place to pick up other men. The next meeting everyone would confess, cry, pray, and then adjourn to pair off again.

"It was just like that, but I kept telling her to go — I was that ashamed. Her hair was falling out, she wasn't eating. I didn't care. I didn't want to be ashamed of her. She was an honors student in high school. She wanted to be a doctor. She even got a pre-med scholarship. And I was ashamed of her."

Reyna knew what was coming. She'd heard this story before as well, but it never made it into the anecdotes offered by ex-gay ministries as a known result of their services. Unwillingly, she felt pity for him.

He couldn't seem to stop, now that he'd come this far. "That last night, after the last support group she went to, she told me she only wanted two things — for me to be proud of her, and to be able to lie down with another woman and not feel like a diseased freak. And she knew she could never have either." He took a long, ragged breath. "Then she blew her brains out."

She gulped at his unsparing recital. She'd written press releases based on unsubstantiated anecdotes and unverified statistics, helping those people sell their lie. She helped them for her mother's sake, but that didn't keep the blood off her hands.

"There's an air about you, and it's gotten more pronounced. You've lost weight. I never see you eat anything but Raisinets, and she'd be your age, maybe a doctor by now. And I can't let it happen again."

"I'm not going to kill myself," Reyna whispered. "I don't hate that I'm gay. I hate that I have to hide it." He'd trusted her with his pain so she told him the truth in a few flat, unvarnished sentences. "And if I'm not a good girl, all that care goes away. I think he really is convinced he has my best interests at heart, that some day I'll be glad to have no known skeletons in my closet. But I don't think being gay is a skeleton. He'll never understand."

Ivar put his head back on the seat and took a deep breath. "So you want the best for her, but what you have to endure to get it makes you wish for . . ."

"In my weaker moments, I can't help it. God help me."

They were quiet for a long while and Reyna felt an unwinding in her spine. Her headache eased. It had felt good just to tell someone, though she knew it was a risk. She couldn't possibly trust this man. "How did you know? About the first Friday of the month?"

"Kubrick night. Can't stand him so I waited out here. Everybody was leaving the theater around one a.m. but there was no sign of you. Turns out the film broke. Long about three-thirty you came out of the alley. I've never been quick enough to follow you, though, so I don't know where it is you go."

Her habits of self-preservation kicked in. This all could have been an elaborate, well-acted ruse to get her to reveal where she went. "And I'm not going to tell you."

"Just as well. Listen, though. I'm not on every Friday. And most of the time there's nobody on you Sundays, but not always."

If he was sincere, then he was taking no small risk.

"Thank you," she was able to say. "I don't intend to take any more chances than I'm already taking."

"Maybe not now. But how much longer can you keep it up?"

She didn't answer as she got out of the car. She kept her head down as rain seeped under her collar. She supposed she ought to feel relieved that at least one detective wasn't looking for any little thing to bring her down, but thinking she had more freedom than before was dangerous. Mark Ivar had never said he would help her beyond turning a blind eye to her monthly disappearance. It would be a serious mistake to think of him as an ally.

Her thoughts turned in circles as she drove home, and it wasn't until she was shedding her wet clothes that she remembered the woman at the theater. It all came back in a painful, aching wash of desire. Eyes dark with anguish eased by sudden desire. Soft hair framing a kind, open face. The lushness of her body, the sweetness of her mouth. The curve of her waist, the swell of her breasts — all offered in a moment of elemental honesty. There had been more, or at least she had thought so at the time. But that could just be her heart talking, and it had no right to be thinking about such things.

How was she supposed to resist what her heart craved? It was the witching hour and the black hole waited. She let herself fall and shuddered in the dark until sleep came over her like a thunderstorm.

10

"It'll be fun," Tori urged.

"It sounds like a meat market."

"Well, it is later on in the evening, but you can leave by then if you don't like it."

Holly chewed on the inside of her cheek. "I don't have anything to wear."

"As if. Black jeans and that black silk shirt — and you're done."

"I don't know how to dance."

"You don't have to know if you do it right." Tori smirked. "Ask that friend of yours — she sounds like a hoot and a half."

She could ask Jo to go with her. It was a thought.

"Murphy will be there. I'll probably end up with her." She bit her lower lip, sorry to have brought up the subject.

"Avoid Murphy like the plague. It's easy with practice."

Geena, who was chopping broccoli at the counter, shrugged. "You know, babe, if you don't stop having a thing about not wanting ever to see her, I'll start thinking you're not over it." She looked over her shoulder, her expression serious. "I don't care about it. I have no regrets. So why do you still care?"

"Because —" Tori's face reddened. "You know why."

"We were almost there anyway. Don't give her credit for improving our sex life, because we'd have figured it out on our own, honey."

There was a pause, so Holly volunteered, "I just want you to know that I don't understand what you're referring to, and I don't expect you to explain. I don't think I want to know anyway."

Geena laughed. "It's no big mystery. Just something we do that nice girls aren't supposed to talk about. Murphy made us talk about it." Geena seemed unperturbed, but Tori's face was flaming.

"Nice girls don't talk about it in front of third parties," Tori muttered.

"As I said, I have no idea to what you are referring. I am a babe in the woods here." Holly gave Tori a look of pure innocence that was not feigned.

"Murphy's hands are apparently more slender than mine," Geena offered. "We learned to work around it."

"Geena! Oh my gaaawd . . ." Tori put her face in her hands.

Holly could not for the life of her think why the size of a woman's hand might — oh. She felt her own blush begin. "Okay, I've got a clear picture on the radar screen." She gulped. "Can I help with dinner?"

Geena assured her she needed no help, and she had a devilish smirk that made Holly abruptly realize that there was another side to Geena hidden under the serious professor. She felt honored to have seen it.

"I can't believe you told her," Tori spluttered.

"I'm not shocked," Holly protested, but she was. She

had thought, well, hadn't known what to think when Jo had blithely described her escapades. It was time to get over being a prude. If they both liked it, what the hell did it matter? It was possible that she might like it, not that she had a chance of ever finding out since she couldn't seem to get a woman to take a second look at her.

Except for the woman at the theater. Even now, almost a week later, she thought of that electric moment and didn't know what she wanted but knew that she would have been willing to try just about anything with her. Her eyes . . . her mouth . . .

"Babe," Geena said, still smirking. She dried her hands and then cupped Tori's face and kissed her tenderly on the lips. "I don't know why you're so embarrassed about it. So you like it. I like to do it. We're still decent people."

"I know that. You just like to make me blush."

"Yeah," Geena admitted. "Because you look gorgeous all red and shy."

"I'll just take this opportunity to go to the potty," Holly said. She didn't think they noticed her departure.

She took her time, and when she returned Geena was tossing vegetables into the wok and Tori looked thoroughly kissed.

She'd spent the previous evening with Audra, who, as it turned out, was in a burgeoning relationship with another teacher also nearing retirement. They were full of plans to travel, perhaps buy a motor home together and visit every single Civil War battle site. Holly was happy for her. She was happy for Geena and Tori, and happy for Flo and Nancy, who needed to close their blinds more often than they did. Nancy had an amazing back. Flo's voice carried when she was particularly excited.

She was happy herself, alone. She felt as if she'd entered a cocoon, and someday she would break out to fly free. She would find the variables and constants that formed the equation of her life.

She'd sent out about twenty form letters to universities all over the country and felt she had entered a period of waiting for something to happen. After so much occurring so quickly, she was learning to be patient again. She did not have to remake her world in a week, or a month, or even a year. She would really — really, really — enjoy a night with a woman, but she wasn't desperate for it.

At least . . . well, not recklessly desperate.

They were finishing up the stir fry when Tori asked, "So you'll come tomorrow night?"

Geena snickered.

"I don't know about that." Holly discovered she could bat her eyelashes, if she concentrated. "But I guess I'll go to the bar with you guys. If you really don't mind my tagging along. I'll ask Jo if she wants to go, too."

Ginger Rogers *sans* Fred Astaire was on the marquee, and if it hadn't been the first Friday of March, Reyna would have stayed all night. As it was she had to tear herself away from *Vivacious Lady*, with the lady vibrant and Jimmy Stewart befuddled. She walked slowly to the end of the alley, then waited. She'd seen the tan sedan behind her on the way and had thought she'd seen Marc Ivar's silhouette during the film's opening credits. But she was alone in the alley, and no one seemed interested when she walked down the block toward the motorcycle repair shop.

It felt different, tonight, dangerously different. She had always gone to escape, to lose herself, to experience renewal. Tonight she could not shake the feeling that she was going in search of something, something she could not have. She didn't know if it was the pounding headache that never seemed to stop that drove her, or the awareness of the growing void inside her. She'd once thought that the black hole was a place she fell, but now she carried it with her.

The weather had turned to spring, but the night wasn't warm. The chill lacked bite, however, and she left her jacket unbuttoned and imagined the wind blasting her free of hypocrisy and self-contempt.

Another bike passed her, slowed up, and they were side-by-side long enough for the other rider — a woman — to sketch a low-key biker greeting. Then she revved her Ninja into high and was gone in a heartbeat. Reyna wanted to take her up on the implied chase, but the consequences of a traffic ticket were too extreme to risk it. She was taking enough chances tonight.

The music was too loud for talking, but Holly stayed near Geena and Tori. She tried not to look alone and desperate. Jo was dancing with her Sandi, lost in the pulsating sea of women which seemed to cheer each new song as long as it was faster and louder.

Struggling to be heard over the siren wails in a souped-up version of the *Charlie's Angels* theme, she shouted into Tori's ear, "Is it always this loud?"

"It's just the beginning," Tori shouted back.

She didn't want Holly's Orgasm Quest to turn into Holly's Loss of Hearing. "I'll be back," she mouthed, and she moved toward the bathroom, which was as far away from the giant speakers as she could get without actually leaving the club. The line was long. No one seemed inclined to talk, though the volume might have allowed it when the music finally keyed down to something pulsating and sultry.

She was on her way back toward Tori and Geena, who were spooning as they watched the dancers, when a voice said in her ear, "Hello, mouse that roared."

She didn't have the same reaction she had before, thank God, so she could smile when she turned to Murphy. She said, "Roar."

Murphy grinned. "I'd heard that you were family now. I had you pegged from the moment I met you, of course." Smug, but somehow likeable.

"I supposed you did. Congratulations."

"Would you like to dance? I'll be good."

Holly shot a glance at Tori, not wanting to be disloyal to a friend by consorting with the enemy. Recalling Geena's point of view on the matter, however, she decided what the hell. It was better than being a wallflower. She had barely nodded when Murphy whisked her onto the floor.

She forgot she did not know how to dance.

Murphy good-naturedly clamped her hands onto Holly's

hips and helped her find a simple swaying rhythm. She murmured in Holly's ear, "Like a lot of things, it comes naturally if you don't fight it."

"Shut up," Holly said, not expecting to feel so fond of the woman. She saw now the easy charm that could slip behind even carefully guarded defenses.

"Say that again and I'll have to dip you."

She laughed. The song was winding down and it was time to put some distance between herself and Murphy's charm. "You're nice when you're not being bad, you know."

"I know." Murphy smiled with perfect equanimity. Holly was struck with how content Murphy was with herself. For better or worse, Murphy understood herself, and giving the devil her due, she seemed to be completely honest about who she was.

"If I thought you'd go on being nice to me I'd probably fall in love with you." Holly hadn't realized she knew how to flirt.

"Can't have that."

"Why not?"

Murphy's eyes were a dark greenish blue and were temporarily empty of their habitual teasing light. "My heart is taken. Sorry."

"Oh, okay."

"Don't tell anyone." She swung Holly in a circle. "You're dangerous, you know that? You inspire truth out of me and I can't have that."

Holly stumbled, collided with Murphy's hip and let Murphy catch her before she fell. She ended up crotch to crotch with Murphy, who grinned knowingly. "Sorry," she muttered.

"Come to bed with me," Murphy suggested. She nuzzled Holly's ear.

"It's tempting."

"But no."

"Sorry."

"Why not?"

"Because I'm not ready to be a conquest. I hope that doesn't sound bitchy."

"You're ready for something." Murphy ran her hands up

Holly's back. "I have excellent instincts. I told you the truth, why don't you tell me the same?"

Holly frowned. "What do you think the truth is?"

"I'm not your type."

"Oh." Holly began to laugh. "Yes, I guess that's right."

"Common deal with the newly out. See, you're thinking that since you're now a lesbian you have to love all lesbians, take them all to be your sisters and desire them equally, but it's okay to find some lesbians attractive and others not. In fact, it's essential."

"Why essential?"

"Because until you're willing to see other lesbians as just people, forgetting they're gay and never forgetting it, you won't see yourself that way either. At the bottom line, we're human beings first."

"That's an impossible equation — two mutually exclusive propositions equaling a resolution."

"Welcome to life. I've been out since I was twelve, and I just gave you the prime wisdom gathered over the twenty-five years since."

"Thank you."

"I should charge you." The devilish glint in Murphy's eyes was back.

"Such as?"

"This, of course."

It was a quick, light kiss, which had a warming effect on Holly's skin, but did nothing more. She could see now that Murphy wouldn't be all that unpleasant to wake up next to, especially after a night of guilt-free sexual expertise.

But just someone was not enough.

Jack's was packed. Perhaps springtime brought out the women. Reyna checked her coat and helmet, shook out her hair and headed for the dance floor. As usual, no one cared that she danced alone, but she felt the difference. Every previous visit she had danced to find a partner, but tonight she shied away from eye contact. She was afraid of what might happen if she made a connection. She couldn't make herself leave. The black hole was inside her, a vast emptiness of loneliness and anger. She needed ... more than sex. She needed ... more than escape.

An arm wound around her waist. She opened her eyes and was face-to-face with Irene.

After a stunned moment of recognition, fear surged through her. Mark Ivar had said she was going to get caught. Then her brain cleared enough for comprehension. Irene wasn't here to catch her. Irene was her for her own desires.

"I hoped you'd be here." Irene had to shout as Reyna fought down her panic.

"I didn't know —" Coherence was impossible at that volume level. She pulled Irene toward the patio. Once they were outside she found a corner where they wouldn't have to yell. "I wasn't sure I was getting signals from you."

"I almost told you I'd seen you here when we were alone in your office. But it was too soon. I had to think it through. How it would work."

"How what would work?"

"Us."

Irene was presuming a lot. "I don't understand."

"We're here for the same thing, aren't we? Wouldn't it be easier, nicer, if we didn't have to let some bar determine our schedule? All it would take is a research project we're working on together. No one would suspect a thing."

Irene was suggesting ... Reyna wasn't sure. "What about ... I'm confused."

Irene tipped her head as if she couldn't fathom what Reyna didn't understand. "We're both the same. Here for ... something a little dangerous, a little kinky. But it's not as if we're ..." She glanced to the side where two women were entangled in the dark. "Like that. We're normal." She shrugged. "It's just a little naughty sex."

Reyna had to close her eyes. All the papers she'd written, the press releases she'd composed, the research she'd misrepresented floated up at her. What else could Irene think of her?

It was something she couldn't pretend. She could live in an airtight closet but it didn't change what she was. Of all that he had demanded of her, Grip had never asked her to say she wasn't a lesbian, or to say that she was straight. She was seen in social settings with men; it was a lie of implication. Her moral lines had gotten so muddy, but this one she was sure of. She would say nothing if possible, for her mother's sake, but she would not, could not pretend to be like Irene. Here for sex, yes, but she was not contemptuous of the women she seduced.

"Think about how easy it'll be. We can stop coming here."

"No, it won't work."

"Why not? When I realized who you were, and I saw you leaving with a woman, I thought it was a perfect arrangement." Irene's voice grew husky. "The woman you left with? She came back a few hours later and was happy to talk about you. From what she said, I'm sure we would have a good time together."

"I can't. It won't work."

"This is better?" Irene was incredulous.

"It is for me."

"But I —" Irene studied her for a long moment. "You're not trying to tell me that you're one of them, are you?"

"I've said all I'm going to say."

"Does your father know?"

Irene might have simply been curious, but the question broke Reyna's nerve. She backed away, wanting the woman's hands off of her.

Irene made a grab for her arm. "You can't be serious."

"Nothing will work between us, Irene. You're not looking for anyone like me."

"Because you're a lesbian."

"And you're married."

"Is that the problem? My husband and I have a sound working relationship, and many shared goals. We agreed long ago that we didn't put a high value on a shared sex life. People wouldn't understand, so we're discreet."

"Sounds like an ideal arrangement for both of you."

"And it can include you."

Stop talking, Reyna told herself. Walk away. She said,

"Someday you're going to fall in love with some woman you fuck."

"Don't be ridiculous."

"And then you'll realize that you can't substitute shared goals for a shared life, a complete life, the future. You can try like hell to make it work out, but in the end you'll have two choices: make the leap to honesty or blow your brains out." She thought of Marc Ivar's tortured daughter and felt overwhelmed by her responsibility for the lies she helped perpetuate.

Irene's mouth was pinched as she regarded Reyna. "Honesty, a quality you wouldn't know much about, it seems. If you are a lesbian."

"You're right. I have my reasons." She swallowed hard. "But you're right. I'm in no position to judge you."

Irene stared at her for a long moment, then her mouth softened, but only slightly. "I seem to have miscalculated, then. I assume we have each others' discretion?"

Reyna nodded. "A lot depends on it, for me."

Irene apparently had no compunctions about judging her. "I'll bet it does." Her gaze doused Reyna with contempt.

Stung, Reyna said, "At least I wake up knowing who I am."

"At least I wake up normal." Irene shoved off from the railing and stalked back into the bar.

Fear-induced adrenaline seeped out of her, leaving her shaking. She took some deep breaths, then headed to the bar for water, club soda, anything. She felt too off-balance to get back on the bike just yet.

The music had toned down, along with the lights. Melissa Etheridge crooned how much she wanted to be in love while bodies pressed and twined, parted and merged in what at times seemed an utterly random pattern of dance. Kisses were shared, shoulders bared, teeth flashed. She reached the bar in time to push back the faintness and close her eyes.

She felt as cold as a statue, and empty of all feeling. A glass of water was all she wanted before she left, because she wasn't entitled, hadn't earned, didn't deserve anything more.

"I think I'm going to go," Holly shouted in Jo's ear. Geena and Tori had left more than a half an hour earlier.

"You haven't given anyone a real chance. Just ask someone to dance. Anyone at all."

"There isn't anyone I want to ask. I don't know how to do the rest."

"It's easy," Jo scoffed. "You say, 'I'm Holly, let's dance and then go to bed together.' "

"Maybe that works for you."

"Not anymore it doesn't." Sandi wagged her finger in Jo's face. "You've used that line for the last time."

"It worked on you."

"You mean it worked on you."

They bickered companionably and Holly glanced at her watch. Maybe if she hadn't waited so long — it just seemed like everyone was paired off for the night.

"What about her?" Jo nudged Holly toward the end of the bar. "She's hot. Ask her."

She followed Jo's gaze, then shook her head. Her vision swam for a moment, and the music seemed to choke her ears. She was panting, all of a sudden, and felt a ripple of heat across her arms and back.

Jo gave her a push — she couldn't know.

One step closer, then two. Look up, Holly thought. *It's me, look up.* You're nobody to her, she told herself, but she couldn't stop her silent plea: *Look up. It's me.*

The other woman's head came up, then abruptly swiveled in Holly's direction with recognition.

Jo and Sandi passed her on the way to the dance floor. "You have her attention, now," Jo said. "Go get her!"

Another step. She stopped, not at all sure she had an invitation to approach. The other woman's eyes — amazing, melting eyes — seemed to be pleading with her to keep her distance, but then one hand raised and turned palm up. Her fingers curled in resignation or invitation. Holly couldn't be sure.

Holly touched the curling fingertips with her own. The jolt shuddered every nerve. It was a new sensation; she had not known skin could hunger.

A tug on her hand, then a moment when they stood toe to toe. It ended with hands on her waist, something whispered that might have been a prayer.

Then, the kiss.

Reyna breathed in the scent of her hair as their lips met, then was lost in the soft, moist heat of the other woman's mouth. She was welcome there, needed, and a moan grew between them, shared, mutual.

Holly knew she could blame it on the music, blame it on the night. Blame it on her body, on her mouth, which had never wanted like this before. She had no choice, but to be here was a choice. Mutually exclusive propositions leading to a resolution. She heard the other woman's low moan, felt hands in her hair. Their mouths parted, then merged again.

Was this a tidal wave? Reyna filled her hands with silken hair, cupped the other woman's face and drank from her mouth an urgent tenderness that left her aching for air and more kisses. She tried to revert to who she needed to be. Sexy, but aloof. Sexual, but not friendly. It was just for the renewal, just to vanquish the black hole. She did not want to know this woman's name, did not need to understand her dreams and hopes, could not want to hear her voice speaking of things she loved. She did not want to hear her name in this woman's sighs.

She could not have these things, so she must not want them. She was here for the sex, something honest and clean, freely given.

She traced those soft, welcoming lips with her forefinger, and when it was kissed, she offered more fingers, then could not bear another moment with her mouth bereft of such sweetness. These kisses were harder as arms coiled around shoulders and hips.

Her lungs clamored for air — she had forgotten to breathe. She gasped to fill her lungs while her mouth begged to return, to taste again.

The other woman said something, but it was lost in the music. Reyna put her ear next to those soft lips. "I've never done this before," she heard.

Reyna answered with the truth. That it was the truth surprised her. "Neither have I."

Part 3:
Glass

Now we see through a glass, darkly.
— I Corinthians (13:12)

11

Holly had a vision of that defining moment when she had launched herself across Clay's office, hoping to find her heart's fulfillment. She had not felt like this, but surely this was no less impulsive, and no less likely to end in disaster. Her mind tried to make her pull away, to find restraint, but her body was saying yes, yes to hands on her breasts, her face, her hips.

Her heart wanted a place in this moment, longed to build on it. Her body pushed her heart out of the equation — she had to explore this mystery, to solve this puzzle, to find new constants for her life. And her body went on saying yes until her mouth said yes, she wanted to go someplace to be alone. She remembered at the last minute to wave good-bye to Jo. She didn't know if Jo saw her and then couldn't think about it anymore.

Yes, she said, yes. Finally, she asked for a name. Reyna sounded like an ancient queen or a Greek goddess. She held the name inside her mouth and knew she would need it, that she would finally know the passion that would force the name out of her along with sounds she had never made before, moans and pleas she could not even anticipate.

"I've never done this before," she said again. Reyna didn't seem to understand what she meant. First she said she hadn't either, then she said she had. Did she mean kissing a stranger or taking a stranger to bed? Holly realized then that Reyna couldn't have understood that she had never done any of this before. She had certainly not ground herself so urgently against someone as to set off a car alarm.

She ran from the noise and for a moment wanted to go on running. She was frightened, not of Reyna, but of the next few hours. She didn't know what to do, didn't even know what she wanted.

What she knew was that she no longer walked a spit of land between past and future. She was in her future, at last. An inferno blazed all around her like a ritual of fire she had to pass through to find her way. Caught by the heat, she could not see what lay on the other side — a mountaintop, or an abyss.

Reyna kissed her again and nothing else mattered but the yes of her body answering the demands of Reyna's mouth.

Reyna was lost in Holly's mouth, which seemed to crave gasps and tongue and feverish lips. It was hard to find the will to end the kiss, but they needed to get out of the parking lot. Holly stumbled on the concrete, but Reyna caught her, setting off another chain reaction of desire.

Holly stopped walking when she must have realized they were heading for the Virago. "I've — I've never done this before," she said again.

Holly's gaze shot up to her face, but Reyna wasn't teasing when she said, "You just hold on. You've already proven you're good at that."

Her voice heavy with meaning and promise, Holly said, "Show me what to do."

Reyna swallowed hard and tried to gesture nonchalantly at the bike. "Just throw one leg across and I'll squeeze in front of you."

Holly used Reyna's arm for balance as she settled astride the bike. "Is this okay?"

Reyna had thought she was the one in control, but the illusion crumbled when she looked down into Holly's upturned face. She was kissing her again, her hand running down Holly's throat, down her arm, her stomach, to the place now so exposed. Holly groaned and tried to stand. Her whole body was shaking and Reyna could barely hold her. This was what they both wanted.

Holly was whimpering, groaning, and Reyna abruptly realized that Holly was on the verge of climaxing while straddling the bike, and that was not what she wanted to happen. Not surrounded by traffic fumes and the stale odor of cooking oil. She didn't want it to be like this. She could not stop herself from wanting more.

Somehow she took her hand away, somehow she once more broke away from Holly's mouth, which was teaching her how to kiss all over again.

Holly was gasping for breath and her arms were shivering. "I've never done this before," she said, and this time it was a plea, not an explanation.

"I want to be alone with you." Reyna couldn't hold back the words anymore. "Alone, together, for the rest of the night." She made Holly put on the helmet and the jacket, though it was a journey of a few blocks. She settled on the bike, vividly aware of Holly's thighs enclosing her hips. She triggered the ignition and Holly's arms wound firmly around her waist. Just before she slipped into gear, Holly's hands moved farther up, and she cupped Reyna's breasts with an earthy moan plainly audible over the purr of the motor.

Reyna shuddered, wished she were naked, wanted Holly's hands all over her. "I can't steer if you don't stop."

Reyna didn't know if it was her heart or Holly's hammering against her ribs, but it subsided when Holly finally lowered her hands and clasped them together around Reyna's waist.

Reyna lost no time getting them to the anonymous motel a few blocks away. Holly leaned with her on the corners as if they were molded together, breast to back. She could imagine riding this way all night. They could be in Mexico before daybreak, and they could keep on running. They could wake up with the sound of the ocean in their ears, and bask in each other and sunshine.

The import of the fantasy finally sank in and she shook herself out of it. Holly was like the others, just a few hours of freedom, a few hours of pleasure. It was bad enough she had told Holly her name. There was no tomorrow for them. Just tonight, which was already slipping into the past.

She turned into the motel parking lot and left Holly on the bike just around the corner from the office, out of the sight of any prying eyes. She didn't know if the clerk remembered her. She paid cash and registered as R. Langston. It was just a minor informational fraud, just the name on her birth certificate.

Holly was standing next to the bike with the helmet in her hands. Reyna took it from her, then took her by the hand, leading her to their room. Holly was still shivering.

She unlocked the door and said, "Wait right there."

Motel rooms were too dark for the kind of intimacy she liked. She turned on the bathroom light and closed the door almost all the way. There was enough light to take in Holly's pale, strained face at the door.

"You can come all the way in," she said gently. "Don't be afraid of me."

Holly's voice quavered. "I've never . . . I don't know what to do."

"Just stand there," Reyna whispered. She pushed Holly firmly against the closed door. "For as long as you can."

Sweet mouth, and demanding. Holly's hands seemed like fire on Reyna's face, then Holly wrapped an arm around her shoulders, on tiptoe, offering her breasts to Reyna's hands.

She was softness and mystery, and her skin burned Reyna's fingertips.

After the kiss Reyna whispered, "There's no hurry."

"I can't — I'm . . ." She crushed Reyna's hand to her breast. "Kiss me."

She realized then how hard Holly's hips were churning, and the reason for her panting, rapid breath. She ached toward orgasm as well, but Holly was far ahead of her. Holly had admitted to being a novice at anonymous encounters and so Reyna listened to her own experience. "I was going to go slow toward the first one, baby, but I don't think you can wait." Her hands went to Holly's zipper.

Holly whispered, "Reyna, please."

Her name as a prayer — it had been so long. She finally managed to get Holly's pants open, then slipped her fingertips down while Holly groaned out her name again, then her hips were slamming back against the door.

"Is it okay?" She was crying. "I can't stop — please!"

"Hold on to me, you're okay. Make it what you need, and hold on to me."

The heat and wetness that surrounded her fingers was a searing pleasure for her as well, but nothing compared to what Holly was obviously experiencing. Reyna held her, helped her, stroked urgently, then stopped when Holly was too rigid for more. Her hand cupped beauty and she could never stop wanting it. Holly's mouth parted with a final cry and Reyna heard her name again, like a prayer.

"I'm sorry," Holly said. Her head swam while her ears felt as if they were on fire. She had not known she had such muscles, nor what they could do, contracting over and over as if to take the pleasure and let it spill outward through the rest of her body.

"About what? I was more than happy to do that for you. It's only the beginning."

Her body said yes even as Reyna took her hand away. She shuddered as Reyna unbuttoned her blouse. "It's just — I've never done this before," she said again, willing Reyna to understand. She lowered her gaze to Reyna's hand as it swept over the tops of her breasts.

Reyna's hand stilled. Holly could feel the wet fingertips on her hungry skin. For a long minute Reyna didn't say anything. Then her hand slipped under Holly's bra strap, baring her shoulder. "You mean with a woman you just met?"

Holly shook her head and Reyna stilled again. "I mean with a woman."

Reyna's hand trembled. "You mean you've never done this before."

Holly felt a tickle of laughter. "That's what I've been trying to tell you."

"Dear God." Her mouth grazed Holly's shoulder, then she drew back. In the dim light she stared into Holly's eyes as if searching for Holly's past.

"I was with a man for eight years and never — what just happened, that was the first time." She felt her cheeks stain with color, but it was hardly the time for shyness, not with her pants open, her shirt undone and Reyna's hand on her breast.

Reyna murmured, "He was a fool," then shook her head as if the matter was closed. "A fool."

Her hands were inside Holly's shirt now, slowly easing her bra straps aside. Holly sighed as Reyna massaged her shoulders where the straps had marked them. Clay had never done that. Would a man even know that a woman's shoulders craved it? She felt as if she were melting into Reyna's hands. If she was on the bed she'd probably be asleep. Drowsiness was claiming her.

Then Reyna cupped her breasts.

All the passion burned through her again with a gasp that echoed between her mind and mouth. Fingertips found her nipples through the fabric and gently squeezed, wrenching another gasp from her. This gasp was lost in Reyna's mouth as she kissed Holly again. There was a promise in the kiss, something in the steady, deliberate exploration of her mouth. The hands on her breasts were a promise as well. Their rhythmic teasing was a prelude to the unknown that left Holly faint.

"I can't stand up . . ." She could hardly speak. Her heart

was between her legs, throbbing a deeply aroused pulse that made her legs tremble in response.

Gravity shifted. She felt weightless until she realized she was on the bed now. Reyna straddled her and was slowly undoing the remaining buttons of Holly's blouse. She massaged Holly's stomach when she was done, then her hands returned to Holly's breasts until Holly could not stop her own hands from pulling her bra down, baring herself.

"Show me what you want," Reyna whispered. She offered her hands to Holly, who cupped them on her naked breasts. "Yes," Reyna said. "I know."

"I can't believe . . . I didn't know how good this would feel." All her wondering about the way a woman would feel and she had not stopped to think how she would feel with another woman's hands on her.

It was glorious and a wonder. Her body had been made to love another woman's touch. She had a key, a constant for her life now. A woman's touch was what her body would always crave.

Holly found the strength to open her eyes and was surprised by the pain in Reyna's expression. She cleared her throat. "What's wrong?"

Reyna shook her head. "Nothing. I just didn't expect — I didn't expect it to feel like this. For you to feel like this."

In a whisper, Holly asked, "Like what?"

Reyna closed her eyes briefly and her hands paused in their massaging of Holly's skin. "Like tomorrow."

Reyna moved off of Holly, suddenly standing up. Her gaze followed Holly's hands as Holly removed the rest of her clothing. She wanted to be naked for Reyna's hands, for whatever came next. Her blouse, her bra — she heard Reyna swallow hard. An impulse deep within her stirred. She had gone through life covering herself up, trying not to be desirable. She got to her feet, somehow, and slowly pushed down her slacks, turning so Reyna saw her first in profile. She eased off her shoes, then bared her hips, her thighs, her calves, all of herself.

She turned to Reyna, stepping into the circle of her arms, naked, a gift.

* * * * *

Just sex, freely given. Holly was giving herself and Reyna should have been relieved. But she wasn't.

Tonight will not be enough. Reyna pulled Holly to her and kissed her hard. She wasn't sure a hundred nights would be enough to take what was offered and to give what was needed. Holly was returning her kiss and she reeled, a moment away from falling onto the bed and offering herself as unequivocally as Holly had.

But they had no tomorrow. There was only tonight.

Holly sank down on the bed, pulling Reyna after her. "Touch me," she breathed.

Reyna let herself get lost in the lushness of Holly's curves, the soft dimples of her skin. She explored every inch, rolling Holly in the bed until Holly clutched the sheets facedown as if they were her only grip on the world. She writhed in response to every caress, panting. Reyna traced the supple line of her shoulder blades. Thumbnails down her spine drew a choked cry. Holly pushed herself up, her body a sensuous curve of desire, and Reyna circled her ribs to caress Holly's sensitive breasts.

"My God, oh please, Reyna."

"What do you want?"

"I don't know."

"You do — of course you know." She slid one hand down to the small of Holly's back, then moved her hand to Holly's calf and slowly brushed it up the back of her thigh.

Holly went to her hands and knees, her face in the sheets. "Yes . . ."

"What do you want?" Reyna knew, and she longed to be inside Holly, feeling her strongest and most intimate muscles responding to the pleasure Reyna ached to give her. There was no need to make Holly ask, except that asking was yet another step on a ladder of arousal. It was her first time — nothing before even counted — and if this was to be their only time Reyna wanted Holly never to forget her.

"I want you inside me," Holly whispered.

Reyna felt a clenching response and realized for the first time that as she was working toward Holly's pleasure her own was building. Trembling, she turned Holly onto her back and began a final massaging descent from face to hips. Holly's hands were on hers, pushing them down. Her legs were spread in need. If Holly's moans, the shimmer of perspiration on her arms, her taut, swollen breasts, the jerking of her hips all were not enough proof that she wanted this, the copious wetness that Reyna's fingertips found removed any final doubt. It was what Holly wanted, and what she wanted, too.

Her fingers slipped in, learning the shape of Holly's receptive body, memorizing it, because — all lies she might tell herself set aside — she wanted to be here again, and again. She knew nothing more about this woman than how she felt in her arms and that private moment of history she had shared at the theater. There was no tomorrow for them, but the time she took to listen to Holly's groans, to interpret them to flutters or thrusts, told her she did not believe it. There had to be a tomorrow.

Holly could not believe that this hunger had always been a part of her, that this need to feel hard pressure deep inside her was her natural, long-denied desire. She had not even known she had such depths, with nerves that could explode in ecstasy. For a minute, maybe two, she could focus on everything Reyna did, everywhere Reyna touched, but it was soon too much to handle, not when emotions spilled out behind the pulsating physical sensations.

Her mind spun to what also gave her unspeakable joy and she considered how a formula could express the exponentially cascading pleasure that surged through her — the constants were the muscle and sinew and size of Reyna's fingers, and the variables how hard, how long each stroke.

Her head exploded with the unbearably beautiful numbers of chaos, burning behind her eyes. She cried out, heard Reyna cry out too. They were identical but different drums, resonating to the same frequency. She lost control of her body, and let it say what her mouth could not: harder, deeper, take what you want of me, it is what I want, too . . .

It ended with a stillness broken only by her realization the she had forgotten to breathe. For some time, air was enough.

Silence took on life and she finally heard Reyna's sobbing breaths. It took conscious thought and planning to move, but once she lifted one knee she found her arms would shift, then she could turn her head.

Reyna was shuddering, but her gaze—those startling, fathomless eyes — seemed never to have left Holly's face.

Holly cleared her throat, tried to speak, but her throat was still too dry.

Reyna was a sudden flurry of action, bringing them both a glass of water and helping Holly to sit up so she could drink it.

Holly found that she was suddenly too shy to talk, now that she could. She studied the glass, the water, the sheets and blankets on the floor.

"Are you okay?" Reyna finally broke the silence.

"God, yes." Holly could look at her then. She wondered how to convince Reyna to take off her clothes. She had no idea if she could do anything for Reyna that was as powerful and satisfying as what Reyna had done for her, but she wanted to spend the rest of the night trying. She dropped her gaze to Reyna's breasts and could not stop herself from licking her lips.

Reyna moved suddenly. "I'll get us some ice."

She was only gone for a moment and returned with a full ice bucket. Holly let her drop cubes into what water remained her glass, though she could have gone without, and marveled that she had the power to make Reyna nervous. That had to be it — Reyna wouldn't look at her now, and stood by the window drinking her water as if she could see out the drawn curtains.

She finished the refreshing, replenishing water and set the glass down. "Come back to bed," she said, her voice husky with desire. "That is, if you want to."

Reyna turned sharply. "I do." She took the two steps needed to stand next to the bed, and looked down at Holly.

Holly felt for a moment that Reyna was going to do something to cycle them into another round of lovemaking, something sexy and calculating. But as she moved to take Holly's face in her hands she brushed the ice bucket off the bedside table and it spilled its contents onto the thin carpet.

Laughing, Holly helped her gather the cubes, their hands tangling and shoulders bumping.

Then Reyna drew one red and chilled finger down Holly's throat. The cold shocked her skin and the sensation of being alive traveled over her body. She wanted again and was amazed at how stirring one finger could be. Then Reyna's hands, cold and purposeful, massaged Holly's ribs, slipped forward to her nipples. Holly was flooded again and could not think what her body could stand. She wanted to know, what could there be? She said, raggedly, "I want you."

She stayed where she was, kneeling, and watched Reyna's hand slowly move to the refilled ice bucket. The melting cube was the color of Reyna's eyes and Holly stared into those eyes when Reyna pressed the cube to the hollow of her throat. Holly thought she heard it sizzle. Drops trickled down her chest, merging and separating. The random dance was for her skin's pleasure.

When the ice moved to her breast, rested for a moment on her nipple, she felt her nerves stretching to cope with new sensations. The cold was almost painful, but from that grew a hunger for pleasure. A singing joy surged in her ears and she knew this was what her body was made for.

She gasped for air and watched with a flutter high in her throat — *my God, my God, my God* — as Reyna put what was left of the cube in her mouth.

It was Reyna's mouth that had brought her here, lips and tongue teaching her new sensations inside her own mouth, but the power of Reyna's hands had made her forget the pleasure Reyna's mouth could draw from her.

She drew Reyna's mouth to her breasts, and the cold brought another shock, another flood in anticipation of an intimacy she could only now envision.

* * * * *

The cold of her mouth melted against the heat of Holly's breasts and she drew her chilled tongue over each taut nipple. Holly panted hoarsely, held her, and was rigid otherwise. Reyna sought the water and salt on Holly's chest, then licked the tip of her chin. She hesitated, then flicked her tongue over Holly's parted lips. A promise.

She lifted her to the bed and spread her out on it, a beauty of stomach and legs, lushly female. She covered Holly with her body, kissed her throat, tasted her shoulders, used her tongue and teeth to draw in the eager flesh.

"Reyna," fervently, "Reyna . . . Reyna." Another prayer.

Soft, vulnerable skin was making love to her lips and the scent of Holly was drawing her downward. For her there was no act more intimate than this. Loving a woman was loving the way she tasted, the way she moved toward the moment of connection.

Just before she submerged she remembered that Holly had never done this before, that it would be — no matter how much she anticipated it — completely beyond her expectations. Her tongue reached — *my God, my God, my God* — she tasted. She lost herself and savored every slick and swollen fold, slipping upward, in, then Holly's hands were there, holding herself open so that Reyna could taste every receptive place. Reyna clung to Holly's hips and drank.

There was nothing she could love more than this, nothing that could make her feel more complete. Physically, she wanted nothing more. It had to be enough, it was too beautiful not to be enough. Holly's hands were in her hair now, holding her in place. She had never tried so hard to please a woman. It had to be enough not to need tomorrow.

She cried silently into Holly's thigh when Holly at last let her go. Holly's legs were trembling. The sheets were soaked. Tomorrow — she had to have it. There was almost nothing she wouldn't risk to have it. Her mind churned possibilities as she raised her head and reached out again with her tongue.

* * * * *

"Dear God," Holly sighed. The sensation was like nothing she could have imagined. One moment she felt shattered yet completed, at peace yet yearning. She thought that there could be nothing more, that she understood the ecstasy that had drawn Audra and her mother together, that tied Tori and Geena, that Murphy seemed to be seeking in every woman she met.

Then Reyna's mouth was on her again. The newly discovered nerves inside her shuddered as Reyna's fingers slid inside her. How could anything feel so good after all she had already enjoyed?

Reyna gasped, "Can you? Again? Please, please try."

"Yes — don't stop —"

"I won't —"

"I can feel you there, inside me."

Reyna was groaning as she pressed her mouth into Holly and her fingertips swirled over a knot of nerves that drew a hoarse cry in response. All that had gone before was making it take that much longer, and Reyna stayed there, knew she would stay there, for as long as it took. She was aware of time slipping away. The last movie was undoubtedly in its last reel. This would be the last orgasm, all Holly's, and Reyna didn't care if it took an hour or a day for Holly to get there.

Holly wasn't aware that she was cold until Reyna covered her with her body. The heat was so welcome. She was so sleepy now. But — there was something missing from the night. She couldn't, at that moment, think what it could possibly be.

Reyna kissed her thoroughly, but so tenderly that Holly felt a faint, persistent stirring of desire. "I want to be with you again."

"Yes," Holly answered. "I want that, too."

"Look at me."

Holly forced her eyes open. Reyna was gazing into her face. She smiled at her. "I'm looking."

Reyna's thumbs swept over her cheekbones. "This is all there can be. I can't give you any more than this."

"Believe me, it's enough." Holly put a fingertip on Reyna's lips.

Reyna shook away Holly's hand. "There can be nothing more than nights like this. I'll be here next Friday night at eleven. If you want me to make love to you again, then be here."

"I don't understand." Reyna suddenly seemed cold and aloof.

"It's the way it has to be. I'm sorry, I have to go."

Something did not compute. Her tired mind tried to form an equation that explained Reyna's behavior. "I don't — why?"

"I can't explain. It's just the way it has to be. Next Friday at eleven. It's all I can give you."

Holly just stared at her, puzzled and torn. She would be a fool to say no to another encounter with Reyna, but she didn't like the mystery. Possible explanations for Reyna's behavior were unpalatable. A lover waiting for her at home was most likely, and Holly didn't want to be part of that. She should refuse. Her pride alone ought to reject Reyna's take-it-or-leave-it attitude.

But just as she opened her mouth to speak — not at all sure of what her answer would be — Reyna said raggedly, "Please say yes."

She said yes because Reyna's eyes were not aloof and cold, and because although she felt like she had done all the taking tonight, Reyna had need of her. She owed Reyna that much, to answer her need.

Reyna had opened the door when Holly grabbed the blanket from the floor. Holding it in front of her she stumbled to the door. "Wait."

Reyna looked down at her and drew a shuddering breath. "I have to go. I don't want to."

"I know," Holly murmured. The blanket slipped to the ground as Holly coiled her arms around Reyna's shoulders. "Kiss me."

Reyna did, stinting nothing, and then Holly let her go, taking some comfort in the fact that if she had drawn

Reyna back to the bed Reyna would have stayed. She knew she would have stayed. There had been something more than sex between them.

She rescued the blanket and sheets and wrapped herself in them before tumbling back onto the bed. She felt wonderful and tired. She found a pillow and curled up.

Sleep swept in like the tide, but as Holly went under she realized what had been missing. Next week, she thought, next week I will touch her. Next week I'll know the taste of her and what she likes. Just a week to wait . . . only a week . . .

12

"You're looking rested and well, sweetie."

Reyna settled into the chair next to her mother's bed. "I'm so glad you're home again. I slept late or I would have been with you."

"Jean looked after me. I'm glad you had some extra rest. It did you good." Her mother's eyes were searching her face from the soft depths of many pillows. She seemed so slight that she made the pillows and the lightweight down comforter appear massive and smothering by comparison. "Were you out late?"

She nodded, not wanting to offer the lie of having been

at the movies. She didn't like to lie to her mother. "I had a good time, but it made me quite tired."

Unfortunately, her mother seemed to want details. "Was it with anyone in particular?"

"No one you know," Reyna said lightly. "Those flowers are magnificent." The arrangement was lavish. She didn't have to check to know they were from her father. Her mother loved gladioli.

"Those purples almost hurt my eyes," her mother said. "If there's someone special . . ."

"No —" Reyna stopped because it would be a lie to say there was no one. There was not an inch of her body that didn't quiver at the memory of Holly last night, of the way she had sounded, had moved, had wanted, had taken, had given herself. The swooping sensation in her stomach was growing familiar. She got up ostensibly to smell the flowers

"There is." Her mother sounded almost girlish. "Tell me all about him."

"Mom . . ." Oh God, she thought. I didn't want to have this conversation.

"Reyna, sweetie." Her mother was trying to maneuver herself into a more erect position.

"Don't, Mom."

"It's not so bad right now. I've still got hospital drugs running around in my blood." Her grimace belied her words.

"Mom," Reyna admonished. "Lie back."

"Reyna, honey. Oh, all right!" The flash of anger in her mother's eyes startled Reyna. She drew back from offering assistance. "I will if you'll sit down again."

Reyna perched on the chair, alarmed by the high color in her mother's cheeks. Her cheeks had once been like fine porcelain, but now they were crusted with the distinctive butterfly rash of her illness.

"I don't have time for silence, Reyna."

Reyna's eyes filled with tears. She had not thought of it that way.

"There's something you're not telling me. Are you going

to let me die without knowing? Is it so terrible that you think I'll stop loving you?"

Reyna shook her head. "No, no Mom. I just never wanted to add to your burdens. I don't want you to worry about me, ever. Because I'm fine. I'll always be fine."

"I know." Her mother gazed at her. "But I'm your mother. Thinking that you spend every night alone, that you work too hard to have friends. Of course I worry about you. I might be dead next week —"

"Mom, don't —"

"But it's still my job to worry about you."

Reyna blinked rapidly, trying to quell her tears. She thought of Holly and the chance she had taken arranging to meet her again. She had jeopardized her mother's care to do it and felt as if she was being forced to choose between two primal desires. She loved her mother and wanted her to have as little pain as possible. She loved — no, she thought. She did not love Holly. A night together, even an incredible one, was not a foundation for love. To think that way was disaster, an absurdity. No, it wasn't love. "You should save your strength for yourself. I'm okay."

"It doesn't work that way." Her mother's stillness made her voice all the more piercing. "The pain is always there. And for a long time, because its always being there was new, and because I had no idea that it could be so much worse, I let the pain into my head. I let the pain be in charge. And then it got worse. I had a choice — let it be in charge and spend all day, every day, crying in bed. Or I could let it have my body and keep my mind for myself. So that's what I did." Her mother's gaze was intense and Reyna wanted to look away but could not. "Remember I told you that the pain brought clarity?"

Reyna nodded.

"That's what I meant. When I let my body go, when I told myself that I was dying —"

"Mom —"

"When I told myself that I was dying, I was suddenly free to think again. It wasn't until then that I realized how much you had changed. I had been so caught up in the pain that I stopped seeing you. You walked in one day and I didn't recognize you because in my mind you were still the girl who had left for Berkeley. But you're not a girl any longer. And you're not happy anymore."

"I wish you wouldn't worry about me." Reyna fidgeted and wished desperately that Jean would come back to distract them.

"Like I said, it's my job and will be until the day I die. Which is going to be sooner than I had planned. So I don't have time to wonder." Her voice faltered and she suddenly sounded exhausted. "If you want me to stop worrying, then tell me the truth."

She was too raw from her encounter with Holly to find the acuity to counter her mother's logic. She was right about there being no more time for evasions. Reyna had not considered that her mother might die not really understanding who her daughter was. "I met someone last night. Something happened."

Her mother had given up fighting gravity, and the pillows claimed her. She looked almost as if they would swallow her at any moment, and only her eyes would remain vibrantly alive. "And yet you look so rested today. Is he nice?"

Reyna tried to say it easily, but the words caught in her throat at first. "It's a — it's a woman, Mom. There's only ever been women for me."

Her mother closed her eyes. "Oh, sweetie."

"I'm sorry if it disappoints you, but it's the way I am."

"You don't know how long I've waited for you to tell me that."

Stunned, Reyna put a hand to her mouth. "How did you know?"

"How could I not know?"

"I — I wasn't serious about anybody until I went to college."

"I had thought for sure you'd come home with a girlfriend. But when you finally came home I was letting the pain do the thinking, and I didn't notice how alone you were."

Choked, Reyna managed to say, "I never meant to lie. I just didn't want you to worry. I was afraid you'd think I was ruining my life. And you would worry."

"If you had told me before lupus I honestly might have felt like you needed help. I would forget — you went out with men, but those were arranged by your father, weren't they? But I would forget that I had been so sure you weren't interested in men. But now . . ." She sighed and Reyna saw deeper lines of pain settling into her face. "What does it matter? If it makes you happy, that is what I want for you."

"Thank you, Mom. I — I don't know what to say."

"Can I meet her?"

"No — we have a date next Friday, but I don't have her phone number. I . . ." She blushed. "I don't know her last name."

"Reyna," her mother admonished. "That's not exactly sensible."

"I know —"

"You should have gotten a phone number. What if something comes up?" Incredibly, her mother laughed.

Reyna joined her. "I'll remember your advice. Last name not important, but phone number is."

"So I can meet her after that."

"I don't know if she will —" She stopped then, because the fantasy of bringing Holly to meet her mother stopped dead. It would never happen. Just seeing her again, for just one more night, was risk enough.

Sternly, she told herself the hard facts. You know nothing about her, and love isn't part of the equation. There's no reason to even want her to meet Mom, just get that through your head.

"It's too early?"

"Yes. I'll get Jean now."

Her mother nodded tightly and Jean came right away with the syringe that would bring sleep. Reyna waited until her mother was all the way under, thanked Jean, then stood on the porch of the house where she had grown up, feeling the sunshine on her cheeks.

It should have been a joyous moment. She had come out

208

to her mother and her mother had already known and lovingly accepted it. But it only intensified the cage she endured, because even if there was someone special to her, she couldn't let her mother know. Because just down the street sat a tan sedan, and she had no guarantee that Mark Ivar would overlook her bringing a woman to her mother's home. Her father would find a way to ask who it was and her mother wouldn't know how much depended on a shameful lie. She did not want her mother to know about that.

And what if her mother knew, and was willing to risk her care, the loss of her house and the nurses, what about Hol — what about that someone special? Her father would find a way to ruin her or remove her from Reyna's reach, the same way he had found ways to pressure Margeaux into simply moving home again.

At home she stepped over the clothes she had stripped off in the early morning hours. She took off the clothes she was wearing now and got into bed, though it was not even four in the afternoon. She wrapped her arms around a pillow and decided that bed was the only safe place for fantasy. She closed her eyes and Holly was there with her. Holly's hands were on her as they had never been last night, and their bodies twisted together, naked and eager. It was just sex, she told herself, then stopped. This was a time for fantasy, and so it was okay to imagine that Holly liked muffins for breakfast and Bergman films. She lost herself in a beautiful dream that had no sex in it, because sex no longer mattered. After last night, her deepest fantasy was about tomorrows.

Jo was delighted to hear that Holly's Orgasm Quest had succeeded, and demanded full details. Holly put her off, promising more news when there was any. She didn't want to explain that she wasn't going to see Reyna again for a week, that she had no idea where Reyna lived, didn't have a phone number or a last name. It didn't seem, well, like something anyone else would understand.

As the next few days went by, she began not to understand it herself. By Tuesday the days seemed endless, and she was back to her old life of reading online journals and thinking that her dream of going back to school was a foolish one. As foolish as her idea that she had some sort of relationship with Reyna, just because she'd agreed to meet her again at a motel for another night of sex. It was just for the sex — Reyna had said there would be nothing else. That did not equal a relationship.

She wondered if there was a cure for the U-Haul Syndrome, but she didn't want to ask Jo. Not yet. Another night with Reyna might change how she felt. She would wait and see. In the meantime, she would celebrate that she knew who she was. She would face her future without flinching. So maybe going back to school was a pipe dream. She would start looking into a teaching credential.

She made up her mind to lower her expectations for the future, and then everything changed.

She almost didn't read the topic — stochastic walk was interesting enough, and the stock market gurus loved the subject. But it wasn't her favorite, and sleep was calling to her. It was actually a slip of the mouse that opened the new message instead of removing it from her to be read stack.

She read, "Since they solved Ramsay 4,5, has anyone else considered that the original Ramsay formula of $1+2^{(k-2)}$ might be more accurate than previously supposed?"

She didn't read the rest of the message, which detailed the writer's theory that Ramsay's stranger-friend design had applications for calculating stochastic walk. All that mattered was the first sentence. Not even that. The first clause: Ramsay 4,5 had been solved.

She deployed all her search engines, trying to find the published paper that would have described a discovery of such huge interest to mathematicians. Ramsay theory, which primarily dealt with inevitable patterns in very large numbers, also advanced the concept that any given set of circumstances had a minimum universe in which to exist. Discovering that minimum universe would naturally reduce random chance and coincidence. The concept informed a wide variety of science and engineering applications, chief among them telephone and server networks where random connections made chance a significant factor in planning.

She had written a paper about Ramsay theory and the formula that Ramsay had suggested when she'd been a freshman in high school. It had been the basis of her application to go to U.C. Irvine for advanced mathematics courses. In it she'd proposed a solution for Ramsay 4,5, based on further refinement to the original Ramsay formula. Using her proposal, she'd predicted that the smallest possible gathering of people that allowed for a certainty that four people were acquaintances and five people were strangers was twenty-five. She'd lacked the computer processing power to prove her theory. Cracking Ramsay 4,4 had taken two years of nighttime use of the available capacity in several university networks, and the result was only 18. If Ramsay 4,5 was 25, it would take twice that computing power to solve. But apparently somebody had done it.

She flipped from link to link, looking for the answer. Finally, she found herself at the site for the Australian National University Mathematics Department, which had announced the solution to Ramsay 4,5. She waded through extraneous Web pages that listed faculty and accolades and finally found her way onto a file transfer page. From there she downloaded the Ramsay 4,5 paper, written by Brendan McKay of the Australian National University, Stanislaw P. Radziszowski of the Rochester Institute of Technology, with attributions to Anonymous, Research Assistants, et al.

Lots of theory — she couldn't wait to read it all. But right now, no longer in the least bit sleepy, she just wanted the answer. And she found it, on page seventy-three.

Four years of devoting all off-capacity hours of individual networked computers at two universities had tested every possible permutation of Ramsay 4,5.

The answer was twenty-five.

That was her answer, in a paper she'd written eleven years ago, when she was fifteen.

* * * * *

Wednesday afternoon found her at her old high school. She'd talked it over with Audra in an early morning phone call, and Audra's practical position had been that she had nothing to lose from asking her old teacher if he recalled the paper and would be willing to authenticate her copy of it.

The school seemed smaller, of course, and more run-down, but she remembered the musty hallways and had no trouble finding the math department. When she'd called at nine to ask if Mr. Frazier still taught there, the school secretary had told her that her old teacher would be finishing his last class for the day at about that time.

The kids looked so young, but they were almost adults. The bell rang and teenagers poured out of the room, only noticing her as an obstacle to get around on their way to freedom for the day.

Mr. Frazier was packing up his case. It might have been the same one he had used ten years ago. He seemed older than she remembered, but younger than she expected — perhaps forty. She pushed away an illuminating revelation. Larry Frazier was an attractive man, in some ways much like Clay. Had Clay been a substitute for an adolescent crush on her math teacher? Poor Clay, she thought. *He never had a chance to have any part of me I valued.*

Mr. Frazier looked up. "Can I help you?"

"I don't know if you remember me. I was a student of yours about ten years ago. My name is Holly, Holly Markham."

"Holly Markham," he echoed, looking stunned. "I wouldn't have recognized you, but I've never forgotten the name. You've come about Ramsay four-five, finally."

It was Holly's turn to be stunned. "Yes, that's why I'm here. You've been expecting me?"

"For the last three years, yes, since they proved your theory." He grinned.

"I'm . . . confused, to say the least."

"You're not here because you finally heard from your aunt?"

"Uh, no. I read about the solution just yesterday. I want

to go back for my master's. I left college after my under-grad work. So I thought I might be able to get you to write a letter for me, authenticating my paper." She held out the copy she'd found in one of her boxes with her Irvine application.

He spread his hands, unconsciously offering the gift of knowledge. "But Holly — you're Anonymous. On the paper they published. Anonymous is you."

She groped for the nearest desk and sat down. "How did they know?"

"So your aunt didn't tell you? I found your old phone number in the school records and left several messages with her. She got quite exasperated with me. Ramsay numbers have always been a pet game of mine, and I never forgot your paper. It was so intriguing, but there was no way to prove it. So about five years ago, a friend of mine was heading Down Under for a research grant to work with McKay, the Ramsay guru. So I asked if he'd take your paper along. He was happy to, especially after he read it."

"I don't believe it." Holly had to clear her throat. "What possessed you to do something so kind?"

His eyebrows came together slightly, as if he didn't understand why she would have to ask that. "I did it because I could."

She heard the echo of her telling Clay the same thing, that she had quit to support Tori because she could. "So they liked the paper?"

"Liked it? They were ecstatic. They altered their rou-tines for a test set of the computers and shaved a year off the entire compilation. They wanted to talk to you, give you full credit, and see what you were working on. So I called your aunt."

"She never gave me the messages," Holly said numbly. Another black mark on her aunt's tallies.

"I wondered. I tried to find out where you had gone from Irvine, but there had never been a request for your transcript from another university except for MIT, and you weren't there. There was no local phone listing for you."

"I — wow." What if they'd put the phone in both their

names instead of just Clay's? She would have known about this miracle sooner. But would she have recognized the magic of it then?

He grinned at her. "This has just made my day. My week — heck, my semester. It bothered me, not knowing if you'd ever gotten your due. They're working on Ramsay five-five now. I know they'd still like to talk to you."

"I'm having trouble taking it in," Holly admitted. "I've been desperately wondering how to get anyone to take an interest in my transcript, which is four years out of date."

He laughed with a shrug, a gesture she remembered from her struggles with problems he had lobbed at her. "Before they published the paper they told me if I found you to let you know you had a ticket to Australia waiting. I don't know if they still have the funds, but I'll send an e-mail the moment I get home. Do you have an e-mail address?"

"Yes." She wrote it out on the notepad he proffered.

"I'll cc you. So you never went on for your master's?"

As they walked together to the front of the school, she told him a little bit about what she had been doing, not owning up to her bad choices because it was too personal to share. They parted with a promise to keep in touch and she watched him whistle his way to his car. He was just a high school math teacher and yet had given her a large part of her future, all because he could. Teachers had a magic all their own. She felt a transformational obligation to pass the magic along, one that could shape the rest of her life.

"I missed you at church." Her father adjusted his tie in his bathroom mirror while Reyna waited near his desk.

Reyna had expected him to tax her about it first thing Monday morning, but last-minute details for the summit had apparently kept him occupied. "I spent the day with Mom. Besides, I knew I'd be here today, in the presence of an abundance of righteous fervor. It seemed like my quota for the week."

He ignored her sarcasm, too caught up in the entrance they would both soon make to the gathered clergy in the institute's boardroom. Day one of the Values and Faith Summit was tightly scripted. "How's your old man look?"

Honesty compelled her to admit, "Handsome." The hand-tailored suit, just a little too large, gave him the physique of a young Orson Welles. The matching silk tie and shirt were exceedingly elegant. She had never had any trouble understanding how he had seduced her mother. Nevertheless, he compelled her to work for him, and she had managed to meet his exacting standards without giving one iota more than was required. So why did she volunteer information now? "But you're not even a candidate yet. You look like a victor, not an ally."

He glanced back in the mirror, then regarded her again. She wore an everyday plain business suit. "Thank you," he said. "Give me a minute."

He disappeared into the recesses of his closet, which Paul kept meticulously stocked with every possible combination of attire. Grip Putnam didn't always have time to go home to change.

Paul bustled in and frowned at her. "The press representatives we wanted have all arrived. They understand that the photographers will have to leave before anyone sits down."

"Good," her father said from the closet. He emerged in different suit trousers, and with a workaday but pristinely pressed white cotton shirt half-buttoned. "Reyna has convinced me I was overdressed."

Her father was too busy with his cufflinks to watch Paul, but Reyna saw the massive effort of will it took for Paul to stop watching her father dressing. He turned blindly away and fumbled toward the door.

She followed him, swept away with compassion. She had many reasons to hate herself, but none of them had to do with something as elemental as what made her happy sexually. She had Holly tucked away in her mind. No matter what the future brought, she had Holly and Kimberly and

Margeaux and her pride. Paul had only a lie, a lie he'd perpetuated on a wife and family. "Self-hatred will kill you," she whispered.

He hadn't heard her behind him. "I'm busy." His voice was shaking.

"You only feel that way about him because you won't let yourself feel it for an ordinary man. You're telling yourself it's hero worship, not love based on homosexual feelings."

"Shut up," he snapped.

"I don't know why I'm bothering," Reyna said quietly. "But I'd stop to help an animal by the road in pain. Abideth faith, hope and charity, Paul. The greatest of these is charity. You have mine if you want it, but you need to find some for yourself."

"You don't know what you're talking about. How dare you quote Corinthians to me, you of all people?"

"You're right, St. Peter has his flaws. But what about Jesus, Paul? He gave us two commandments, and said they are more important than anything else, even more than believing in him. You know what they are, don't you?" She'd written so many papers quoting explicit scripture that seemed to unequivocally condemn homosexuality, but she knew the simple words that balanced the scales of hatred and abuse. Christ's commandments negated all else as the cornerstone of true Christian philosophy. She'd never wanted to speak them before, never thought her truth would help anyone but herself.

"Stop." His breathing was ragged.

"You love God, don't you? That's the first. You wouldn't be suffering like this if you weren't trying to love God."

"Please, don't."

"You know the second commandment from Christ, I know you do. But you can't love your neighbor as yourself if you don't love yourself first. That's all you have to do to find the reward of heaven. Love God. Love your neighbor. But can you do either if you are consumed with hatred for yourself? Hatred for anyone?"

He walked out of the room without answering. The door closed behind him just as her father's office door opened. "Is this better?"

She turned and realized that this was the first time he had ever taken her advice on a personal level. "Yes, that's much better. You look like one of the people, not their king."

"Where did Paul go?"

"I'm sure he has many things to take care of," she hedged.

"I'm ready, then. Shall we?"

They had done this before, walked side-by-side into important meetings. She had always resented the inference that she was his heir apparent, that she supported everything he did and said. It wasn't as sharp today, possibly because she was living in denial that he would act as he always had before when her behavior conflicted with his goals. He had acted as if he respected her, but that would change the moment he found out about Holly.

Stop thinking about her, she told herself. Put it away. You have to survive this summit before you should even be thinking about Friday. You don't even know for sure, not for certain, that she will be there.

But Holly was there, in her mind, when they walked through the double doors into the pop of flashbulbs. She needed the memory of Holly to shake Danforth's hand, and to find even a cool smile for other men she detested even more for their frothing vilification of gays and women, immigrants and non-Christians.

Her smile became more natural for others, particularly people she had been able to form a respect for in past meetings. Terence Hallorood from the central Methodist convention was especially welcome, as was Judith Giles, who had come all the way from her Episcopal diocese in Newark, New Jersey.

They let the photographers do their work, then a pale-looking Paul shooed them out of the room. The central table had been carefully set with working materials for every participant and two side tables provided workspace for the attending reporters. Reyna had worked out most of the choreography herself, with requisite emphasis on sound bites from her father's opening speech.

She prepared to fade into the background, believing that the success and failure of the summit meant nothing to her. But if that was so, she asked herself, why had she cared what her father wore?

He was as well prepared with the speech as always. His voice had a magic all its own, rich and compelling. It was hard not to listen, harder still not to believe that this group of people could change the world if they let their hearts and faith guide them.

After the opening speech several reporters left, but a few remained, quietly tapping on their laptops.

As was usual practice at meetings like this, approval of the agenda, which had been worked out in advance with everyone, was a mere formality.

"Unless there is dissent, I'll take it that we're ready with agenda item number one," her father said. "Let's begin by —"

"Mr. Putnam."

It took Reyna a moment to track down the source of the interruption. Judith Giles raised her hand to confirm that it was her.

"Yes, Judith?"

"This is the third such summit we've had." She rose and alarm bells went off in Reyna's mind. Judith had something very important to say. "I would like to be very clear that I am here to discuss universal values that can be employed to the enrichment of all families, all people. Our last two gatherings were mired in discussions about how to segregate some people, some families, from our compassion and our ministry. I cannot countenance in silence any more ridicule and denigration of some people —"

"Speak plainly, Judith." Danforth got up to pour himself a cup of coffee, a casual counter to Judith's intensity.

"Plainly then, Danforth, I am not interested in crafting a policy statement about core human values with footnotes that exclude homosexuals. Either we are here for everybody or I cannot take part."

"Hear, hear." From farther down the table, a Baptist

minister, newly representing a northwest convention, leaned forward. "If my esteemed Episcopalian colleague had not brought it up, I would have. My time and budget are too short for bigotry. We have more important work to do."

Panicked, Reyna looked at her father. Part of her rejoiced at what was said. She wanted to applaud, to dance, to thank them, but the summit was about to tear itself apart. Her father's gaze flicked down the table, weighing options and considering damage control.

"Are your time and budget too short for the Lord's work?" It was one of Danforth's allies, the shrill and hateful representative from Focus on the Family.

"Peace." Terence Hallorood rose not far from where Judith Giles still stood. "If we begin to question each other's personal faith then we are not ready to work together. I can only say from where I sit that the issue of homosexuality and how my own church regards it is tearing the church apart. People are leaving our congregations in droves, disenchanted by ugly talk. I will do nothing here that will pour more oil on the fire. I want to find a way to put the fire out. We must come together. It is time to reconcile the bitterness." His gaze sought Danforth, who in turn looked at her father, the glue that had held them all together in the past.

She had never seen him at a loss. She interjected, "Perhaps we could establish some ground rules about off-limit topics."

"I'm sorry, Miss Putnam, but that's not good enough." Judith turned toward her. "We have been hoping to build an inter-faith statement about core human values, about what makes a strong family unit. When there are thousands of children who need stable homes, we can't support adoptions for only those families we like. We can't encourage fidelity within marriage if we won't let those who wish it to marry."

"How can you condone such things?" Danforth left his coffee, having never taken a sip, and came back to the table. He was taller than Judith by at least a foot and he looked down at her with naked contempt. "Scripture is clear —"

"I am not here to debate scripture." Judith raised her

hands. "Perhaps I have not been plain enough. I am here to help craft an understanding of a universal belief in certain values: compassion, truth, fidelity, loyalty. I will contribute to that based on both my life and my faith. I believe there is a common ground that does not by definition have to exclude homosexuals. But I will not help — in fact I will fight — anything we do that is spiteful hate-mongering. I was silent in our previous gatherings when I should have spoken. I asked God for guidance and this is how he has moved me." She looked pointedly at Grip. "So I want clarity on the tone and scope of our discussion. I need to decide if I am staying."

"Is that a threat?" Danforth shrugged, then also looked at Grip.

Reyna was aware of the rapid tapping on the reporters' laptops. This was not what her father had wanted.

He waited too long to speak. Danforth sat down smugly, assuming the day was his. Judith took a deep breath and gathered her things. Terence Hallorood did the same. Then it was clear that several more people were going to leave with them.

Reyna leaned toward her father and whispered in his ear, "Do the math. If you can't have the whole pie, keep the larger portion."

"Judith, wait. All of you, please sit down."

Reyna sat back in her chair, gripping her pen under the table to hide her white knuckles. Her father had always covered the bases, always seemed to be a step ahead. He would find a way to have it all his own way, because he always did.

"When I lost my wife and son I took it as a sign. I had to redefine what family was. I had to be more open." He touched Reyna on the arm. "Looking past rigid definitions brought me more than it has ever cost me. Nothing so tragic as death has happened here today, but I feel a similar moment in the air. I went through life thinking that nothing would change, and God taught me that I was wrong. I think he is trying to teach me that lesson again today. Change happens."

Reyna gasped. She felt the room focus on her, but she continued to stare at her father.

He blinked like a man who had just had a revelation. "I want to hear more of what Judith and the others have to say. I think she is right — it is time to find common ground, to reconcile, and to exclude no person of good faith."

Was it genuine? Had she just watched him change? Or was he playing the moderate early, planning to woo Danforth and his ilk privately?

"What is the point of teaching your children everything you know, of sending them out into the world to learn all they can and then refusing to listen when they return to teach you?"

"Grip, you can't mean this." Danforth seemed frozen in place.

"I'm sorry, Dan, but I do. I do. I am amazed that in such a small passage of time God gave me a clear choice to make. I realize that you now have choices forced upon you as a result, and I am sorry for that."

"After all the years of fighting together, trying to keep our schools free of taint, to rid television of homosexual propaganda — was that for nothing?"

"I am taking Judith's point, I think. If we win that war we lose in the end. We can't . . ." Reyna had never seen him forced to search for words. Her heart hammered so loudly that she almost didn't hear what he said. "We can't preach hate to foster love. It's as simple as that." In seeming wonder, he echoed, "It's as simple as that."

13

Holly woke on Friday morning with a happiness she had not known since she had been a child. If she'd been a character in a musical no doubt she would have burst into song at the sight of the brilliant sky or the smell of the freshly brewed coffee.

All her joy showed in her voice when she answered the phone a little past nine.

"Holly, is that you?"

It took her a moment. "How have you been, Clay?"

"I've been good. You sound different."

In another mood she might have taken it for an accusation of some sort, but no way was she going to let him spoil her day. "I'm happy. How about you?"

Perhaps someone else would have replied in kind, eager to show her that he had not missed her for a second. Instead, Clay said, "It was hard for a while. I did miss you."

"I'm sorry, then," she answered. "And now?"

"Well, it's better. I have to admit that making my own meals made me realize how much you did." There was a hint of self-deprecating laughter in his voice.

"I'm sure that's good for you, then." She didn't bother to hide the fact that she was smiling.

"Anyway, I called because I'm drowning in tomatoes."

She laughed outright. "Yeah, that's what happens this time of year. It's only the start."

"You did all the work, so you should share some of the bounty. I just wanted to tell you that if you wanted some, I'll leave a box on the porch for you."

Touched, Holly agreed. "That would actually be wonderful. Even the organic market tomatoes aren't the same."

There was an awkward silence, then Clay asked, "Are you really happy?"

"Yes," she said firmly. She found herself telling him all about Ramsay 4,5 and her paper, and the e-mail she'd gotten from Professor McKay in Australia, who had asked her to decide nothing about her future until he had checked his scholarship budget.

"That's really wonderful news," Clay said heartily. "I am thrilled for you."

Holly knew that if he had said things that supportive when they were together she might never have realized what was missing from her life. Nevertheless, it was good to hear. There was so much more he didn't know about — Audra, her mother — but she didn't want to share that with him. She would be happy to maintain an arm's-length friendship with him, and discussing her academic pursuits was a start.

She waited until she knew he had left for his classes, then popped over to the house to get the tomatoes. They were gloriously red and ripe. She'd make a tomato salad for Jo to go with lunch.

She bounded to the door to let Jo in when she knocked.

Jo's classes and papers had kept her busy until today, and Holly couldn't wait to tell her all about Ramsay 4,5 and Professor McKay.

Before she could say more than hello, Jo waved the morning *Orange County Register* at her.

"Look close, would you?" She held a photograph in front of Holly's nose. "I'm sure that's her. I thought she seemed familiar, like I'd seen her in a picture, maybe on TV, but not as an actress. It's her."

Holly stared at the picture. Metro section, page twelve featured an article about something called a Values and Faith Summit at the nearby Putnam Institute. The photograph was of Grip Putnam, the famous radio pundit, and his daughter. His daughter was named Reyna.

"I don't think so," Holly lied. She just couldn't admit it to herself. Reyna. She was Grip Putnam's daughter. Grip Putnam, the most hated man in radio. Irrational, rabidly conservative Grip Putnam. Reyna worked at the Putnam Institute, which made her his accomplice in spreading misinformation and lies about liberal policies and conservative goals. The Institute was tightly linked to something Holly had never heard of before: ex-gay ministries. Clay had foamed at the mouth when he talked about Grip Putnam and the Putnam Institute. They passed themselves off as a place of learning, he'd explained, but they were just political hacks spewing out flawed findings and out-and-out propaganda.

Reyna had loved everything she had done that night, Holly could not be wrong about that. The caption on the picture had to be wrong. *Oh damn it, damn it.* Reyna. Reyna Putnam.

Jo tapped the picture. "How many Reynas do you know?"

"One," Holly answered, honestly. She was amazed at how quickly dreams could turn to dust. She blinked at the photograph and didn't want to believe it. She made herself read the article more closely. It sounded as if the summit had taken some sort of unexpected turn toward moderate policies, but it was likely to be just spin to bolster the early whispers of Grip Putnam's intentions to run for office — very high office.

She wanted Jo to go because she wanted to cry. She had thought, had hoped, that maybe Reyna was more than just a fantastic lover. If all she had wanted was great sex then she might as well have gone with Murphy. Murphy had references, after all. Instead she'd gone with a complete stranger.

But she had felt something when she looked at Reyna, something missing with Murphy. Sure, she'd had flashes of lust for Tori and for Nancy . . . and for Flo and Geena and the woman at the organic market who had hoisted a fifty-pound bag of millet on her shoulder with ease. She'd probably have happily gone to bed with Galina, if she had ever called. But none of that had been like what she felt just looking at Reyna. They had shared something that started in that moment of shared honesty in the theater bathroom. The connection had been with more than their bodies.

Or was she just a fool? Had she fallen again for someone who would turn out to be another intellectual fascist, only this time as conservative as Clay had been liberal? She had changed so much, so quickly, but this was one direction she would refuse to go. Audra had paid the price, accepting security as a substitute for family. She herself used to think being needed was the same as being loved.

"Hey, don't cry," Jo said. "I'm sorry, Holls." She wrapped one arm around Holly's shoulders. "Trite but true, there are plenty of other dykes in the sea."

She dashed the tears off her cheeks. "I know. But she —"

"She was good, I understand. I'm glad your first time was great. But you can't possibly go back in the closet for her, and that's what it would take." Jo stabbed the paper with her finger. "What a hypocrite. They work for American Values for Family, the Traditional Values Coalition, Focus on the Family — the scum of the earth, as far as I'm concerned. She's making money off of gay-bashing when she secretly likes muff-diving as much as I do. Typical rich-privilege thinking."

Holly wiped her eyes and tried to make a joke. "Gee, tell me how you really feel."

"There's nothing that can possibly justify hypocrisy on this scale, nothing."

Holly knew it was true. She had been so happy, far happier than she had thought possible. Reyna, Audra, Ramsay 4,5 — her cup had overflowed.

"Forget vegetables. Let's go get a hot fudge sundae," Jo suggested. "We could go to the movies, too. Have a wild Friday afternoon. Then, if you want to, we could go get drunk and disgrace ourselves in downtown Irvine."

"I don't think so. I'm ... too depressed." She ought to go out with Jo and somehow find a way to be anywhere but the motel tonight at eleven. She wasn't going. She couldn't.

"And you were on top of the world — I'm sorry, Holls. It's a tough break."

"I'll mend," she said, though she didn't think she would, at least not in the near future. She could close her eyes and see Reyna's face watching every reaction as her fingers explored deeper. Reyna had loved doing it and there had been no shadow of shame.

Lunch wasn't a lot of fun, though Jo tried to distract her. Talking about the possibility of going to Australia was somewhat distracting. She'd never been out of southern California and agreed with Jo that it was high time. Australia could prove a godsend, if she couldn't get over wanting to see Reyna again.

She waved good-bye to Jo and sank back down on the sofa. Alone with her computer and her books, she didn't know what to do with herself. Hope had gone right out the window.

The walls seemed to close in. She needed to do something. And as before, when the future seemed untenable, she concentrated on the past. She was not in the best of moods when she set out for her aunt's.

* * * * *

"So even though you're now willing to distance yourself from gay-bashing, you'll still do it in your own household." Reyna twisted her hands around a pencil, envisioning his neck. His epiphany had been a well-acted ploy, at least as far as its impact on her life.

"Don't muddy the issues, Reyna. What you do with your life has repercussions for me. I may have realized that it was time to moderate my positions, but that doesn't change my protective instincts. The Putnam name is part of what I have to work with. It's what I've given you."

"I never wanted it. You never asked if I wanted to be a Putnam. You just made me into one." The pencil Reyna had been gripping suddenly snapped. "And to think I respected you for a moment."

"I thought I was meeting you halfway, Reyna." He flipped closed a file on his desk and gave her his full attention. "You no longer have to work with Danforth and the others. I realized at the summit that that was probably hard on you. I had thought you would change —"

"It's not something that will ever change —"

"I thought you would change, but I see that I was wrong. But that doesn't mean you can do as you please. You have a responsibility to the family. I thought you knew that all along —"

"You said your daughter wasn't going to be a biological error," she reminded him.

He sighed. "I admit that. I don't believe it anymore. But neither will you be a detraction from the Putnam family name."

"I get it," Reyna said sarcastically. "I'm no longer diseased, but I am still a freak. Do you know what being a Putnam has turned me into? Do you have any idea?" She threw the broken pieces of the pencil on the desk. She knew she was going the way of the pencil and there was no holding back. "I've done everything you asked, and I lived with the detectives watching me, endured never being really free to do anything without wondering what it might cost someone I loved. I let you blackmail me with my mother's illness and I hate you for it. I hate myself for ever agreeing. I should have just exposed you —"

"There was no blackmail, just a clear understanding of actions and consequences."

She choked and then cleared her throat. "But instead I did what you wanted because I love my mother, and yet I'm sitting here wondering when she's going to die. Do you understand? I don't want her to die but I wonder when it'll happen." She pressed her hands to her stomach. "When it does I'll tell you to go to hell. When it does I won't be a Putnam anymore, not for any price you might put on it. You've made me look forward to a time after my mother dies, you bastard."

"Reyna, calm down!"

"I can't!" She pressed her hands to her eyes. "And now you tell me that I still have no choice — no dating unless they're with men you have preselected. Nothing changes for me except that I no longer help people persecute people like me."

"When you calm down and think it over, you'll realize how much is at stake —"

"What do you want, Father? Do you want the media to report about a daughter who is queer or one in a mental institution? Do you want a daughter you can be proud of because she's happy and at peace with who she is, or no daughter at all? Would you really prefer that I be dead to you rather than be gay? Because I'm always going to be gay."

His eyes had narrowed. "As far as I know, you haven't been with anyone since that unfortunate incident at Georgetown. Or have you?"

She was too irrational not to panic. "It doesn't take practice to know that I am still gay."

"Answer the question."

"No! You can have people watching me every minute, you can tap my phone and screen my e-mail, but that doesn't mean I'll answer your questions." She struggled to her feet, feeling like a hundred pounds was strapped to her shoulders. After the initial schism, the summit had been a huge success for her father. She had thought the summons today had been to thank her and let her know that her cage door was finally open. But he wasn't even going to

228

take the current copout for certain highly placed Republicans and say that his daughter's sexuality was a private, family matter. Her sexuality was to remain invisible.

"You have always made things so difficult."

"When you were sleeping with my mother, when you got her pregnant, were you just thinking you had a right to do it? An extramarital affair, and bastard child — okay for you as long as you said 'sorry' afterward. But I can't have any kind of affair. I get to be Caesar's wife, but never Caesar."

"I can't talk to you when you're like this."

"Good."

She turned on her heel and walked out. Paul didn't look up as she passed his desk. She didn't have any compassion left for him, not right now. The fight with her father had lost her all hope of Holly and all that Holly represented. Nothing had changed.

She ran out into the twilight and wanted to keep going. She remembered the fantasy of taking Holly to Mexico. Holly, a woman she knew nothing about. A mystery that could be so much more.

She drove toward home, but passed it by, winding into the canyon, then out again. She didn't know where to go, how to start over. She had thought the cage was open and had let her mind fly free. Tonight at eleven she had been going to tell Holly who she was, suggest they go back to her place to talk and make love and talk, and wake up in the morning to a tomorrow full of promise.

But the cage door was still locked and she didn't know how to cope. How could she be with Holly tonight and then walk away?

Her cell phone chirped. She almost didn't answer it.

"Reyna, it's not serious, but we're at ICU again. Can you come?" Jean's steadiness beat back the panic Reyna had felt when she had first heard her voice.

"I'll be there as soon as I can." She quickly turned in the direction of the hospital and made herself forget about everything else for a while.

In his usual careful way, Dr. Basu explained what had happened, but Reyna was having trouble taking anything in. Her mother was not in any danger, but the episode only proved she was getting worse. How could two opposite things be true at the same time?

"It's an electrolyte and sodium imbalance. It's not life-threatening. But the stress it causes her system is so extreme that her other conditions are escalated. The imbalances are then more pronounced, adding to the systemic stress."

"Okay," Reyna said. "I guess I understand. She's having these little problems, and they're not the real danger."

"Right. It's her kidneys most of all, as we've known for some time. I'm going to order another functionality test —"

"Do you have to? It's so painful for her."

"I don't think I have a choice," he said, not unkindly. "I think we're in final stage. But this stage can be quite long with proper treatment, and she gets that."

"I just wish we could do something about the pain."

"We're learning more every day. But something that short-circuits the most important safety feature in the human body — the nerves that say *ouch, stop, pain is bad* — that doesn't also turn off consciousness is a long way away. I wish there was more I could do."

"I know," Reyna assured him. "You probably feel more helpless than I do."

He regarded her in his gentle, professional way. The lilt of his New Delhi accent had always soothed her. "Speaking of you, when was the last time you saw your own physician?"

"Why? I thought lupus wasn't —"

"No, I'm not implying that there is something you should be watching for. But I have eyes, and you don't look well. I am guessing it's stress, and you appear to have much stronger coping mechanism than your mother, but we all have limits. How much weight have you lost in the last six months?"

"I forget to eat," Reyna admitted. "I'll try to do better."

"I'm just recommending that you take better care of yourself. You can't help anyone if you're ill."

"Thank you. I'll keep it in mind." You're not unbreakable, you know that, she told herself. Maybe your father doesn't, but if you do have a mental or physical breakdown, he wins. That is not a choice.

She sat with her mother for an hour, watching her sleep and feeling all the while as if she was drowning. She had to leave before her mother woke up. She had led her to believe that some sort of happy ending was in the offing, but that wasn't the case. One look at her drawn face and her mother would want to know what was wrong.

She showered and changed at home, pulling on black jeans and a thin white shirt. The black leather jacket accentuated her pallor, but it was part of her shield. She couldn't stay with Holly tonight, but she wasn't going to leave Holly sitting in the parking lot, wondering why she didn't show. She knew there could not be a tomorrow. Easier, then, if there was no tonight, either. Her mind knew it, even her body seemed to know it. Only her heart didn't believe it, and her heart, so far, was never right.

It was a quarter to eleven, and Holly resisted the urge to check her watch. She sat in the dark of the motel parking lot reliving the final confrontation with her aunt and telling herself she did not want Reyna.

In the end, her aunt had told her nothing she did not already know. She had denied keeping the messages from Mr. Frazier from her.

"I don't know what you're talking about," she said. "I have a bridge game in half an hour, so if that's all you wanted to know..."

"There's more," Holly said stubbornly. "I know everything now."

"I'm sure whatever it is you've decided, it's my fault. You've been blaming me for everything lately."

"You aren't to blame for everything. You didn't rape my mother, you just married the rapist and made me call him my uncle."

Her aunt turned so pale that it looked like she would faint. Holly found it hard to care, in that moment; then, when her aunt's pallor didn't improve, she fetched a glass of water.

She set it within reach and said, "I told you I know everything. I just can't fathom why you did it."

"I did it for you. Where do you think the money to pay for college came from? You were owed something, and I got it for you."

"Wonderful," Holly said sarcastically. "Do you expect me to be grateful?"

"He made a mistake, but your mother drove him to it. She drove me to it — she thought only of herself."

"I won't listen to this. I only wanted to know the truth. I didn't want to believe that you knew exactly what you were doing when you married him, but you did. Fine. I won't see you again. I can't."

"This was her fault. She refused to behave in a decent manner. People were whispering all the while we were growing up, and it was always on me to be the normal one. It wasn't enough for her, she had to make men want her anyway —"

It had been too much to bear, and Holly had left without another word, leaving her aunt alone, which was what she had always seemed to want. There was no resolution to be had, and no amount of arguing would change the reality her aunt had constructed to justify her actions.

Headlights swept over her, but it was a car that pulled into the parking lot. She illuminated her watch — ten more minutes.

You can't want her, not knowing what she is. You're here to tell her, no more. A quick Web search had found her numerous links about Grip Putnam, many of them unflattering. There were also a few news articles that mentioned his daughter's role in the Putnam Institute. More recently there was a gossip item connecting Reyna with Jake Graham, another conservative scion of a political family.

She would say, just like Galina had, that she didn't fuck straight women. That was what she would say.

She heard the muted rumble of the motorcycle before she saw it, and the sound made her remember the feel of it between her legs a week ago, when she had felt as if her body was fused to Reyna's.

She got out of the car and waited. She tipped her head back to look at Reyna while she took off her helmet. The poor motel parking lot light was still sufficient to illuminate Reyna's eyes.

Reyna seemed to want to say something, and the words Holly knew she should utter were in her mouth, too. Then Reyna dropped her helmet and took Holly's face in her hands.

Hard, raw want coursed through her because her body didn't know better. But her mind knew she should pull away. She had rewritten her life in the last month, but some parts of her had not changed. She had only contempt for what Reyna represented, and so she could not go to bed with her, not again.

She tipped her head back with a low whimper as she opened her mouth to Reyna. She was washed with desire and conflict, voices in her head screaming at her to push Reyna away. All the while her heart pounded with an escalating passion that made her arch hard against Reyna's thigh. She had conflicting answers to the same equation. She bit Reyna's lower lip even as the part of her that saw the world as a puzzle reminded her of a simple axiom. If statements that ought to be equal are in conflict, then there isn't enough information for a solution.

It was a thinly veiled rationalization, she knew, but it was enough. She clutched Reyna to her, saying yes and yes again. The car was unyielding and cold at her back. Reyna was all heat and fierceness. Between the two extremes Holly felt far too pliant, but she waited in the dark while Reyna went to get a room.

She was going into the motel room to gather more information, she told herself, lying through her teeth and not caring. There could be no future, she thought, because her foolishness would have a price. But at least they would have tonight.

She was the one who turned on the bathroom light, then closed the door almost all the way, giving Reyna enough illumination to watch as Holly undressed. Reyna seemed frozen in place when Holly went to her, naked again. Reyna was still dressed, including her jacket, and appeared poised to run for the door. But her gaze never left Holly and Holly knew Reyna would not go, not yet.

Reyna drew in a shuddering breath. "I only came here to tell you I couldn't stay."

"So did I," Holly admitted. She drew Reyna's hand to her ribs and shivered when fingertips grazed her nipples a moment later. "But I want this."

"So do I. I'm sorry — it has to be this way."

Holly almost said that she knew who Reyna was, but Reyna was kissing her shoulders, then her neck, and Holly felt the deep stirrings of arousal just as she had before. She would not be this woman's lesbian plaything. She wanted to say no, but there was only yes in her. She wound her hands under Reyna's jacket, thrilled by the feel of Reyna's clothing against her hungry skin. Reyna asked, she said yes, and she was on the bed. Reyna's mouth was on her, Reyna was inside her, and she begged for more. Hated herself and begged for more.

They came to a rest at last at the foot of the bed. Reyna stretched over Holly for a lingering, deep kiss. She told herself that this shouldn't have happened, but every part of her was rejoicing that it had. She put her head on Holly's shoulder and rested. Everything she had learned last week had come back to her. Every place she stroked and licked had been familiar and longed for.

Holly jerked. "Something's scratching me."

Reyna raised herself to see that the zipper of her jacket was responsible.

"Take off your jacket," Holly whispered.

Her head felt hot. She knew what Holly wanted and hadn't realized that keeping her clothes on had been an unconscious attempt to maintain some distance. If she felt Holly's skin against her she'd never give it up.

Holly pushed her over on her back and her hands went

to the buttons of Reyna's blouse. "As sexy as I seem to find it, you're not keeping your clothes on this time."

Reyna said, "No." She trapped Holly's hands in hers. "I can't stay."

Holly pulled away and sat up, her face turned from the light. Her voice was harsh and distant. "You can't stay, or you're just done?"

"I can't stay." Reyna's fingers went to her blouse and it took all her will not to unbutton it.

Holly's voice took on an edge of anger. "I don't understand all the nuances of this yet. Is it that you're not a lesbian if all you do is fuck me? But I can't fuck you because that would make you gay, too?"

Reyna wanted Holly's hand back on her. She could not stay. "No, no, that's not it."

More gently, Holly asked, "Then what?"

"I can't explain. But I can't see you again. I only came here to tell you that."

Holly turned her face back to the light, but her eyes were dark and unreadable. "And I led you astray."

"No," Reyna said quickly. "No. I wanted to do that. I told myself I couldn't, but I knew all along I would, if you said yes."

"And you think you can leave now?" Holly leaned over her. "I don't understand why you have to go, but you promised me that you would make love to me, and we're not through."

Reyna's mouth parted when Holly straddled her lap. "What do you want me to do?" She had to swallow to be able to speak. "I'll do it."

Holly murmured, "I want you to make love to my hands with your body. My fingers need to touch you."

Reyna shivered, but this time she didn't stop Holly when she went to unbutton her blouse.

"I want you to make love to my mouth with your skin." Holly kissed Reyna's jaw, then trailed her tongue down Reyna's throat. "Let me know all of you."

"Last week, you were enough. It's not that I didn't want you to. I didn't need it." Her words were staccato, punctuated by short, hard breaths.

"Do you need it now?"

Reyna had to close her eyes. "Yes." The word tore through her. Her shirt was open and she felt Holly's naked breasts against her stomach. She had what she wanted and felt utterly lost. She whimpered when Holly's skin left her.

"Am I hurting you?"

"God, no. Touch me." Reyna pulled at her clothes. "I want your body against me."

She lifted her hips so Holly could push down the sleek black jeans. "Stay there," Holly breathed. "Please." She slowly went to her knees next to the bed as she kissed Reyna's belly, her thighs.

"Is this what you want? My mouth . . . here?"

"Yes," Reyna said brokenly. "Yes."

She felt poured out, like wax, as Holly learned her. She began to talk, as she had not with any of the others, letting her desires voice themselves after such a long silence.

"There. Please," she begged. "Please." She said much more and didn't know if Holly could hear her. She was choking on the words, on fire to tell Holly how good her mouth felt, then how much she needed fingers in her now. She could not stop groaning out her need until she arched hard against Holly with a desperate shaking that continued even after she had slumped into Holly's arms.

"There's more," Holly whispered. "You want more."

"Yes," Reyna said. She would never stop wanting more. What more could there be, you fool, she cursed herself. There is no more. But my lord, such wonder, such ecstasy, and knowing it was Holly who moaned low in her ear.

"Tell me." Holly caressed the side of Reyna's breast as if she wanted it in her mouth again.

I will never be able to leave, Reyna thought. I can't stay. I can't go.

Holly nuzzled at her breast. "Tell me. I'll do it."

"I want . . . I want tomorrow." Reyna was off the bed as she spoke, gathering her clothes. She did not know where she found the strength. "I have to go." In a panic, she buttoned her shirt and yanked on her pants. If she didn't leave now she never would. Tomorrow would come and with it her future smashed to bits again. Holly's future, and her mother's future, too.

She stumbled to the door, but hesitated when Holly said, "Wait," behind her.

"I have to go. Now." Reyna stood in the open doorway, knew if she looked back she would be lost in Hades forever. She walked out into the empty night.

Holly chased after her, not yet buttoned, and caught up to Reyna as she threw her leg over the bike. "I'll be here next week. Say you'll be here."

"I can't."

Reyna kept her gaze on her hands and fought the desire to look up at Holly one last time. She put on her helmet and chanced a sideways look. Holly hadn't buttoned her shirt and she was naked underneath. Reyna's mouth watered and she was dizzy with heat.

Holly kissed her then, a hard, demanding kiss, a kiss meant to get Reyna off the motorcycle and into bed again.

Reyna whimpered with the pain of saying no. "I can't." Holly said something else, but the bike's ignition drowned it out. In a heartbeat she walked the bike backward enough to clear the parking space. In another heartbeat she was gone. Her heart wasn't even beating, she thought, not anymore. There was no air, no tomorrow, not even a tonight.

Holly sat on the motel bed, her mind a whirl of information she strove to sort and quantify so she could make use of it. She tried to draw up equations to explain Reyna, but nothing made any sense. Reyna was a closeted conservative, who sought out anonymous lesbian sex from time to time. Otherwise, she was deeply involved in promoting antigay organizations. Wouldn't the result of such conflict produce either shame or a tissue of rationalizations that the sex meant less than it did?

Reyna was clearly not ashamed of liking sex with a

woman. She acted like someone with a secret, but not one based on self-hatred or denial. She loved sex and had not afterward tried to characterize it as less that it was.

The rejection Holly felt was intense and humiliating, but if she just knew why maybe she could bear it. Who was Reyna Putnam really? How could she find out?

She felt powerless, and it had been less than thirty minutes since she had felt powerful for the first time in her life. Leaning over Reyna, listening to the rhythm of Reyna's breathing and feeling the pulse of Reyna moving under her — she had never felt so connected to anyone, never sensed that she could have such an impact on someone else. She had loved the feeling and hated the way she felt now. And she did not know what she could do about any of it, except live with it.

"Miss Putnam."

The voice came from far away.

"Miss Putnam."

Reyna waved one hand to make the voice leave her alone.

"You can't stay here."

Why was her head so heavy? She reached up and touched it. Oh. Her helmet. She loosened the strap. It was easier to breathe.

"You have to pull yourself together."

Hateful voice. It belonged to . . . someone not hateful, but not a friend. She had no friends. She wasn't permitted.

A hand touched her elbow and she slapped at it. She wanted to stay here. Where was here?

She opened her eyes. She was lying on a bus stop bench. Her face felt a mess, her eyes like sandpaper. She had been crying.

Holly.

She was seized by a torrent of sobbing, and the hand became an arm, levering her off the bench and into a car that smelled of stale coffee in styrofoam cups.

They were driving, where she didn't know. "My bike," she was able to say, finally.

"It's hanging most of the way out of the trunk. I think you fell off."

"I stopped for the light and I couldn't hold it up anymore. I had to sit down." So I could cry, she could have added. So I could try to survive this pain. Not even giving up Kim had hurt like this.

"Do you just leave the bike in the garage? Is there a key?"

She looked out the window and realized finally that they had come to a stop. Marc Ivar had obviously been able to follow her, finally. "Under a mat at the top of the stairs."

"Trusting guy." He went up to get the key. Reyna got out of the car to help ease the bike out of the trunk. She was amazed that it had fit at all, and as Marc had said, it was more out than in.

"Let me take you to your car," he said when they had locked the garage again.

"I'll walk."

"No," he said firmly. "I'll take you."

"You're not my father," she snapped.

He made no reply, so she got back in the car. He circled the block, then idled next to her car where it sat at the curb. "Get some sleep," was all he said.

She made it to the parking garage in her building, and stumbled up to the apartment. She doubled over several times, holding her stomach against the grief. Once inside she let go again, and cried into the carpet. It was where she was when she woke up hours later, with a blinding headache that, in the end, she thought she deserved.

14

"You'll never guess who just called me."

Tori sounded excited, but Holly had to dig down to find even a meager level of interest. She felt dead inside. She'd felt that way for the last three days. "Since I'll never guess why don't you tell me?"

"Sue from Alpha, who, you may be surprised to learn, is a lesbian."

"I had wondered about her," Holly admitted. "What did she want?"

"Well, she's out now. Jim Felker has been sent to diversity training and relocated to the Shreveport office. Sue has been authorized to offer me not only my job back, but, without admitting any wrongdoing, a track in their in-house actuarial training. And back pay."

"Wow." The possibilities for Tori did perk her up a little bit. "But I thought you'd accepted the offer from United Indemnity."

"I was going to call them this morning. I had my hand on the phone when it rang. And Sue is going to call you, too."

"I'm not interested in going back," Holly said. "I mean, I'm happy for you, if that's what you want."

"I think I do. Geena says it's up to me. Everything will be like it was, except I'll get a promotion, eventually, and I'll work for an out lesbian. Sue is so closed-mouth, but I think she ripped Jim Felker a new one, and didn't stop there. She just handled things in her own way."

She might never have needed to quit, Holly thought after she had hung up. What a mind-boggling thought. She might still be with Clay, not knowing the physical ecstasy of being with a woman. She might not have this almost unbearable ache wearing her down. Reyna Putnam was the ache. Her mysterious behavior just compounded it.

She'd read all she could find on the Internet, even bought Grip Putnam's autobiography. Reyna was his illegitimate child, and had grown up here in Irvine as a part of a small, closed society formed by the conservative politicos of the area. But there was little more than that to be known. She had an impressive educational background, including a Ph.D in governmental policy from Georgetown. None of that explained why she would stay in the closet. Solve for the simplest answer, Holly told herself for the hundredth time. She stays in the closet because it's personally expedient.

That solution worked until she remembered the anguish in Reyna's eyes when she'd ridden away.

The phone rang and it was indeed Sue, offering her old job back. Holly explained that she was going back to school, but congratulated Sue on being able to patch things up with Tori.

She had just hung up the phone when it rang again. After she said hello, a gravelly voice said, "U.C. Medical

Center, fourth floor ICU, room four thirteen. It will be worth your trouble." The line went dead.

What on earth? It had to be a wrong number. What could possibly be of interest to her at the medical center?

Her mind wouldn't leave it alone. Because she spent most of her time listlessly thinking about Reyna, she began to assume the call was about Reyna. After all, true coincidence is rare, she told herself. A mysterious phone call probably does relate to a mysterious woman in your life.

It was ridiculous, and contrary to common sense. Sometimes, common sense was more valid than formulas and axioms and unproven theories. She wasn't going to go running about on the proverbial wild goose chase.

Of course she went.

She'd been to the emergency room once, when she'd cut herself with a kitchen knife, but she knew nothing more about the hospital than that. She found the fourth floor intensive care unit easily, though, and then felt foolish and conspicuous. She walked the corridor slowly, trying to find where room 413 was without prompting anyone to offer help or ask who she was.

Two women in white were conferring at the nurses' station, and didn't look up as she passed. She heard one say to the other, "Next patient. Langston, Gretchen, updated meds order," before launching into a string of indecipherable terms. Holly kept going, and considered retracing her steps to the elevator when what she had heard suddenly clicked. Langston had been Reyna's birth name. Her mother . . . The name had been something Germanic starting with a *G*. Gretchen could be it.

She found herself in front of room 413. It seemed bizarre to be here. The door was propped open, so she peered inside, having no idea what she would find.

There were two women asleep in the room. The one on the hospital bed had to be Reyna's mother. They shared cheekbones and a jawline, and the same dark hair and brows. She looked as if she would float away in even the gentlest of breezes. Her skin was tautly stretched over her

242

frame, and even in sleep deep lines of pain were etched into a face marked with vivid red patches.

The other woman was seated in the room's only chair, resting her head on her arms on the bed, and breathing steadily and deeply. She'd never seen Reyna asleep, and even now she couldn't see her face.

This was a clue, but not one she could comprehend. She remembered Reyna saying at the theater that her mother was dying from a long and painful illness; she felt the only thing she could do was work to pay the bills. There was an answer here, but one so private she felt abruptly that she could not pry, even though her heart begged her to try. And who on earth had called her? She turned to go.

"What are you doing?" The nurse at the door had a no-nonsense directness. "Who are you?"

"I'm lost," Holly whispered. "I think I got the room wrong."

"What patient are you looking for?"

"Maternity," Holly stammered. She was a bad liar, and knowing she was didn't help.

"Maternity is on eleven."

"I didn't know." That, at least, was the truth.

Someone stirred behind them and Holly froze. There was the rustle of someone getting to her feet.

"What's going on?" Reyna's voice, sleepy and unfocused.

Holly had no choice but to turn. Recognition hit Reyna like a sledgehammer. She literally staggered.

"I'm sorry," Holly whispered.

Reyna recovered, then crossed the room toward her. "You have to go," she said tautly. "I don't know what coincidence brought you here —"

"There's no such thing as coincidence," Holly told her.

"Should I get security?" The nurse seemed poised to do so.

Reyna shook her head violently at the nurse, but spoke to Holly. "You have to go."

"Reyna?" The thin voice stopped them all. Holly saw Reyna close her eyes. "What's going on?"

"Just someone lost, Mom." Her eyes opened again and silently pleaded with Holly to go, and quickly.

Reyna's mother said, "You must be Holly."

Reyna was faint with fear. Her mother gestured to Holly to come closer, and Holly was going. All she had suffered, all she had done would be for nothing if Holly was discovered here.

"Who told you I was coming?"

"A nice detective who dropped in earlier today," her mother answered. "He used to work for the agency Grip has always used. He told me an interesting story."

"Mom, he was just a troublemaker." Marc Ivar was a dead man.

Her mother ignored her. "When did you meet my daughter?"

"Last week," Holly answered. "Wait, two weeks ago, but the first time didn't count. I've only known who she was for about a week."

"Yes, she said you didn't exchange last names."

Holly had known who she was when they had last met, Reyna realized. She had known. Some of the things she had said now made sense. Her confusion and that flash of disdain when Reyna had at first refused to get undressed — my God, she thinks I'm like Irene. She thinks I like the kicks, but I don't consider myself gay.

And yet, she had stayed, and had made love to her, knowing who Reyna was and what she did for a living.

Her mother's inquisition had not stopped. "I do apologize for the fact that the detective delved into your background a bit. Apparently, that was a standing order when Reyna was involved — no matter how casually or how seriously — with anyone. He said you lost your mother when you were young."

"I did." Holly went on answering her mother's questions, questions Reyna had longed to ask but couldn't, not when there were no tomorrows.

She was desperate to get Holly out of the building. The hospital's nurse was listening avidly, but she left abruptly when her beeper sounded. Reyna quickly shut the door.

"Mom, you need your rest."

"I just woke up, dear. What exactly does a conceptual mathematician do?"

"We play games a lot." Holly had a patient smile. "I say we, but I'm not actually one, not yet. I'm going back for my master's though."

"That's a good idea. There's no substitute for education."

Holly glanced up at Reyna, who was trying to figure out how to drag Holly out of the room. Out of the room and into the nearest bed. *Stop it*, she willed herself. This won't work.

"Well, very few things." Holly ran one hand through her hair. Reyna couldn't help but remember that hand and how it had felt on her. "I didn't finish my studies because I thought I was in love, but that didn't actually turn out so well."

Holly's eyes were dark with a misery that Reyna recognized. Behind the dark was a kind of silvery light, as if some dim glory was nurtured and would someday be set free. Was that pity? No, she didn't want that from Holly. She didn't want it any more than Holly had seemed to want it, when she explained the circumstances of her conception. Neither of them wanted anything founded on pity.

"We all make mistakes when we're young."

"Mom, Holly has to go."

"No, she doesn't." Her mother spoke with surprising asperity. Reyna hadn't seen her so animated in a long while. "Have you ever seen a detective here in the hospital? I think we're safe, for the moment. The detective seemed to think so, since he *is* assigned to you this weekend and no one in his office yet knows he has resigned."

Fuck Marc Ivar. Fuck him and his pension and his meddling. "I don't know what he told you, but you don't need to worry about it," she said tersely.

"That's my job. You should have told me."

"I think I should go," Holly said.

"Oh, fine, now you want to go," Reyna snapped. "Great."

"Don't leave yet, Holly. Please sit down." Her mother reached for the water, but let her arm fall back to the bed with a grimace of pain. Holly quickly picked it up and offered the straw. "Thank you. I have more questions and sometimes it's hard to talk."

"You should save your strength," Holly suggested.

"You're probably right, I'm going to need it. Stop flitting about, Reyna. You're giving me a headache."

"Mom, you don't have to be involved in this. It's between me and him." She could feel Holly's gaze on her. She couldn't cope with pity and would not meet her gaze.

"But it's all about me."

She should never have told Marc Ivar the truth. Damn him, he had had no right. He didn't know anything about her mother's condition or what the stress of this encounter would do to her. "You don't need to worry."

"I thought after we talked last week that I would see you happy again. But you only look worse. I've never seen you so depressed. I knew there was a reason and I knew I'd never find out from you. You keep secrets, just like your father. I didn't know he was married for the first three months we were together."

"I'm not like him." The very idea was repellent.

"When it comes to the stupid certainty that nothing can be done in this world unless you do it yourself, you are exactly like him." Her mother stopped abruptly and turned her gaze toward the water. Holly brought it to her without speaking. "Thank you," her mother said again.

There was a knock at the door. Reyna hurried to tell whoever it was to go away.

"If that's the stenographer, have him or her come in."

Stenographer? Mother of God, what was going on? It *was* a stenographer. He was neatly dressed, and tucked under one arm he had a transcription machine like those used in courtrooms. She let him in because he was expected, but she didn't know for what.

Holly gave up the chair as he settled in.

"I'm afraid I racked up quite a phone bill this morning." Her mother introduced everyone to the stenographer, whose name was Scott, then said to him, "When we're done each day how long will it be before I get copies back?"

"Less than twenty-four hours if you like."

"If I asked you to deliver another copy to someone else, could you do that?"

"Certainly. It's often done."

"That's wonderful. Let's begin then."

Holly was standing in the corner near the window and she looked as dazed as Reyna felt. Reyna was furious with her for staying when she had pleaded with her to go. Her mother didn't have energy like this to spare. She was all stirred up because of Marc Ivar and now meeting Holly. She didn't know what was going to happen when her father discovered what had transpired. And he would find out, and when he did, everything would shatter, starting with her.

"Why couldn't you have just left?"

"Because she asked me not to. And I didn't want to." Holly wouldn't look at her.

"Mom, my father is not going to like this."

"And he holds the purse strings, I know that now." She glanced at Reyna, and Reyna knew the pain had to be bad if she wouldn't even turn her head. "Scott, please go ahead now." She paused while he lifted his hands to the keys. "My name is Gretchen Langston, and when I was twenty-three I met Grip Putnam for the first time. I was a small-town girl, and I'd never heard of him, or his father, or his grandfather. I didn't know he was married. But I knew that I loved him from the moment he stopped to help me change a flat tire."

"Mom, what are you doing?"

There was a knock at the door. Reyna threw her mother a helpless glance.

"That'll be your father. Let him in."

She was so stunned she couldn't move at first.

She reminded herself that he would never make any threats in front of witnesses. Her mother had no idea what she was getting into. She had never seen Grip as he really was. Reyna let him in, but turned her head away when he looked to her for some sort of explanation. She felt utterly helpless, with nothing left to defend either her mother or Holly. Holly — she had no idea what was about to happen to her, just as Margeaux hadn't known.

He glanced about curiously as he walked toward the bed. Reyna knew he would forget nothing he saw, including Holly's ashen face. "Gretchen, you are looking lovely for someone in the hospital."

"Thank you, Grip."

"What did you want to see me about? Is there something you need?" He looked pointedly at the stenographer.

Reyna watched her mother raise her hand in a graceful gesture that must have cost her an enormous toll in sheer agony. None of it showed in her face. She looked as if she had an inexhaustible supply of energy. From very far away, she heard her mother say, "Grip, this is Holly Markham. She is studying to be a conceptual mathematician. She's Reyna's lover. And this is Scott. He's a stenographer — well, you can see that. I'm writing my memoirs."

Holly wanted to tell Reyna she now understood, but the room was filled with a furious crackle of silent conflict. She had not expected Grip Putnam to be so dynamic in person, and she could see that Reyna's incredible eyes came from him. He was flustered. Gretchen appeared to have caught him completely off his guard.

"I know that all my life I've let you take care of me. When you didn't, Reyna did. But things have changed for me." Gretchen gestured broadly at her body, and Reyna made a sound that might have been a whimper. "Both of you have to realize that I have changed. I want what concerns me to be discussed with me."

"Of course, Gretchen. We were wrong not to discuss how your bills would be paid with you."

Gretchen gave him an exasperated but fond look. "You're not going to tell me what I want to hear and then make some sort of deal with Reyna when you leave. Either you commit to paying the bills — and truly, Grip, I wish I

248

didn't have to ask, but you're the only wealthy person I know — or I shall sell my memoirs and pay them that way. You probably didn't know that I had turned down offers to sell them in the past. I've read hints that you're considering running for office. I'm sure I'll get a good advance."

"That sounds suspiciously like blackmail." Grip didn't seem angry, though. It was as if he accepted that matters are sometimes resolved through coercion. They were communicating in a language Holly had never wanted to understand.

"No, dear. It's your choice. I'm happy either way. And either way Reyna is free to live the life she chooses."

Reyna made a helpless gesture. She took a step toward her mother, and then like a puppet whose strings were suddenly cut. she collapsed. Her head hit the floor with a frightening crack.

"Reyna!" Holly's cry was a match to Gretchen's. Holly was instantly at Reyna's side. She didn't know what to do. A bruise was forming on her forehead.

She was suddenly pushed aside by nurses and then she made way for a gurney. Grip Putnam kept saying, "She's my daughter, only the best."

Reyna came around while they were wheeling her away. "I'm okay," she said weakly. "I don't need to go anywhere."

Holly wanted to follow the gurney but she had no right. Reyna wouldn't want her there. She had been so angry about Holly's even being at the hospital in the first place.

"What have you done to my daughter?" Gretchen, who had managed to pull herself to the edge of the bed, sounded irate and exhausted. The stenographer had retreated to a corner and both Gretchen and Grip ignored him.

"I'm only trying to give her the best in life, including a Putnam name worth having."

They had forgotten she was there as well, and Holly decided that she was far better off with Reyna's anger than a bitter family quarrel. She ran after the gurney and squeezed into the elevator at the last minute.

The doctor was shaking his head over Reyna's answers to his questions. "I thought you were going to make an effort to eat more regularly."

"I tried." Reyna's voice was steadier. "No food and a shock, that's all it was."

"We'll see about that," the doctor said. His eyes narrowed as he realized Holly was listening to every word. "Can I help you?"

Holly shook her head and then felt Reyna's attention shift to her.

Reyna held out her hand for something. Holly looked around, wondering what it was she could get for Reyna in the elevator.

Then she realized what Reyna wanted. She took her hand in her own and felt a rapid shifting of the puzzles she had been trying to solve. The equations resolved themselves. Chaos became predictable, all because she held Reyna's hand.

So it seemed, for a moment. Then chaos ruled again.

When the elevator doors opened, Reyna dropped her hand. "Please go. Don't make me ask again."

"I understand," Holly said, and she did. Reyna was done with her old life and she was a part of that. She watched the hospital staff wheel Reyna through an employees-only door. She had told herself that if she understood Reyna's behavior she would be able to cope with the rejection. Understanding did not help one bit.

She made herself go home. Reyna didn't want her there. Reyna didn't want her.

Australia wanted her, and right away. She read the e-mail again slowly. In a fog she sent back her acceptance. She hoped that being on the other side of the planet would be far enough away to forget.

15

Like many times before, Reyna and her father stood outside the institute's main conference room and prepared for an entrance. Today was different. Reyna smoothed her plain black suit with shaking hands. Today was so very different.

Paul wouldn't look at her as he signaled that it was time to begin. Reyna faced the doors and lifted her chin.

"Wait," her father said. "One last thing."

She turned to him, wondering what more there could be after four days of endless strategy meetings and draft after draft of press releases, talking points and position papers.

"I really did want what was best for you."

She looked at him, noting again the similarity of their

eyes. "Only when what was best for me was also best for you."

"I thought they were the same thing."

He embraced her for the first time in a very long time. She couldn't bring herself to return the show of affection. "There aren't any cameras."

"I'm well aware of that." He let her go.

"I can't forgive you yet," she said baldly.

"So be it." His eyes narrowed and she realized that when she walked through those doors she would on her own for the first time in many years. "Good luck," he added.

"And to you." It was as close to forgiveness as she could get, at least today.

"Miss Putnam! Miss Putnam!" The blinding pops from camera flashes punctuated the hubbub. Reyna blinked in the white glare of television lights.

She let the noise subside and steadied her nerves, then pointed to the woman in the front in the yellow suit.

"Miss Putnam, how do you feel about your father's chances in the New Hampshire primary?"

"At this stage, his intention to run is mere speculation, but if he should decide to do so, I would wish him the best of luck. For now, however, I'd like to address questions about my past and future. By the way, my name is now Reyna Langston in honor of my mother. Reyna Putnam no longer exists."

The reporters went on asking questions, and Reyna went on answering them as she had agreed she would.

She never dreamed she'd see her father beaten, but even if she had thought it possible, she would never have conceived that it would be by her mother. Her mother hadn't been able to cope with burnt toast, sometimes, but her illness had completely changed her. It had taken a monumental effort of will to orchestrate her coup d'Putnam.

She called on the reporter from the *Register* next. "What did you mean when you said that Reyna Putnam no longer existed?"

"I am honoring my mother by changing my last name back to hers. At the same time I'm changing my life focus. Reyna Putnam's work is over. I'll be stepping away from politics for a while."

"Is it because you don't want to support your father?"

She had a carefully scripted answer for that question, the one her father had dreaded most. She was aware that many of the press representatives were here hoping to catch a nuance of his future intentions. "My father will not be surprised to learn that my ideology differs from his on many issues, particularly those surrounding full and equal civil rights for gay Americans. Nevertheless, as I said, I wish him the best of luck should he decide to run for public office."

When she had gone back to her mother's room, after a completely unnecessary CAT scan and other obnoxious tests, an armistice had been reached. Her father had only one stipulation. Reyna's coming out would be handled carefully, allowing him time to prepare. They had spent the next three days overhauling all of the Putnam Institute's position papers on gay rights, moving carefully toward more moderate positions. Reyna still hated the words she wrote, but there had been some healing for her in the exhausting process. On Thursday afternoon she had given an exclusive interview to *The Advocate*, which had then leaked it to the *Los Angeles Times* in time for the Friday morning news cycle. Her announcement of a 3 p.m. press conference had brought the media running, eager for a story for the evening news.

"Now that you're a lesbian, do you have a girlfriend?"

Reyna knew for a fact that the A.P. reporter who asked the question was a lesbian. She happily told her the truth. "I have been a lesbian for my entire adult life. I'm not answering any questions more personal than that."

Reyna had not wanted a media circus, but her father had convinced her that if she wanted to be left alone she had to get the inevitable confrontation with the press out of the way. Grip Putnam's daughter coming out of the closet was news enough, given his well-known ties to groups like Danforth Hobson's. But the media interest had been carefully stirred up by persistent rumors that her father was going to run for president. Reyna thought of it as the beginning of her penance. After all that she had done to lure gay people to ex-gay ministries, to argue against their rights to legalize their relationships and form their own families, becoming an emblem of the changing times was fitting. If her father was lauded as an example of compassionate, tolerant, loving fatherhood, then so be it. Let him be an example to other parents. The irony would always secretly amuse her.

The A.P. reporter lobbed follow-up questions at her. "Didn't you do research for American Values for Family? Didn't you write position papers on their behalf against same-sex marriage, against gay adoptive parents and against hate crimes legislation?"

"Reyna Putnam wrote those on behalf of clients whose politics mirrored that of the Putnam Institute's." What a cop-out, she thought. She quickly added, "Those groups are no longer clients and I disavow every word I ever wrote on those issues. I say that personally. I am not speaking for my father. As I said, there are some issues we disagree about." She shot him a glance where he stood unobtrusively to her right.

His lips twitched and she saw what could only be a glimmer of pride in his eyes.

She grinned. "I suggest that you ask him all about that when he takes the microphone in a few minutes. Lots of questions about exactly where he stands on his daughter's civil rights."

There was a ripple of laughter as her father returned her smile. They could be adversaries without being enemies, she supposed. When she stopped hating him.

Her press conference came to a close when her father took the stage. She stood behind him while he fielded questions about her, then stepped off the dais when the questions turned to his political future. He tantalized the reporters with maybes and no one seemed to notice that she was slipping out the door.

She left the echoing halls of the institute for the last time, she hoped, and left Reyna Putnam behind as well.

There was sunshine on her face. All the pressure of the last few days seeped away.

She was alone.

She was free to think, to want, to dream. And her dreams turned to Holly. She had buried her dreams, but the memory of Holly had kept her moving forward. She had desperately needed to put this life behind her before there could be any tomorrows that meant anything.

She had asked Holly to go away, just before they made her get undressed for their stupid tests. She had started to explain, but Holly simply said, "I understand." But how could she have understood anything? She couldn't have known that Reyna's mind had already turned to the inevitable media circus and protecting Holly's privacy. She didn't want anyone to know Holly's name or who she was to Reyna.

A light spring breeze cooled her cheeks and she closed her eyes for a moment. Who was Holly to Reyna? More importantly, who was she to Holly? They hardly knew each other and yet Reyna could picture them twenty years in the future, sailing into a rising sun. She did not deserve it, but had to find the courage to reach out for it. But Holly could easily want no part of Reyna's tainted history, or the politics and the media.

She opened her eyes and let the green of the canyon soothe her. She did not even know where Holly lived. She was so tired. Something to eat, some sleep and then she would find her.

There was a man leaning against the car she would shortly be returning to the leasing service. She hesitated, then recognized him.

She waited to speak until she was leaning against the car next to him. "I suppose you're happy with yourself."

"As a matter of fact, I am."

"You had to quit your job."

"A point of honor." He lit a cigarette.

"Those are bad for you," she said primly.

"I know." He put away his lighter and pulled a piece of paper out of his pocket. "This is her address. I wrote out the directions."

Damned, interfering man. She could grow to love him. "Thank you. I didn't know how I was going to find her. I asked her to go, but I'm not sure she understood why."

"Probably not. I have a file on her if you want it."

"Not interested."

"I didn't think you would be, but I thought I'd make the offer. When were you going to see her?"

"Tomorrow. I need some sleep really badly."

Marc finished his cigarette and ground it to powder on the asphalt. "You might want to go now."

"Could you be more specific?"

"She bought a ticket to Australia two days ago. She leaves around midnight."

Stunned, Reyna fumbled for her keys. "What's in Australia?"

"I thought you didn't want her file."

"I don't — get off the car." She got in and slammed the door. Once the engine was running she lowered the window. "What's in Australia?"

"Her future, I would guess."

"Damn." She backed out quickly and screeched for home. She wouldn't go to Holly in a business suit that epitomized what Reyna Putnam had been. She made a lightning change, then drove to the bike shop.

"I wouldn't want to forget to send a check, so I thought I should just pay four months in advance." Holly handed the check to Flo, who tucked it into her account book.

"It's been lovely having you about. Nancy is quite smitten."

Holly laughed. "That's a flattering idea, but not true."

"She's been a big grouch since you said you were going, but she'll be relieved when I tell her that you've paid the rent, so that means you'll be back sometime."

"It could be in a few weeks, or maybe not for months.

It depends on their funding, what I know and what they want to learn."

"It sounds a treat." Flo held out a sheet with some names and addresses on it. "These are old friends who moved to Australia years ago, and I've told them you might call. You won't know a soul and they're all nice women."

"Ever the matchmaker." Nancy had come in from her studio in the garage. "She's not happy unless the world is paired off."

"Which is lucky for you," Flo said.

Nancy wrinkled her nose at her, then turned back to Holly. "Hey, I found a new joke on the Internet. How do you know you've been living with a mathematician too long?"

Holly snickered. Nancy had been peppering her with jokes ever since she had told her about dart theory and Ramsay numbers. "I have no idea. Tell me."

"Her habit of converting everything to base seven is getting on your nerves because she does it thirty-three hours a day, ten days a week."

Holly laughed. She felt happy inside, at least the part she let feel anything. She was glad to be going to Australia, glad for an opportunity to prove herself and begin more serious studies. The cocoon had burst and now she knew she could fly. She would not let anything put a shadow on that. She would not look on her future through a dark sadness. It took monumental effort to think positive, but she hoped it would get easier when she was airborne.

Nancy reminded her of when they had agreed to leave for the airport that evening. Holly was saying good-bye when she heard the slow rumble of a motorcycle. The pitch seemed familiar. Her spine stiffened as she realized the sound came from directly in front of the house.

She hurried back to her cottage. Her thighs remembered the vibration of the bike. If it was Reyna . . . It couldn't be. Reyna had asked Holly to go, without tears or apparent regrets. She was free of the trap she had been in, and Holly accepted that Reyna had no reason to pursue anything with her. She was no longer required to find comfort with just anyone who happened to agree to go to a motel with her.

She was closing the door when the bike turned into the driveway. The vision of Reyna in her long, leather jacket shattered her composure. What could Reyna want? Not . . . not anything Holly could possibly give her.

The bike suddenly ceased its rumble. Holly realized that Flo and Nancy would have heard it. They'd be wondering who Reyna was and why she was sitting on a motorcycle outside Holly's cottage. Not that it would take a mathematician to discern the answers.

She opened the door. Reyna was hooking her helmet onto one handlebar. She looked up as Holly stepped into the sunshine.

Holly thought Reyna wanted to say something. She knew she should speak, be civil, ask her to come inside. But anything could be construed as an invitation for more, and she didn't want Reyna to think that was all she was. She was more than a hungry, eager woman, and she wasn't thinking only about how to get Reyna naked and into bed, and quickly. Oh damn.

She took a step forward just as Reyna did, then another, and faster, until her arms were around Reyna and Reyna's mouth was on hers. The kiss rocked her like the first one had, like every kiss since. It shocked her breasts, her toes, her heart, and she gave herself over to it without reservation.

It mattered more, this time, that she was acting in conflict with decisions she had made. Her mind had more strength of will than before, and she finally lifted her head, intending to say that her future was in Australia.

Reyna murmured, "I didn't mean to start here, but every time I see you I want to kiss you first thing. But I came here to talk. About us."

"There's an us? You wanted me to leave, so I did."

"I didn't want you to leave, but it was necessary."

"Why?" Then she kissed Reyna again because she couldn't stand having her so close and not be kissing her.

Their mouths tangled and teased. Holly realized she was panting.

"You had to go. If you had stayed I would never have

let you leave again. You'd have been discovered by the media." She gestured at Flo's garden. "They'd have trampled all this while waiting for a glimpse of you, or the chance to ask you vapid questions about me. I wanted to spare you that, if I could."

"Oh." That had not occurred to Holly as a possible reason for Reyna's behavior. "I wasn't . . . I didn't know if . . ." She kissed her again, lips so soft and somehow taut, pressing against her own with a firm intention that made Holly tremble. She remembered those lips moving in more intimate places.

Reyna's tongue began to tease hers, hinting at what might be possible if they went inside. Holly could feel yes building in her again, and didn't want it to be this way. She searched her desire and she wanted Reyna in every way she could imagine, but if it all happened she would still want more. But there was no more than the sex.

"You're going to Australia," Reyna murmured. "I had to see you before you left."

She didn't know how Reyna found out, and ought to have been at least a little bit outraged that someone had been snooping into her personal affairs again. But she was also oddly touched that Reyna had cared enough to find out what she was doing. Reyna's hands were like fire through her shirt. Holly loved the sensation. She wanted to have it again and again, but she was going away. From far off, sounding kissed and eager for more, she heard herself say, "There's a good chance I might be able to get a scholarship to do part or all of my master's studies there." She swallowed, wanted Reyna's fingers on her lips. "I don't have to go."

"Don't be ridiculous," Reyna said. "Of course you have to go."

Two mutually exclusive emotions swamped her, making it hard to think. She was angry that Reyna did not want her to stay and relieved that Reyna understood and supported how important it was for her to go. "I know. I don't want to get on the plane right now. But when I wake up tomorrow I might feel differently."

Reyna blinked back tears. "I know hardly anything about you. I can't believe that you still respect me after what I've done —"

"I understand why."

"I want you," Reyna said brokenly. "Can we go inside? I understand there's no tomorrow. Do you have a few hours?"

"Yes," Holly said, glad she was already packed. She pulled Reyna after her and they twined behind the closed door, eager and hungry, hands unbuttoning and easing zippers down until they were skin to skin, need to need.

It was what she wanted, but the pressure of time was too much for Holly. Her tears would not hold back. Abruptly, she realized they were mingling with Reyna's. "I can't go." She cried into Reyna's shoulder.

"I won't let you give up this chance. You have to go."

"Come with me, then."

"I want to. I have no job now, just a strong desire to write about the disgusting people I helped and why I did it, and the truth about how ex-gay ministries are run." Reyna stroked Holly's face as if she would never stop. "I have to get all of that out of my system. I can do that anywhere. Australia — with you — sounds like heaven ... oh ..."

Holly brushed her fingers over Reyna's breasts, then her mouth was on them, eager for the way they seemed to swell when she kissed them. It was such a brilliant vision, to explore a new land and a new future with Reyna.

But she knew that Reyna couldn't leave Irvine. When she could bear not to be tasting Reyna's skin, she whispered into her neck, "Your mother needs you. I understand."

"She's dying," Reyna answered softly. "I spent these past years fighting the desire to know when it would happen. I hated myself for it. I can't let anything put me in that place again."

"I don't want to do that to you. I won't go."

"I won't let you stay. I have no right to stand in the way of your dreams."

Holly fought back the tears, her heart still fighting with her head. It was a seventeen-hour flight. Not exactly a weekend jaunt that either of them could hop on even once a month. She had wondered how what she felt for Reyna was different than the impetuous emotions that had led to a dead end with Clay, and now she knew. Reyna wanted her to become who she dreamed of being. That Reyna would let her go away made her want to stay.

Stay or go — the equation of her future wanted solving. She had all the information she needed. Reyna was kissing her again, her mouth suggesting so many sensations that Holly could not resist. She offered what she could, having grown up enough to finally understand that dreams have no substitutes. "I have a few hours," she murmured. "The bedroom is upstairs."

Reyna gasped. "Thank you," she said, and followed her up the stairs, never letting go of her hand. They didn't let go of each other for a minute, not once, always touching, prolonging the connection that would be too soon severed. Their tears became a part of the way they loved each other for the few hours they had. Holly tried to make them enough, but no matter how she constructed the formulas, they did not add up to tomorrow.

16

Holly, Four Months Later

"Anything to declare?"

Holly handed over her itemized list. She had a lot of souvenirs after four months, everything from clothing to books to an awesome aboriginal mask that she knew Audra would like.

She was tired in every pore. The seventeen-hour flight was grueling, even with three movies and comfortable seats that reclined almost enough for proper sleep. Her MP3 player batteries had died two hours ago, but she doubted that even the Gypsy Kings at full volume could perk her up.

She used a credit card to pay the duties on her declaration and slung her backpack onto her shoulder. With effort she got the luggage cart moving, precariously balancing her suitcases and the extra boxes she had brought with her.

Nancy had e-mailed that everything was fine in her cottage. The weather was all southern California summer, hot and glorious. Through the thick airport glass she could see that it was true, but she had left behind the mild beginnings of the Australian autumn. Her eyes wanted vivid blue sea, too, and a sky that was open and immense overhead. It was confusing to her body, but bodies were meant to adapt. She would still have strawberries whenever she wanted them.

If everything went as planned, Nancy would be waiting at the curb to take her home. If anything had come up since the last time they had connected, it would be Tori waiting.

Thoughts of Tori made her grin. Tori's last e-mail had relayed amusing news. Murphy finally got hooked, and by an Irvine professor she had apparently been in love with for some time. The professor was divorcing her husband and she and Murphy were living together. Tori and Jo had gone out of their way to forward articles and links to the latest stories and events, but that bit of gossip had been by far the most salacious.

The brief moment of glee was overrun by jet lag as she propelled the cart up a long incline toward the front of the terminal. She was going to have to find a way to travel with less stuff, that was plain. When she went back, after four months in the States, she did not want to be lugging around so much junk with her.

After discussing it at length with Audra, using the wonder of private chat rooms, she had decided that U.C. Irvine would be the university of record for her master's program. Audra's sensible advice had been a godsend, and worth every bit of trouble she and her new partner had gone through to get her online. Audra had been suspicious of computers, but was now addicted. Holly still couldn't find anything dehumanizing about it — her laptop and modem allowed her talk to Audra once or twice a week. They were more connected, not less. They had so much time to make up for.

She had to take a minimum number of courses at Irvine, though her work with Professor McKay in Australia would also provide a lot of her course credit. She had turned down several offers from other universities because she wanted to be here, in Irvine, for a while.

She had not had any contact with Reyna, and had not expected any. What was the point of keeping in touch when just being friends wasn't a possibility? They had parted in tears, not wanting to give or take more than the other could honorably afford.

When she finally got her Internet access set up and started receiving e-mail again, she'd found scads of articles forwarded by Jo, all about Reyna's coming out and the subsequent frenzy surrounding her father's possible presidential campaign. Only then did she really understand what Reyna had spared her by sending her away from the hospital. For a few weeks after the big announcement Reyna did television and radio interviews. Holly was even able to download streaming video of one. And only then did she realize that she did not really know who Reyna was.

She had never seen this poised, cool woman, who listened calmly while interviewers asked pointed, personal questions. Reyna appeared to be firmly on the path to her new future. They'd made no promises. She was meeting a lot of new people, Holly theorized. There was no reason for Reyna to remember her as more than a body.

She told herself that hard fact, over and over, and tried to make herself believe it. The articles about Reyna had finally fizzled out. There had been no news of her for two months.

Holly had sometimes forgotten about her, when she was deep into the other thing that she loved. After several weeks of looking at the data already accumulated on Ramsay 5,5, she had made her prediction about what its value would be, based on laborious work with the formula she'd suggested in her high school paper. Only time would tell if she had got it right again.

Then she had left Ramsay numbers behind and submerged herself in the joy of chaos theory and the universe of randomness, where it seemed her best instinctive efforts were centered. The goal of mathematics was to reduce randomness, to shine knowledge on uncertainty, to quantify what could not even be described. Professor McKay wanted her to concentrate solely on conceptual theory, but she had not forgotten her strong desire to teach. She still wasn't quite sure what she would do. In the meantime, she would divide her time between home and Australia, and never flinch from the future she had chosen.

There were nights, however, when she had left behind the endless puzzle-posing and dart games of her fellow students, and she had gazed up at unfamiliar constellations. With two mirrors, the horizon and a star map she could tell exactly where she was. She longed to know where Reyna was, who she was with, if she was happy. Reyna could not see these stars, she knew that, and yet she had felt an inexplicable pull inside her, as if a thread in her heart had been forever caught by Reyna. She would wonder if Reyna was looking up at the sky then, wondering where Holly might be.

She stopped the cart for a moment, out of breath and yawning. She wished someone would invent a transporter that first and foremost transported weary travelers from airports to home in the blink of an eye. Of course, if they could do that, she mused, there would be no need for airports. When she got home she would shower and sleep, and then she would somehow track down Reyna. Just call her, just say, "Hi, it's me," and see what happened. She would never forgive herself for not trying.

It was vivid in her mind, the way she had willed Reyna to look up that night in the bar. Her head was suddenly full of Reyna, and she didn't fight it, now that she was home.

She was about to muscle the cart back into motion when she shivered. Gooseflesh dusted her arms. She seemed to hear a voice, longed-for, whispering in her ear. "Look up," the voice said, "it's me."

It was a startling sensation and might have been the product of her weariness and wishful thinking. She wasn't used to hearing voices that suggested actions to her, like looking to her left, to the bare stretch of wall just beyond the airport lounge, past the blue awning, not that way, back to the left, that's right —

She was caught by those eyes and their melting light. There was no air, nor did she need any.

Reyna had cut her hair. Wearing blue jeans with a simple shirt, she looked about as far away as she could get from the tight-spined woman being interviewed on television. Her mouth curved in a smile of greeting, but more than that, it seemed to relax after the smile, as if happiness of a sort had found her. The lines of strain had been replaced by the beginnings of laugh lines.

Reyna walked quickly toward her, then slowed as she reached the cart. She seemed about to stop a polite distance away but then she kept going, stepping so close that Holly could smell her skin and hair and a faint hint of a complicated cologne.

"Welcome home."

"I . . . Why are you here?"

"There's no such thing as coincidence. You told me that," Reyna said. "I remember everything you've ever said to me."

She wanted Reyna to kiss her. It was as if the last four months had been a day. They were sharing air, sharing light. She tried not to close her eyes and raise her mouth with a hunger that seemed to know no propriety. "How did you know when I'd arrive?"

"I had help. A friend."

Whoever it was, she wanted to give thanks. "How is your mother?"

"Her condition has deteriorated somewhat, but not as rapidly as we feared. The pain management has improved and we're able to spend a lot of time together every day, reading, watching old movies."

"I'm glad." She swallowed hard and caught herself before her gaze had lingered overlong on Reyna's breasts. They made her ache with thirst.

"She wants to see you."

"I'll be happy to visit." What about you, she wanted to add. Do you want to see me? Of course, she does, silly, why else would she be here?

Reyna was standing so close. Her shoulders were rising and falling more rapidly now, and Holly realized that Reyna was staring at her mouth. The trembling between her legs was back. Two minutes and she was a mess. No, not a mess. A mess was chaos and she was not random. She knew exactly what the resolution to her need was.

She could only think about how she'd forgotten the shape of Reyna's hands and the way her body moved. Forgotten the taste of her but not the softness of her mouth. She had forgotten the sensation of Reyna inside her, but not the blazing ecstasy that followed.

"Where do you go from here?" Reyna sounded far too casual.

"Home. A friend is meeting me." She ought to be pushing the cart toward the front of the terminal. Nancy was no doubt wondering where she was.

"And after that?"

"To bed." It was an invitation — Holly knew it as she said it.

Reyna's voice was low from an intensity of emotion that Holly felt as a wave of heat. "I don't have any right to ask for anything from you."

Fiercely, Holly said, "Ask for what you want."

"May I have tonight? If there is no one who's expecting you?"

"Is that all you want?" Holly fought the urge to unbutton her blouse. She wanted to give herself to Reyna, the way she had that first night. Naked, without reservation.

Reyna shook her head.

"Ask for what you want."

Reyna had tears in her eyes, which shimmered like melting ice. The dark distance was gone and the thaw seemed permanent. "I want tomorrow," she said.

"Is that all you want?" Holly put her hand on Reyna's neck, slowly moving around to the back of it, pulling her head down even more slowly. Their lips were inches apart. "Ask for what you want. Don't you know that I'll give it to you?"

"I want all the tomorrows you can give me."

"Yes," Holly murmured. "They're yours."

Reyna kissed the corner of her mouth and Holly forgot where she was until a loudly cleared throat brought her back to the time and place.

Nancy, looking both curious and congratulatory, was leaning on Holly's boxes. "Don't mind me."

Holly disentangled herself from Reyna. It was no easy thing to do when her body didn't want to listen. "Nancy, this is Reyna. I didn't know she was meeting me." She could hardly explain that she and Reyna hadn't communicated at all for the last four months and in less than a minute had picked up exactly where they had left off.

Nancy shook Reyna's hand. Nancy had heard about Reyna on their first drive to the airport, four months ago. "Why don't I take charge of your stuff and you two have a, um, reunion."

"I can't do that to you," Holly protested. It would be rude. "You're not my personal stevedore."

"So you'll owe me," Nancy said. "Besides, you haven't seen the piece I decided to paint on your bedroom wall, and I want you in a good mood when you do. I had all this leftover blue and red and came up with the most bitchin' purple — but we'll talk about that later. Really, I don't mind, especially if you put the time to good use." Her eyes were twinkling.

They all helped get the heavy cart out through the crowds and into the short-term lot. Once the boxes and suitcases were loaded Holly waved good-bye to Nancy, and turned beet red when Nancy whispered that she wanted all the details later.

She looked at Reyna after Nancy had backed out, and all the desire was there. But there was more. There was time for details. Time for honesty. "I'm here for four months," she said. "Then I go back for six months or so. Then I'm back here again for a while. It'll be that way for the next two or three years. I might...I might have good reasons to settle there."

"I understand," Reyna said. She was still on the other side of the parking space and it was entirely too far away for Holly's liking.

Holly crossed the distance that separated them and smoothed Reyna's cheek. Her thumb caressed Reyna's lips and was quickly kissed. "I wish Australia was closer."

Reyna moaned as Holly's hand slid down her neck to her chest, to her stomach. "You have a life to get on with, I understand. I won't stand in your way when you have to go, wherever it may be, with whomever you choose."

Holly's hand stilled. Hadn't Reyna understood what Holly meant by all her tomorrows? "What are you asking for? What are you giving me? I can't be confused about it. I need to know."

"All you want of me, of this," Reyna answered. She kissed Holly with a bruising hunger and Holly felt her body ignite. Reyna pushed her against a hard concrete column and her mouth was demanding, then tender. She broke away with a low moan. "I'm sorry. I want you so much."

"No," Holly said. All the blood in her head had drained to places south. She felt faint and yet she could still think. "No," she repeated.

"Did I hurt you? What —"

"It's not good enough." Holly tried to steady her voice. Her heart and mind were in total agreement about the future.

Reyna looked wounded to her core, and turned so pale that Holly was afraid she would faint. "I misunderstood, then."

"Look at me." Holly captured Reyna's face in her hands. "I'm going with you tonight, wherever you want to go. I know that before you're done with me I'll be screaming and dying, and begging, and I'll do all I can to make you feel the same way, and there will be nothing you ask of me I won't try, and I'll learn every inch of you again, and it will be magnificent."

Reyna was moving against her as she spoke and Holly could hardly see for the pulsing between her legs.

"But it won't be good enough. Because as bad as I want it, I'm not going with you if you didn't mean you wanted all my tomorrows, even when I'm away. Because that's what I want. No matter how long we have to be apart, I can bear it if I know that I have your future. I give you mine, right now. It's the only thing of value we can give each other."

Reyna's eyes shimmered. "I didn't dare hope. I can't imagine what you thought of me, the way I lied, the hypocrisy of it all."

"We're agreed on tomorrow, right. All the tomorrows?"

Reyna nodded and swooped in for another hard kiss.

"Then we'll talk about that tomorrow. Tomorrow I'll prove to you that I'm not just about sex. Tomorrow. Because tonight sex is all I can think about, you and sex and you —"

Reyna's mouth was on her, traveling from forehead to chin, to her throat. "We have to get going or we'll get arrested."

Holly murmured her agreement, but it was several minutes before they parted, clothing askew.

Reyna pulled her quickly toward the elevator to the next level of the garage, then toward the section where motorcycles were parked. The Virago was at the end.

"You really weren't planning on suitcases, were you?"

Reyna looked chagrined. "I didn't think for a minute that you would want me. I just had to see you. I wasn't even going to speak to you, but then you saw me." She laughed shakily. "But I had hopes of seeing you soon." She unlocked new compartments on each side of the bike and withdrew two helmets and two leather jackets.

Holly blinked away tears. "You sure know how to romance a girl." She shrugged into one of the jackets and then slid across the bike seat.

Reyna bent over her to secure the helmet, then kissed her again. "Would you mind going to the same place as before? I want to finally have a tonight become a tomorrow there. I think I'll believe it then, that the past has actually led to this future. With you."

Holly wrapped her arms tightly around Reyna's waist and let the wind blow away the past. She felt fused to Reyna again, one body, one heart, one skin between them. Tomorrow was subject to random chaos — her intellect told her it was unquantifiable. But she had the constant she needed to solve the equation, at least for herself. The constant was their future. It was the only solution that mattered.

LOOKING FOR NAIAD?

**Buy our books at
www.naiadpress.com**

**or call our toll-free number
1-800-533-1973**

**or by fax (24 hours a day)
1-850-539-9731**

SHE WALKS IN BEAUTY by Nicole Conn. 304 pp. Meet
Spencer — she is talented, handsome, and driven to succeed.
ISBN 1-56280-269-0 $14.95

SUBSTITUTE FOR LOVE by Karin Kallmaker. 288 pp. Take one
look and fall hopelessly in lust.   ISBN 1-56280-265-8   12.95

OUT OF SIGHT by Claire McNab. 240 pp. 3rd Denise Cleever
thriller.   ISBN 1-56280-268-2   12.95

DEATH CLUB by Claire McNab. 224 pp. 13th Detective Inspector
Carol Ashton Mystery.   ISBN 1-56280-267-4   11.95

FROSTING ON THE CAKE by Karin Kallmaker. 272 pp.The
answer to every romance.   ISBN 1-56280-266-6 $11.95

DEATH UNDERSTOOD by Claire McNab. 240 pp. 2nd Denise
Cleever thriller.   ISBN 1-56280-264-X $11.95

TREASURED PAST by Linda Hill. 208 pp. A shared passion for
antiques leads to love.   ISBN 1-56280-263-1 $11.95

UNDER SUSPICION by Claire McNab. 224 pp. 12th Detective
Inspector Carol Ashton mystery.   ISBN 1-56280-261-5 $11.95

UNFORGETTABLE by Karin Kallmaker. 288 pp. Can each
woman win her true love's heart?   ISBN 1-56280-260-7   12.95

MURDER UNDERCOVER by Claire McNab. 192 pp. 1st Denise
Cleever thriller.   ISBN 1-56280-259-3   12.95

EVERYTIME WE SAY GOODBYE by Jaye Maiman. 272 pp.
7th Robin Miller mystery.   ISBN 1-56280-248-8   11.95

SEVENTH HEAVEN by Kate Calloway. 240 pp. 7th Cassidy
James mystery.   ISBN 1-56280-262-3   11.95

STRANGERS IN THE NIGHT by Barbara Johnson. 208 pp. Her
body and soul react to a stranger's touch.   ISBN 1-56280-256-9   11.95

THE VERY THOUGHT OF YOU edited by Barbara Grier and Christine Cassidy. 288 pp. Erotic love stories by Naiad Press authors. ISBN 1-56280-250-X 14.95

TO HAVE AND TO HOLD by Peggy J. Herring. 192 pp. Their friendship grows to intense passion . . . ISBN 1-56280-251-8 11.95

INTIMATE STRANGER by Laura DeHart Young. 192 pp. Ignoring Tray's myserious past, could Cole be playing with fire? ISBN 1-56280-249-6 11.95

SHATTERED ILLUSIONS by Kaye Davis. 256 pp. 4th Maris Middleton mystery. ISBN 1-56280-252-6 11.95

SET UP by Claire McNab. 224 pp. 11th Detective Inspector Carol Ashton mystery. ISBN 1-56280-255-0 11.95

THE DAWNING by Laura Adams. 224 pp. What if you had the power to change the past? ISBN 1-56280-246-1 11.95

NEVER ENDING by Marianne K. Martin. 224 pp. Temptation appears in the form of an old friend and lover. ISBN 1-56280-247-X 11.95

ONE OF OUR OWN by Diane Salvatore. 240 pp. Carly Matson has a secret. So does Lela Johns. ISBN 1-56280-243-7 11.95

DOUBLE TAKEOUT by Tracey Richardson. 176 pp. 3rd Stevie Houston mystery. ISBN 1-56280-244-5 11.95

CAPTIVE HEART by Frankie J. Jones. 176 pp. Love in the fast lane or heartside romance? ISBN 1-56280-258-5 11.95

WICKED GOOD TIME by Diana Tremain Braund. 224 pp. In charge at work, out of control in her heart. ISBN 1-56280-241-0 11.95

SNAKE EYES by Pat Welch. 256 pp. 7th Helen Black mystery. ISBN 1-56280-242-9 11.95

CHANGE OF HEART by Linda Hill. 176 pp. High fashion and love in a glamorous world. ISBN 1-56280-238-0 11.95

UNSTRUNG HEART by Robbi Sommers. 176 pp. Putting life in order again. ISBN 1-56280-239-9 11.95

BIRDS OF A FEATHER by Jackie Calhoun. 240 pp. Life begins with love. ISBN 1-56280-240-2 11.95

THE DRIVE by Trisha Todd. 176 pp. The star of *Claire of the Moon* tells all! ISBN 1-56280-237-2 11.95

BOTH SIDES by Saxon Bennett. 240 pp. A community of women falling in and out of love. ISBN 1-56280-236-4 11.95

WATERMARK by Karin Kallmaker. 256 pp. One burning question . . . how to lead her back to love? ISBN 1-56280-235-6 11.95

SILVER THREADS by Lyn Denison. 208 pp. Finding her way back to love . . . ISBN 1-56280-231-3 11.95

CHIMNEY ROCK BLUES by Janet McClellan. 224 pp. 4th Tru North mystery. ISBN 1-56280-233-X 11.95

MAKING UP FOR LOST TIME by Karin Kallmaker. 240 pp.
Nobody does it better . . .   ISBN 1-56280-196-1   11.95

GOLD FEVER by Lyn Denison. 224 pp. By author of *Dream
Lover.*   ISBN 1-56280-201-1   11.95

WHEN THE DEAD SPEAK by Therese Szymanski. 224 pp. 2nd
Brett Higgins mystery.   ISBN 1-56280-198-8   11.95

FOURTH DOWN by Kate Calloway. 240 pp. 4th Cassidy James
mystery.   ISBN 1-56280-193-7   11.95

CITY LIGHTS COUNTRY CANDLES by Penny Hayes. 208 pp.
About the women she has known . . .   ISBN 1-56280-195-3   11.95

POSSESSIONS by Kaye Davis. 240 pp. 2nd Maris Middleton
mystery.   ISBN 1-56280-192-9   11.95

A QUESTION OF LOVE by Saxon Bennett. 208 pp. Every
woman is granted one great love.   ISBN 1-56280-205-4   11.95

RHYTHM TIDE by Frankie J. Jones. 160 pp. . . . to desire
passionately and be passionately desired.   ISBN 1-56280-189-9   11.95

PENN VALLEY PHOENIX by Janet McClellan. 208 pp. 2nd
Tru North Mystery.   ISBN 1-56280-200-3   11.95

OLD BLACK MAGIC by Jaye Maiman. 272 pp. 6th Robin
Miller mystery.   ISBN 1-56280-175-9   11.95

LADY BE GOOD edited by Barbara Grier and Christine Cassidy.
288 pp. Erotic stories by Naiad Press authors.   ISBN 1-56280-180-5   14.95

CHAIN LETTER by Claire McNab. 288 pp. 9th Carol Ashton
mystery.   ISBN 1-56280-181-3   11.95

NIGHT VISION by Laura Adams. 256 pp. Erotic fantasy romance
by "famous" author.   ISBN 1-56280-182-1   11.95

SEA TO SHINING SEA by Lisa Shapiro. 256 pp. Unable to resist
the raging passion . . .   ISBN 1-56280-177-5   11.95

THIRD DEGREE by Kate Calloway. 224 pp. 3rd Cassidy James
mystery.   ISBN 1-56280-185-6   11.95

WHEN THE DANCING STOPS by Therese Szymanski. 272 pp.
1st Brett Higgins mystery.   ISBN 1-56280-186-4   11.95

PHASES OF THE MOON by Julia Watts. 192 pp. . . . . hungry
for everything life has to offer.   ISBN 1-56280-176-7   11.95

BABY IT'S COLD by Jaye Maiman. 256 pp. 5th Robin Miller
mystery.   ISBN 1-56280-156-2   10.95

CLASS REUNION by Linda Hill. 176 pp. The girl from her
past . . .   ISBN 1-56280-178-3   11.95

FORTY LOVE by Diana Simmonds. 288 pp. Joyous, heart-
warming romance.   ISBN 1-56280-171-6   11.95

IN THE MOOD by Robbi Sommers. 160 pp. The queen of
erotic tension!   ISBN 1-56280-172-4   11.95

SWIMMING CAT COVE by Lauren Wright Douglas. 192 pp. 2nd
Allison O'Neil Mystery.   ISBN 1-56280-168-6   11.95

THE LOVING LESBIAN by Claire McNab and Sharon Gedan.
240 pp. Explore the experiences that make lesbian love unique.
                                           ISBN 1-56280-169-4   14.95

SEASONS OF THE HEART by Jackie Calhoun. 240 pp. Romance
through the years.   ISBN 1-56280-167-8   11.95

K. C. BOMBER by Janet McClellan. 208 pp. 1st Tru North
mystery.   ISBN 1-56280-157-0   11.95

LAST RITES by Tracey Richardson. 192 pp. 1st Stevie Houston
mystery.   ISBN 1-56280-164-3   11.95

EMBRACE IN MOTION by Karin Kallmaker. 256 pp. A whirlwind
love affair.   ISBN 1-56280-165-1   11.95

HOT CHECK by Peggy J. Herring. 192 pp. Will workaholic Alice
fall for guitarist Ricky?   ISBN 1-56280-163-5   11.95

OLD TIES by Saxon Bennett. 176 pp. Can Cleo surrender to a
passionate new love?   ISBN 1-56280-159-7   11.95

SECOND FIDDLE by Kate Kalloway. 208 pp. 2nd P.I. Cassidy James
mystery.   ISBN 1-56280-161-9   11.95

LAUREL by Isabel Miller. 128 pp. By the author of the beloved
Patience and Sarah.   ISBN 1-56280-146-5   10.95

LOVE OR MONEY by Jackie Calhoun. 240 pp. The romance of
real life.   ISBN 1-56280-147-3   10.95

SMOKE AND MIRRORS by Pat Welch. 224 pp. 5th Helen Black
Mystery.   ISBN 1-56280-143-0   10.95

DANCING IN THE DARK edited by Barbara Grier & Christine
Cassidy. 272 pp. Erotic love stories by Naiad Press authors.
                                           ISBN 1-56280-144-9   14.95

TIME AND TIME AGAIN by Catherine Ennis. 176 pp. Passionate
love affair.   ISBN 1-56280-145-7   10.95

PAXTON COURT by Diane Salvatore. 256 pp. Erotic and wickedly
funny contemporary tale about the business of learning to live
together.   ISBN 1-56280-114-7   10.95

INNER CIRCLE by Claire McNab. 208 pp. 8th Carol Ashton
Mystery.   ISBN 1-56280-135-X   11.95

LESBIAN SEX: AN ORAL HISTORY by Susan Johnson.
240 pp. Need we say more?   ISBN 1-56280-142-2   14.95

WILD THINGS by Karin Kallmaker. 240 pp. By the undisputed
mistress of lesbian romance.   ISBN 1-56280-139-2   12.95

NOW AND THEN by Penny Hayes. 240 pp. Romance on the
westward journey.   ISBN 1-56280-121-X   11.95

DEATH AT LAVENDER BAY by Lauren Wright Douglas. 208 pp.
1st Allison O'Neil Mystery.　　　　　　　ISBN 1-56280-085-X　　11.95

YES I SAID YES I WILL by Judith McDaniel. 272 pp. Hot
romance by famous author.　　　　　　　ISBN 1-56280-138-4　　11.95

FORBIDDEN FIRES by Margaret C. Anderson. Edited by Mathilda
Hills. 176 pp. Famous author's "unpublished" Lesbian romance.
　　　　　　　　　　　　　　　　　ISBN 1-56280-123-6　　21.95

WILDWOOD FLOWERS by Julia Watts. 208 pp. Hilarious and
heart-warming tale of true love.　　　　　ISBN 1-56280-127-9　　10.95

NEVER SAY NEVER by Linda Hill. 224 pp. Rule #1: Never get
involved with . . .　　　　　　　　　　ISBN 1-56280-126-0　　11.95

THE WISH LIST by Saxon Bennett. 192 pp. Romance through
the years.　　　　　　　　　　　　　ISBN 1-56280-125-2　　10.95

FAMILY SECRETS by Laura DeHart Young. 208 pp. Enthralling
romance and suspense.　　　　　　　　ISBN 1-56280-119-8　　10.95

INLAND PASSAGE by Jane Rule. 288 pp. Tales exploring conven-
tional & unconventional relationships.　ISBN 0-930044-56-8　　10.95

DOUBLE BLUFF by Claire McNab. 208 pp. 7th Carol Ashton
Mystery.　　　　　　　　　　　　　ISBN 1-56280-096-5　　12.95

THE FIRST TIME EVER edited by Barbara Grier & Christine
Cassidy. 272 pp. Love stories by Naiad Press authors.
　　　　　　　　　　　　　　　　　ISBN 1-56280-086-8　　14.95

CHANGES by Jackie Calhoun. 208 pp. Involved romance and
relationships.　　　　　　　　　　　ISBN 1-56280-083-3　　10.95

GETTING THERE by Robbi Sommers. 192 pp. Nobody does it
like Robbi!　　　　　　　　　　　　ISBN 1-56280-099-X　　10.95

FLASHPOINT by Katherine V. Forrest. 256 pp. A Lesbian
blockbuster!　　　　　　　　　　　　ISBN 1-56280-079-5　　10.95

CLAIRE OF THE MOON by Nicole Conn. Audio Book —
Read by Marianne Hyatt.　　　　　　ISBN 1-56280-113-9　　13.95

FOR LOVE AND FOR LIFE: INTIMATE PORTRAITS OF
LESBIAN COUPLES by Susan Johnson. 224 pp.
　　　　　　　　　　　　　　　　　ISBN 1-56280-091-4　　14.95

SOMEONE TO WATCH by Jaye Maiman. 272 pp. 4th Robin
Miller Mystery.　　　　　　　　　　ISBN 1-56280-095-7　　10.95

These are just a few of the many Naiad Press titles — we are the oldest and
largest lesbian/feminist publishing company in the world. We also offer an
enormous selection of lesbian video products. Please request a complete
catalog. We offer personal service; we encourage and welcome direct mail
orders from individuals who have limited access to bookstores carrying our
publications.